twisted
MARRIAGE

TWISTED MARRIAGE

FILTHY VOWS SEQUEL

ALESSANDRA TORRE

INTRODUCTION

Let's be blunt for a minute. Let me open the door and bring you into my marriage.

We thought we could branch outside of the norm. Explore my sexual fantasies. Dip our toes in a kinky pond just to see how it felt.

But you can't have sex with your husband's best friend in front of him without consequences. Ripples in the pond. A subtle shifting of events and feelings and triggers that will eventually affect every core molecule of your marriage. Your friendships. Your life.

Once I knelt down between the two of them, everything changed. And now, I'm faced with wading in deeper or drying off my pink manicured toes and trying to pretend it never happened.

They say that three is a crowd, but what about four?

What about more?

This is the truth of what I started when I confessed my desires and my husband gave them to me.

This is the sequel to Filthy Vows. If you have not read Filthy Vows, you can purchase it here.

1

Easton undid his belt and dragged the zipper down, moving closer so that I could reach him. "Take it out."

I obeyed, self-conscious under Aaron's gaze as I worked Easton's jeans and underwear down, then ran my hands softly up his muscular thighs and over his cock. It was already stiffening. I wrapped my hand around the shaft and squeezed it, smiling as it quickly went from pliable to rigid.

"Jesus," Aaron muttered from his spot beside us. "I forgot how fucking big you are."

"She can take it all." My husband's hand closed on the back of my head and gently pulled. "Show him, Elle. Show him how well you suck my cock."

I felt different when I woke up. It was a very similar feeling to how I felt the morning after my first period. Older. More worldly. Like I had secret access to an elite club that had finally accepted me as a member.

I rolled onto my back and stretched. The right side of Easton's makeshift fort had fallen, and I could see a water stain on the joint of the ceiling beam. I studied the water stain with growing concern. Had it been there before? I propped up on one elbow and tugged at the wall of the fort, trying to get a better look. If we had a leak, so help me...

"Hey." Easton ducked under the sheet and grinned at me, his aqua golf shirt a little crooked on his frame.

I reached over and straightened his collar, folding it into place and returning his smile. "Good morning."

He leaned forward and planted a kiss on me. "Already taking down my fort?"

"I wanted to get to it before Wayland did." I scooted to the edge of the bed. "You know him and sheets." Our Great Dane had a vendetta against any white blankets, sheets, or towels—one that worked him into an immediate fervor at first sight. Easton's grandmother wore a white wrap to last year's Christmas party and he had knocked her to the ground, tug-o-warred it off her body, and was pouncing on it like he was giving CPR when I came around the corner and found the scene. Wayland was put in his crate and Grandma Ann confiscated his Christmas stocking out of pure spite.

He pulled a belt from the closet and worked it through the top of his shorts. "I'm going to brew some coffee and see if Aaron is up."

"Okay." I glanced around for further evidence from last night. With the morning sun beaming through the windows, the bathroom air vent on high, the cocoon of sheets dropping around me—it seemed crazy that this room had been the same place where Easton's best friend had stood naked, his dick in hand, waiting to take his turn on me.

Easton stood at the side of the bed, his gaze on me, eyes burning with heat. "Put your fingers in yourself," he ordered. "Show him how wet you are."

I flicked my gaze to Aaron and slowly ran one hand down my stomach and across the thin strip of hair between my legs. I pushed a finger in, then a second, opening my legs and showing him the tight fit around my knuckles. His eyes followed the motion, and his breath shortened as he stroked his cock in rhythm with my fingers. "Fuck me," I begged. "Please."

What had we been thinking? We weren't those kind of couples. We were the forget-trash-day couple. The ones who snuck a flask into football games and didn't send Christmas cards. The kind who paid property taxes late and booked concert tickets early, and argued over parking spots and coupon usage and whether celebrity hall passes were allowed. We were Easton and Elle—not...*ew*...swingers. Not those creepy people who pressured their friends to join them in the bedroom. I knew those sorts of people. My first boss in real estate had been *that* sort of person.

We weren't those people, yet we had done it. Ten hours later, and the memories were still crisp and vivid.

The possessive and aroused look on Easton's face.

His hand tight around his cock.

Aaron's fingers, trembling as they traced around my nipple.

His mouth coming down on my breast.

The drag of his teeth and the hot swipe of his tongue.

His rigid cock, pushing inside of me.

The hiss of Easton's breath.

Their tight grip on me.

The groan of their orgasms.

The intense peaks of mine.

I fisted the sheet and pushed off the bed, needing to get onto my feet and away from the memories before my arousal got the better of me.

I met Easton's eyes as I moved past him, toward the bathroom. His hand closed on my wrist and he pulled me back until I was against him. "Wait."

I resisted. "I need to brush my teeth."

"Is that what you need?" His gaze sharpened. "Because it looks like you might need something else."

It was my body that betrayed me. Trembling with need and still naked from last night, no shirt to hide the diamonding of my nipples in the cool room. No barrier to stop my legs from parting when he ran his hand in between them to verify what he suspected.

His eyes darkened when his fingers easily dipped into me, my body warm and wet, a whimper sliding out of my lips as he curved his fingers into me. He nodded to the bed. "Get back on there. On your knees."

"But—" He unzipped his pants and I forgot my excuse. He got behind me and pushed his way inside, and I couldn't hold back my cry.

I found my first orgasm quickly, then triggered his with my second. By the time I stumbled into the kitchen, a silk blouse and linen pants pulled over lazy limbs, I could barely formulate a sentence, much less feel apprehension over Aaron. Which was good, since he sat front-and-center at our kitchen island, a mug of coffee in hand.

"Morning." He nodded at me, then slid a coffee cup toward E. "How'd you guys sleep?"

"Okay," I mumbled, beelining for the fridge. Opening the door, I hid behind it and studied the shelves.

"Hey, Aaron. Why can't you lose in a threesome with Vietnamese twins?"

I groaned and grabbed the orange juice, ignoring the slightly expired date. "Easton."

"Shush, it's funny." He rested his weight on the counter and waited for Aaron to come up with the punchline. "Well?"

"No idea."

I grabbed a short juice glass from the cabinet and filled it, my gaze pinned to the action.

"Because it's a Nguyen-Nguyen."

There was a beat of absolute silence, then Aaron chuckled.

I risked a glance up from the glass. "It's not funny," I chided him, then glared at Easton, who lifted his hands in innocence.

"Hey, it was a backup joke. The other was better." He grinned at Aaron. "Want to hear it?"

"He doesn't want to hear it," I interrupted. "And listen." I snapped my fingers at my husband, then Aaron. "Let's talk about last night for a minute."

"This will be interesting…" Easton muttered, pulling out the closest stool and straddling it. Aaron smiled, and it was dandy how amused everyone was by this.

"Get all of your threesome jokes and side comments out of the way right now, because we have about…" I glanced at the oven's clock. "Five minutes, then Chelsea is going to be here and we are never *ever* going to talk about this again."

"Can Aaron and I talk about it, just not when you're around?" Easton's brow pinched, as if this was a super important question worth sucking into our five minutes.

"No," I snapped, then reconsidered, aware of how much I'd been turned on by them discussing me. "Only good stuff," I countered. "You can praise my magical vagina but nothing else."

"And your mouth," Aaron snuck in with an almost shy smile. "Can we talk about your mouth?"

"Her hands are pretty good too," Easton pointed out, and my ego inflated further. "Oh, and that middle toe on her right foot."

"It was the left foot," Aaron argued. "You have the sides confused because you were facing her."

"I'm going to dump this orange juice all over both of your heads." I lifted the carton off the counter to accentuate my threat.

Easton held up his hands in surrender. "Fine. Your middle right toe is horrendous."

If we were alone, I'd pour it. I'd pour it over his shoulders and watch his anger grow. I'd struggle against him when he knocked the orange juice out of my hand and pinned me against the fridge. I'd try to knee his balls, and he'd bite into the side of my neck. We'd end up half-naked on the juice-covered kitchen floor, his tongue and dick deep inside of me. It was who we were, what we did, and God, I loved him.

I let out a controlled breath and forced myself to return to the fridge, my hand slightly sweating as I worked it into an open spot on the second shelf. "Chelsea can't know what happened."

"Agreed," Easton said. "Though, you're the one who tells her everything."

"Yeah, well." I closed the fridge. "Not this. No side jokes, no weird looks, nothing that will make her suspicious. Okay?"

Aaron shrugged in agreement and Easton nodded. This was easier than I thought. Adopting a bossy role helped. It was like a shield between me and them, one they were cushioning with their teasing.

I tapped the edge of the counter, daring to take it one step further. "And that was a one-time thing. No getting drunk and trying to feel me up," I warned Aaron.

"Come on, Elle Bell. I've never tried to feel you up." He scowled at me, and that gorgeous mug could've been Instagram-famous if he'd ever wanted to.

"I think you did last night." Easton smirked and I reached over the counter and poked him.

"That right there—those are the things you can't say around Chelsea!"

"Speaking of my future roommate, any tips for living with her?"

I made a face. Late last night, Easton had shared the plan for Aaron to move in with Chelsea. I wasn't in love with the idea, but did appreciate having some physical space from him, given that we'd just had a genital jamboree. "Got a chastity belt?" I said dryly.

"I can handle Chelsea. Though, to be honest, I'm probably the only guy she's never made a move on."

"Never?" Easton raised his brows. "You're kidding."

"Maybe I'm not her type."

I swallowed a snarky response about everyone being her type and searched for some helpful advice on living with Chelsea. We'd shared a dorm room freshman year, then an apartment in our junior and senior years. Other than an annoying obsession with reality TV, she was pretty easy to live with. "She's not a morning person," I managed. "I'd avoid playing loud music or using power tools before ten."

"Not an issue." He took his coffee cup to the sink and rinsed it out.

"And she doesn't wear a lot of clothes around the house." The first time Easton had popped by unannounced, he'd walked in to find her ironing butt-naked in the middle of our living room.

"Also, not an issue." I saw a grin break his profile, one that gave me pause. I'd always heard Chelsea's inappropriate comments about Aaron, but had never thought about his potential attraction to her. I'd had them in the friend zone for so long that cement had dried around the words.

"Oh, my GAWD, take this thing before I drop him off at the pound." Chelsea's entry into the house was punctuated by Wayland's paws, which skittered across the wood floor at a frantic pace toward me. I crouched to receive his love and was knocked back hard on my right hip. His tongue swiped from my chin to my eyebrow and I craned away from the contact right as a paw plowed into my breast.

"Hey!" Easton said sharply, pulling on Wayland's collar and getting the dog off me. The Great Dane gasped against the collar, his nose lifting in the air as he sniffed in my direction. "Here." Easton held out his hand and helped me to my feet.

"Jeeeez, that dog is a pain." Chelsea collapsed on a stool and eyed Wayland, who had latched on to one of Easton's belt loops and was tugging on it with short jerky motions that would quickly snap it off. I opened the back door to distract him, then moved out of the way as he galloped through it.

"Don't get an irrigation system," Chelsea advised. "The sprinklers came on at seven and Wayland clawed through my curtains trying to get through the windows and attack them." She spotted the coffee pot and stood. "Do you have any—"

"Almond milk is in the fridge." I leaned back against Easton's chest as he wrapped his arms around me. "We're out of Splenda."

"Let me guess, Wayland ate it?" She opened the fridge and grabbed the milk. "You guys owe me a box of Wheat Thins and a new head for my toothbrush." She gave me a withering look, and I snorted.

"Hey, you're the one who offered to watch him. I am ninety-nine percent sure I said it was a terrible idea."

"He's my godson," she said indignantly. "I wasn't going to have you stick him in a kennel. By the way..."—she glanced around—"did they fix the vent thingy?"

"Yep. All taken care of." I picked off dog hair off my shirt and hoped the action would hide the telltale blush that crawled along my cheeks. We'd had to invent something that required Wayland to be out of the house. I had been the one to come up with some elaborate issue that required our floor vents to be repaired. Chelsea had half-listened to the flimsy excuse before asking if the Chick-Fil-A near our house was still closed for remodeling. "And thanks for watching him."

"No problem." She poured a generous helping of milk into her coffee. "Making everyone's lives easier is what I do. Right, roomie?" She gave Aaron a bright smile.

"Don't trust that smile," Easton warned. "She's about to ask for something."

"I'm not asking for anything." Chelsea gave E a withering look. "My friendly nature has absolutely nothing to do with the fact that my thermostat control isn't working right."

We groaned and E let out a shout of victory. Chelsea smiled, and I took the moment of distraction to kiss Easton goodbye.

"Meet me for lunch?" he asked quietly.

"I can't. I have an open house." I gave him an extra kiss to make up for it. "But dinner tonight? That Mexican place with the half-price margaritas?"

"I'm getting Margarita Elle?" He smirked at me, and maybe I should lay off the drunk sexual antics if it was earning me my own drinking nickname. "Done. Six?"

"It's a date." I turned away and caught the look that passed between Aaron and Chelsea. "What?"

"You guys are obnoxious," Chelsea intoned. "Seriously obnoxious. You have an old maid and a heartbroken handyman as an audience. Can't you at least pretend to hate each other?"

"We hate each other on Wednesdays," Easton informed her, his face earnest.

"It's true," I chimed in. "It lasts all day. It's on the calendar and everything. It culminates in hate sex, where we shout really mean things at each other during the act."

"I insult her life choices," Easton added in.

"And my friends," I contributed, pulling on a nude slingback that would be kicked off the minute I got into the car.

"She has really shitty friends," he agreed. "Especially the rich blonde with the nice ass."

Chelsea spread her arms. "Hey, I'll take a compliment any way I can get it. Double H, you got your stuff packed? I emptied out my trunk if you need me to take a load."

"Double H?" Easton raised a brow.

"Heartbroken Handyman?" I guessed.

"Seriously, no one picked up on my *take a load* comment?" Chelsea glared at us.

"Yeah, I'm not down with Double H," Aaron remarked.

"It could be Handsome Handyman," Chelsea amended.

Or Hung Handyman. My mind seemed to be the only one that dipped into that gutter. I swallowed the suggestion, along with the visual image of his cock, jutting out from my hand, side by side with Easton's. *Horny Handyman*. Another moniker I should probably keep to myself.

"I've got to run," I said quickly, wanting to change the subject before Chelsea's mind followed the same path. "Aaron, will you lock up Wayland when you leave?"

He nodded, and our eyes met for one brief unfiltered moment. He smiled, and some of my nerves calmed. "No problem."

I gave Chelsea a hug and grabbed my purse and cell. "See ya guys later."

A chorus of goodbyes sounded, and I escaped through the formal living room and to the front door. Opening the heavy oak number, I let out a breath of tension.

The morning after and walk of shame had gone, all in all, surprisingly well.

2

My open house was at an ugly home built in the seventies, back when flat roofs, low ceilings, and wallpaper were all the rage. I stood in a cramped kitchen that still had the original stove and hunched over my planner, making a list in the neat penmanship that consistently earned me the boring job of addressing wedding invitations.

I had decided, mid-Miami traffic, to organize the post-threesome jumble of emotions in my mind into a list. I stared down at the page and added a decorative flourish to the top *Pros and Cons* header.

I considered adding "of a threesome" to the heading, but wasn't confident in my ability not to misplace my planner at some point in time. The bulky organizer had been a gift from my mother, and included a section for article clippings (didn't Pinterest replace those?), my calendar (pathetically empty), contacts (mildly full), inspirational quotes (still blank), and photo sleeves. She'd pre-filled the photo sleeves with pictures from family gatherings, my sister's new baby, and a wedding photo of Easton and me. The spiral-bound book weighed three pounds, which didn't sound like a lot, but was the probable cause of a pinched nerve in my right shoulder.

I glanced around the quiet house, the lights already turned on in every room, the air conditioner set to a crisp 71 degrees, discreet air fresheners plugged in every room. I sniffed. They weren't quite doing their job. I could smell the cigarette smoke hanging in the air, despite my seller's reassurances that they had *"never, honestly Elle, NEVER"* smoked in the house.

I returned to my list. In the PROS column, I had three items listed.

- *It was hot*
- *Made me feel sexy*
- *Grew closer to E*

I added "fantasy and role-play fodder" to the list, thinking of the nights before the threesome, where Easton had whispered the filthiest things in my ear, egging on my orgasms as he'd grown harder.

Now that it was over, I was curious how much it would be discussed. Would he bring it up during sex? Whisper things in my ear during parties? I straightened a stack of folded red dishtowels and reconsidered the list, adding *very* before the word *hot*.

It *had* been very hot. The hottest experience of my life, and I'd been a very satisfied wife already.

The front door creaked open and I stuck my pen in the planner and shut it. Leaving the bulky binder on the counter, I strode around a yellow four-top dining table and moved into the living room.

"Good morning," I said brightly, smiling at the woman who moved cautiously into the home, her purse clutched in front of her stomach with both hands.

I immediately pegged her as a one-time looker. She probably lived on the street and was curious about the inside of her neighbor's home. I couldn't blame her. Easton and I had practically sprinted over to the broker's open for the Maxwell mansion at the end of our street. I'd been burning with curiosity over the elusive couple who had a Rolls tucked in their garage and two security guards stationed at their gate.

I handed her a flyer and let her wander the house, her tentative steps pattering across the carpeted floor toward the first of three small bedrooms. Moving back into the kitchen, I clicked on the touchpad of my laptop, awakening the screen, and watched the live video of her movements.

On my second ever open house, a glamorous couple in Burberry and Chanel pocketed an iPad and a jeweled figurine. I'd realized the theft early because it was *my* iPad, left in the master bathroom to charge. They hadn't filled out the visitor's form, and I'd had to pay for the figurine myself. The next morning, I purchased the cameras and—of course—hadn't had another theft since.

On video, the woman paused before the vanity table and adjusted her braids, then tugged at the front of her shirt, smoothing the material over her generous and potentially pregnant stomach. *Lucky bitch.* Glancing back down at my planner, I considered resuming my list.

The cons side felt a lot more daunting, and I could feel my subconscious resisting the task. My mother would instantly peg the action as evasive and say that I didn't want to face the consequences of my actions. It was true. I didn't want to write the cons down because they would far, far outweigh the pros.

Which was probably why I was writing this list now, and not four days ago, when I could have pre-evaluated the action and squashed it. Then again... four days ago I wouldn't have been able to definitively list the positives. I wouldn't have expected the act to make me feel closer to E. I would have put a giant question mark next to the word *hot*. I would have...

"Excuse me. Do you know the R values of the floors?"

I closed the laptop before the woman had a chance to see the screen, then turned to face her. I'd been wrong. Curious neighbors didn't give a damn about insulation values. "Absolutely." I smiled. "It's R13. And the air conditioner is brand new. Let me show you the utility room where you can take a look at it."

Ushering her toward the back of the house, I left my list behind, that pesky con column still incomplete.

3

"Here's to your offer." Easton lifted his Corona and I shook my head.

"First off, it's bad luck to toast with water and secondly..." I straightened at the glimpse of an approaching waiter with two strawberry margaritas. He veered off to another table, and I slumped back against the sticky booth.

"Secondly?"

"Secondly, it's a low offer with a three-month closing period. My seller probably won't even respond."

"You'll work it out." He grinned at me as if it was done, that commission in the bank, and the issue with wholeheartedly believing this visualization crap is that it doesn't work.

"Two frozen strawberry margaritas?" A man in a saggy sombrero paused at our table, a platter in hand, and I practically swooped forward.

"Yes, right here. Both for me." I cradled the huge glasses close to me, eyeing both before deciding to start with the right one.

Easton chuckled.

"Shut up. I'm drowning my stress." I picked up the right goblet and lifted it toward me. "Plus, I've got you here to keep me from hitting on waiters or doing the Macarena butt naked in the middle of this restaurant."

He dipped a chip into the cheese. "It's been a long time since I saw your naked Macarena. Can I let you do it, and just keep anyone from filming it?"

"Not if you expect to get a sloppy blowjob on the way home."

He crunched through the chip quickly and held his hands up in surrender. "Deal. I'll make sure your clothes stay on, and keep all your secrets." He winked at me.

I set down the giant glass. "If you could just keep our *one* secret for the rest of your life, I'll be happy."

"Ah, so it was a one-time thing."

I very carefully moved my straw around the glass goblet, stirring the contents without spilling them out. "Potentially. I made a pros and cons worksheet during my open house today."

"And?"

"And I didn't get a chance to finish. Jury's still out."

He pushed his phone toward me, and I watched as the device spun across the surface and ran into the bowl of salsa. "Read the text messages from Aaron today."

I picked up the phone quickly, before the offer was gone, and keyed in his passcode. Scrolling down his texts, I found the conversation with Aaron and clicked on it. There were only a few, starting at eleven this morning.

Last night was insane. She's so fucking hot.

You're officially the luckiest man in the world.

Also, Becca is a bitch and she's texting me photos of her with that asshole.

Chelsea has fucking Playboys in the bathrooms. Send help.

I bit on the edge of my cheek and set down the phone, nudging it back to his side of the table. "Hmmm." I glanced at him and found him studying me, an interesting smile playing across his features. "What?"

"I don't know." He tilted his beer to one side. "I've been in an odd mood all day over it."

I leaned forward. "Like how?"

"Turned on." He nodded at the phone. "That turns me on, hearing another man talk about you. But it also worries me." He lifted his beer and pointed one of the fingers wrapped around it in my direction. "That smile on your face, that scares me a little." He rushed forward before I could respond. "But I also like it. I like seeing this side of you. So, I'm torn. I'm feeling this collision of emotions and don't know how to handle them."

I wanted to chug the margarita down in one gulp and hug him at the same time. If the booths at El Calisto's weren't so tight, I'd squeeze in next to him. What he was describing... I got it. I got it because I felt so much of the same things. An electric thrill of arousal. A gnawing weight of dread. This couldn't be just fireworks. Somewhere, an ember would land on something important and burn.

"I get it." I folded the corner of a paper napkin and creased it with the tip of my nail. "I'm figuring out my own emotions on it."

"Do you regret doing it?"

I took a moment to honestly consider the question. "No. Not yet. But I'm still braced for a fallout. I feel like you and I are good, like this didn't hurt us in any—"

"It didn't."

"But"—I glared at him for the interruption—"it might have changed things with us and Aaron. We just have to wait that out and see. I do probably regret that it was with Aaron, versus a random."

He settled back against the red cushion of the booth and brought the beer to his lips. "I don't think you would have ever done it with a random. I think you needed it to be someone you knew, someone you were comfortable with."

I broke a chip in half and considered the opinion. "You might be right on that. I mean, I don't know about *ever*, but I certainly wouldn't have jumped into this so quickly. The stars definitely aligned, with my raging libido and his divorce and living with us."

The waiter approached and we fell silent as our fajitas were delivered. I waved away the steam and took another sip of my drink. Easton hunched over the table and began to unwrap the tortillas. His hair was getting long and a lock of it fell over his forehead. He pushed it away without thought and I tried to imagine him with gray hair. It wasn't too far off. Ten years, maybe? Would we have children by then? Would we be right here at this table with a high chair pulled up to the end, a pile of Cheerios scattered across the plate?

"What are you smiling at?" Easton peered at me and I reached over to dab a smear of queso off his lip.

"Thinking about you with gray hair." I smiled. "It's a good look. Very distinguished."

"I have no doubt that you'll give me lots of them." He held out a rolled tortilla, stuffed with steak and peppers. "Here. No onions."

"Thanks." I reached over my drink and took it, biting into one end and watching as he assembled his own, heaping on the onions he had sequestered from mine.

I reclined the Range Rover's seat as far back as it would go and jabbed at the sunroof button, watching as the glass above me gaped open in a smooth and silent motion.

"Move your arm," E grunted, struggling with my limbs as he stretched the seatbelt across my chest.

"No groping," I warned, and felt him squeeze my right breast in response. "Hey!" I smacked him lightly. "No groping!"

"You love my groping," he scoffed.

"It's true." I toed off one heel, and then the other, putting my bare feet up on the dash. "You are an excellent groper. I'm going to put that on your tombstone. Easton North. A cracked skull. Rugged cock. All-star groper."

"No."

"No?" I closed my eyes. "What do you think your tombstone should say?"

"I haven't really thought about my tombstone. And I don't think they call it a tombstone. It's a headstone."

"Wait." I held up my hand as it came to me. "Gravestone. It's gravestone."

"Yeah, because they're graves. Not tombs, not anymore."

I started second-guessing gravestone also. I reared up off the seat and groped in the dark floorboard for my purse so I could look it up online.

"Woah," Easton brought the Range Rover to a stop and positioned me back into place. "What do you want?"

"Myyphone." The words slurred together and I laughed. "Crap. I'm drunk."

"Yeah, we knew that was coming when you claimed both margaritas." He reached into my floorboard and then handed me my phone. I brought it close to my face to unlock the screen, then peered at the blurry glow, attempting to pull up the Internet.

"E." I let the phone fall to my lap and curled to face him, too drunk to continue the search. God, he was pretty. Even blurry, he was drop-dead gorgeous. "I love you."

"I love you too, Elle." He reached out and found my hand, linking his fingers through mine.

"We're going to be okay," I instructed him. "Rich and successful and with lots of babies."

"I know we are," he said quietly.

I closed my eyes and tightened my hand through his. He pulled onto the street and I relaxed against the leather, blocking out the knowledge that the Range Rover's payment was a week late.

"Elle?" He nudged me and I drifted back to him.

"Yeah?"

"Even if we don't have any of those things, I'm happy, just like this."

"As a groper of drunk wives?"

He chuckled. "Yeah."

"You could be so much more," I whispered.

He didn't say anything and it felt like I'd said the wrong thing. I tightened my hand on his and tried to amend the statement, but fell asleep halfway through the attempt.

4

The following Saturday, I perched on the hood of my car, Wayland's leash looped around my wrist, and watched as Aaron and Easton carried a long toolbox through the front yard and toward Aaron's truck. "You should have put that in first."

Easton shot me a look as Aaron angled his end toward the lowered tailgate. It looked heavy, and I moved to my feet, unsure if I could help. Squatting, Aaron got his shoulder underneath it and then up and high enough to land on the gate. I winced at the bang of impact and Wayland whined, lifting his paw in the air and looking back at me as if trying to offer his own assistance. I sat back down and pulled him closer to me, running my hand over his back and scratching the itchy area right above the base of his tail.

"Damn, that's heavy," Easton grunted as he got his end in.

I expected the back of the truck to sag from the additional weight, but it didn't seem to notice. "How much more is inside?"

Aaron brushed off his palms. "Maybe four more bags of tools. A few boxes of clothes."

"I need a second." Easton hobbled over and stretched his back before sprawling pitifully across my lap. Unlike Aaron's truck, my car did sag from the additional weight. I choked out a laugh and pushed at his shoulder, trying to get his sweaty form off. Wayland's huge paws swung forward through the air, mimicking mine, and Easton yelled at him to stop. "My shoulders are killing me," he groaned, readjusting to sit on the front bumper in front of me. "Rub 'em?"

I did, finding a bed of knots along his left trapezius, and dug into the tight muscles with easy familiarity. After baseball practice, I used to sit him down in front of the TV for a full hour and given his neck, shoulders, and arms a working over. It was a ritual I missed, and I kissed the top of his head, suddenly nostalgic.

"Me next." Aaron rolled his neck and I heard bones crack.

"Okay, no. I'm not turning the hood of my car into a massage table." I gave Easton a light smack on the back. "You guys finish loading up the truck. I'm going to walk Wayland and then I'll give quick neck massages inside, in the air conditioning."

Easton rolled to his feet without argument. "Deal. But watch him on the curve by the lake. There were some baby ducks there this morning."

"I will."

He leaned forward and pressed his lips against mine. I smiled against the kiss, then watched as he returned to Aaron, his sweaty T-shirt clinging to his strong expanse of back muscles.

I'd wasted a lot of time at Florida State, but the massage techniques class I had taken my junior year had been one elective that had come in handy. I flexed my fingers, then wrapped the leash around my hand, tugging on the heavy rope. "Come on, buddy. Let's go."

By the time Wayland and I made it around the lake and back down the tree-lined hill, Aaron's truck bed was completely filled, a bungee cord net stretched across the top. Wayland sniffed at his front tire, then lifted his leg, watching me with quiet detachment as no urine came out. He had run out of juice before we even made it to the lake, which hadn't stopped him from attempting to mark every interesting bush, mailbox, mound of dirt or stick we passed.

I pulled the leash and walked along the front sidewalk, noticing the fresh repair Aaron had made to the gutter downspout—a fix I'd bugged Easton about for weeks, then given up on. There had definitely been some benefits to having Aaron as a guest. The roof leak—fixed. The shower control that had been installed upside down, allowing only either scalding hot or freezing cold water—fixed. The shredded back screen door panel—replaced, though that had been a fairly useless repair and one that Wayland had torn back through with joyous excitement, as if we'd given him a new toy.

As wonderful as Easton was, handy was not an adjective I'd use for him. His parents had been the sort to call a repairman rather than figure out something themselves, and we had a stack of receipts that proved his loyal adherence to that method.

I hadn't exactly helped. In our first year of marriage, I became adept at picking up the phone, my credit card cheerfully in hand. Once he was dropped from the Marlins and our finances grew tight, I stopped making calls and we started to ignore issues. That had been a broken plan that had been saved by the last month of having Aaron as a houseguest. Suddenly dead light switches were working, my ice maker was back in business, and the noisy rattle of the bathroom vent was a quiet purr.

"You look pissed." Easton raised a brow as I entered the kitchen. "Was it the ducks? Did they point and laugh at your shoes? I swear to God…"

I rolled my eyes. "Don't be a douche."

"What's going on with your shoes?" Aaron tilted back the chair he was sitting in, trying to see me from his place at the kitchen table.

"Dude, they're the ugliest things I've ever seen." He took the leash from me and unclipped Wayland. The dog bounded through the hall and toward his water dish. "I swear, a dozen fashion designers got together and figured out the perfect way to kill an erection."

"Hey—they're comfortable." Making my way over to a chair, I leaned over and unlaced my new tennis shoes that Easton had branded, upon first glance, as grandma shoes.

Granted, they did have a big velcro band across the top that vaguely resembled my grandma's orthopedic walkers. But everyone was wearing these right now! And they were super light. The colors *were* a bit loud, a clash of neon pink and lime yellow.

But they felt like walking on clouds, and I liked to push E's buttons by wearing them.

"They do look comfortable," Aaron said, always willing to play Switzerland.

"Sure," Easton agreed. "Comfortable and ugly."

I tried to peel off the first shoe, which had an odd inner sock that got stuck on my heel. I tugged harder. "Do you want me to work on your shoulders or not? Because I'm going to need a lot more sucking up before my magic fingers do any heavy lifting."

"I love the shoes," Aaron offered. "Do they come in size 13? Especially that color. I love that color."

"And... Aaron wins." I used my still-shoed foot to pull the closest chair in front of me. "Take a seat and give me that sore neck."

"Total bullshit," Easton commented, leaning against the counter as he watched Aaron straddle the chair, facing away from me. "I'm the one who has to live with those things." I pulled the other shoe off and flung it at him.

Aaron pulled his baseball cap off and rested it on his lap, tilting his head back as I ran my forefingers down the levator scapulae muscle in his neck. It was tight. Really tight. I thought of everything he'd been through and realized this was his second move in a month. Talk about upheaval. I found a trigger point and pressed on it. "How long do you think you'll stay at Chelsea's?"

"No clue." He dropped this head forward, obeying the gentle manipulation I gave. "I guess I'll see how it goes. If it doesn't work out, I'll grab one of those furnished units they have on 42nd."

I met Easton's eyes and made a face. The 42nd Street lofts were located between a closed Kmart and a gas station that specialized in homeless beggars. I pictured E helping him move that truckload in and wondered how they would get it all inside without the panhandlers helping themselves to the contents.

"It'll work out." I moved higher, kneading a tension knot at the base of his hair. "Chelsea's pretty easy to live with. Plus, you'll be in the guest house, right?"

"I guess. We didn't discuss the logistics—she just said I wouldn't be a bother."

"That guest house is sweet." Easton opened the fridge door and grabbed another bottle of water, tossing it in the direction of Aaron before getting his second. "It wouldn't be a bad place to bring a girl."

"Yeah, that's not exactly the plan right now." He groaned as the muscles crunched, the knot breaking. "I plan to lie low and lick my wounds."

His tongue flicked hot and thick across my nipple before his mouth crushed over the spot, gentle yet needy.

I focused on a freckle on his left trap and fought the blush that worked its way up my neck. If E was watching me right now, he'd know. He'd know in an instant that my mind was wandering, my stomach was twisting, my need growing.

I rolled my own neck and tried to think about something else. Big saggy old lady nipples. Rotten pimento cheese. The smell of Easton's locker room after a practice.

"What's the market like in Glenvar Heights right now?"

I almost missed Aaron's question, my attention skittering between the sexy memories and the nasty images I was trying to counter them with.

"Uh…" I moved to the other side of his neck. "What are you thinking about? A house or one of those townhomes by the mall?"

"I don't know. Something less than two-fifty, if I can help it."

"I'm assuming you want something you could fix up?"

"Preferably."

"I'll pull listings and send them to you this afternoon. But honestly, I'm not sure you should be buying anything right now." As much as we needed the commission, Aaron needed to take a beat and see how he handled running his company without Becca's help, and how the chips fell into place after this divorce. "If you could live with Chelsea for a year and save your money—I'd rather put you in something better, that will appreciate more."

"I'm taking Elle's side on this one." Easton navigated around the edge of the counter and to the back door. Opening up the slider, he called Wayland's name. "Damn dog," he muttered. "He's in your bougainvillea bush."

I groaned and let out my own shriek of Wayland's name. Before me,

Aaron winced at the sound. "Sorry." I kneaded along the upper border of his shoulder blade.

"Keep doing that and you can make me deaf." He closed his eyes and tilted his head to one side. "God, Elle. Your husband know how lucky he is?"

Easton met my eyes and gave me a wink. "I do. Now get up. It's my turn."

5

Four days later, I sipped cheap champagne in a sea of my peers.

"Dr. Witter is the *best*." The woman jumped in place, her magnificent cleavage bouncing in an impressively realistic fashion, and the surrounding cluster of Realtors cooed in approval. "But you've got to get in his books early. I had to wait nine months for these babies."

I took a sip of my champagne and eased around the group, fighting the urge to stare at the woman, who was turning sideways in an attempt to show her lack of facelift scars. Pushing sixty, she had the breasts—and face—of a thirty-year-old. I glanced down at my own chest briefly, then dismissed any thoughts of enhancement.

My breasts were one thing I'd always been happy with. Big enough to fill out a bathing suit, but small enough to avoid back pain. Back in Ocala, they'd earned me a spot on the homecoming court. At Florida State, plenty of admiring looks poolside. In Miami... I walked past a well-timed cluster of tan double-d-sized agents pecking at the open house's lunch buffet.

In Miami, I was considered flat. I tried to resist the urge to compare myself with the naturally endowed Cubans, or the cosmetically enhanced bikini models, but my bras had grown more padded, more push-up, and I'd moved my thinking from an after-baby reconstruction to an after-baby reconstruction with size upgrade.

Assuming I ever had a baby.

"God, this place is a disaster." Tim Rowland appeared beside me, his own champagne flute tight against his Vineyards Vine-clad chest. He peered down at the listing flyer. "Five bedrooms and only two baths? No wonder they're bribing us with alcohol and lunch."

"I can deal with the two bathrooms." I nodded toward the living room. "It's the decor that's going to kill this. They need to move out all the furniture, paint the place, then re-list."

"Honey, old people in Miami love this shit." He set down his drink and picked a gold monkey off a nearby console table, examining it. "I bet this thing cost a fortune."

Maybe he was right. I tried to look at the house through different eyes, but I couldn't find a single thing that appealed to me. All the furniture was pastel. Everything. Lamps, sofas, rugs, art, pillows, and curtains. What wasn't pastel was gold. Gold light switches. Gold kitchen fixtures, lights, doorknobs, and appliances. Where had they found a pink and gold fridge? I could have possibly dealt with the palette if it had been offset with white, but they'd chosen black as the staple color. Black painted concrete floors. Black marble countertops. Black wood accents on the furniture. It was Miami Vice dipped in noir.

"At least the view is nice." I looked through the sea of realtors and out at the Intracoastal.

"True," he drawled, setting down the monkey. "If you like staring across at someone else's backyard."

"Well, we can't all live beachfront." I poked him playfully in the side. "The beggars can't be choosy."

Tim dismissed the dig with a careful sweep of his freshly highlighted hair. "I work for that view every night. Don't you forget it."

"Please." I held up a hand. "I really, really don't want the details."

Tim picked his champagne back up and winked at me. When I'd first met him, I'd assumed that the Porsche Carrera and Patek Philippe watch were family money. And they were, but not his. He was three years into a relationship with Fredrick Mount, III. To an outsider, he was a boy toy of the handsome and older shipping heir. But I'd spent enough time around them to realize they had a deep friendship and were truly in love, despite the thirty-year age gap. And Fred took Tim's real estate career seriously, supporting him both financially and emotionally as Tim worked his bubble butt off to grow his business.

It had been a slow growth, like mine. We were both desperately clawing for a piece of the market and an ounce of respect. And we were both fighting stereotypes. Me, that any of my eventual success (oh, please let it happen!) would be attributed to my looks. Him, from business fed by (or bought by) his sugar daddy.

We didn't care. We wanted this career. My motivations were almost strictly financial, his deep-seated in earning his father's respect. I looked around the room. We weren't special. There were hungry eyes everywhere, all with different stimuli behind them.

He tapped at the front of the flyer, where they'd hidden the price in 14-point font. "Look at this. Three million is way too high. At that price point, I'd be on the ocean or on OLT. And speaking of which…" He glanced around furtively, then pulled at my elbow, drawing me away from the crowd. "I need to talk to you about something."

Our options for privacy were limited in the crowded home. By the time he'd led me through the sunroom and out onto the side deck, my curiosity had swelled. Closing the screen door behind us, he moved to the railing. "I have a lead for us."

For *us*? I straightened in my coral wedge heels. I'd never worked a listing with Tim before, but his leads came straight from Fred's Rolodex, which was literally dipped in solid gold.

"It's an Olive Line Trail listing. They haven't started interviewing brokers yet—aren't even sure they want to list it yet. I already prepared a CMA, but this client..." He huffed out a breath. "Let's just say my chiseled looks are wasted on him. While you..." He gestured down the length of my body, then shrugged, as if everything was clear.

"He likes women," I clarified.

"According to Fred, he *loves* women. But he knew him back when he was single. He's married now. Still... I want to put my best foot forward. And that foot looks better in four-inch stilettos versus Ferragamos. Got me?"

I gave a slow nod, processing the information. Olive Line Trail homes were a rarity. They were never available, and most had been squatted on by wealthy Miami families for the last three decades. It'd be a quick sale, one with multiple offers and a six-figure listing commission. He'd been wise to take our conversation outside. If any of the realtors knew of the potential, we'd be clawing through them just to reach the ivy-lined gate.

"What did the CMA come in at?"

"Three-point six million. But there hasn't been an OLT sale in three years, so that's using other comps in the area. You know what that street name is worth. I think it'll fetch closer to four."

Yep. If Olive Line Trail was a zip code, it was in the 90210 prestige range. I studied his perfectly enhanced features and tried to understand what he was offering me. A co-listing seemed like too much, given that all he needed was a pretty face to accompany his market analysis. "Okay... so you want me to go with you on the listing presentation?"

"No, I want you to handle the listing. Start to finish. Make the introductory call, secure the listing, and maintain it."

I frowned. "You don't want to co-list it?" That didn't make any sense. Not when our future at Blanton & Rutledge lived and died with our sales stats. Our positions on the board determined everything from our parking spaces (or lack of) to our up rotation. He needed a four-million-dollar bump as badly as I did.

"I want to refer it to you." He pitched back the glass of champagne and then placed it on the deck railing. "For a seventy percent referral fee."

The halo floating above his head dimmed by half. A seventy percent referral fee was unheard of. Twenty-five percent was standard. Then again, no agent in their right mind would refer a listing on OLT. Not that we even had the listing. Right now, all we had was a lead. A lead that we believed to be secret, but who knew. Maybe this seller was blabbing his intentions all over town. Maybe we were one of a dozen realtors with a market analysis in hand, already mentally depositing their commission checks.

A four million dollar sale at a three percent listing commission. $120,000. I struggled to do the math on my cut of that. Giving seventy percent to Tim would cut it down to thirty-five thousand dollars, give or take. Our brokerage would take another thirty percent, but I'd still get at least twenty thousand dollars. Twenty thousand dollars in our bank account and a four million dollar jump in my sales tally for the year.

I couldn't turn it down. I also didn't understand why Tim was giving it to me. We could have co-listed it with a 70/30 split and he could have still gotten the sales stat bump. I verbalized the observation and he gave a short but firm shake of the head. "It's yours. Honestly. I don't need my name on it."

"Why?"

He wrapped an arm around my shoulders. "Love, it's an Olive Line listing. Stop overthinking this and say 'thank you Tim, I love you dearly'."

I looked up at him and smiled. "Thank you, Tim. I love you dearly *if* we get the listing."

"If *you* get the listing," he corrected me. "Which you will. Just flash that beautiful smile and don't piss off the wife. Piece of cake."

"Will you get me the introduction from Fred?" I kept my voice low as he herded us inside, his thin arm still tight around my shoulders. He smelled like peaches and ocean, an odd but delicious combination.

"Fred already gave them your number. He said they'll call you this week."

I stopped just inside the door, the voices of the crowd magnified by the vaulted ceiling and concrete floor. "How did you know I'd say yes?"

"Because you're like me," he said, not unkindly. "Frantic and desperate."

6

"Frantic and *desperate*." I tore a piece of paper towel off the roll and laid it out on the counter. "That's what he called me. And he said it nicely, as if he wasn't insulting me to my face."

"Truthfully, we are a little desperate." Easton crouched beside the fridge, pulling Coke cans out of the case and adding them to the door. "And I don't know if frantic is the right word, but it's not too far off."

"When's your next call with Nicole?" I pulled a stack of graham crackers out of the box and broke each one in half, laying the squares out on the paper towel.

"Monday. And it's getting to the point where I need to be a dick."

"I don't get it. She's got the money, right? This isn't a case of her being broke and not wanting to tell you?"

"Her agent confirmed that they closed the Nike endorsement deal. That was seventy million, with fifteen at signing. Even if she was destitute before, she'd have that."

"Good point." I stuffed a marshmallow in my mouth, then put another on top of the graham cracker.

"What do you know about the Olive Line sellers?"

I chewed for a minute, getting enough of it down to speak clearly. "He's an attorney who handled Fred's divorce a few years ago. He married another attorney, so they're probably going to be complete bitches over the listing contract."

He straightened and shut the fridge door, the empty Coke case in hand. Moving to the trash, he started to stuff it in.

"Uh-uh." I shook my head. "Break it down and put it in the blue can."

He dropped it on the floor and stepped on it, letting out a sigh of irritation. "Okay, so they're attorneys. And Tim said he likes women?"

"Yeah. Will you grab the chocolate?" I bit into another marshmallow, chewing through the gooey texture as I watched him open the pantry doors and stare at the contents. "Somewhere near the top."

"Got 'em." He reached up, then tossed the package to me without turning. The two Hershey's bars arched in perfect synchronization through the air and toward me.

Cupping my hands against my chest, I caught them easily. "Nice throw."

He shrugged and shut the cabinet doors. "So... some rich attorney. Should I be worried?"

"A married rich attorney," I pointed out. Ripping open the first Hershey package with my teeth, I eyed him curiously. "But no, you shouldn't be. Are you ever?"

"Not about you." He settled against the counter and crossed his arms over his chest. "But a man doesn't marry a woman like you without being aware of the situation."

"What situation?" I bent off a piece of the chocolate and watched as he crossed the kitchen toward me.

"The situation where every man who meets you wants to fuck you."

I tried hard not to smile, but I warmed to the compliment like a panhandler to rush-hour traffic. "You know that's not true."

He stopped before me and pulled at the white tie of my drawstring pajama bottoms, then hooked his fingers in the sides of them. "It is. Every single man."

He crouched, dragging the pants down, my panties coming along for the ride as he slid them to my ankles.

"E…" I resisted his attempts to spread my feet.

"I need this." He tilted his face up, his eyes meeting mine in the brief moment before his mouth settled between my legs, his chin working them open, his light beard tickling my thighs. "Sit on the counter."

The chocolate hit the floor somewhere near his feet as he gripped my waist and lifted, setting me on the cool granite. I parted my knees, my ankles held together by my pants. I was relatively smooth from my preparation for Aaron, still bare to his eyes, and he let out a low groan of appreciation. "I love you like this." He pushed his fingers inside me and I gripped the edge of the counter tightly, letting out a soft moan as the tips of his fingers gently teased over my G-spot. "I want you to prepare for me like you prepared for him."

I wanted to argue, to say that I hadn't done it all for Aaron, but I had. I had waxed and shaved and done extra Kegels and gotten a mani and pedicure… all in preparation for Aaron. When was the last time I'd done that for E? When was the last time he'd seen me so well groomed?

"I want you to beg for me like you begged for him."

"I wasn't begging for him." I bit back another moan as his fingers quickened inside of me. Leaning back, my shoulders hit the cabinet and I tensed to stay in place. "I was begging for both of you."

His knees hit the kitchen floor and my pants were pulled off. He pushed my legs farther apart, his fingers wet against my thigh, and his warm mouth settled on me. I dug my hands into his hair, grinding against his mouth. He was greedy and unrelenting, fucking me with his tongue, journeying down to my taint, then back up through my folds, his touch softening as he circled my clit and then hummed over it. My hand fell slack on his head, my hips freezing in place as he focused in on the sensitive bud.

"Yes," I gasped. "Yes. Oh God, yes."

"The front curtains," he grunted. "Are they open?"

I turned my head, focusing on the formal living room to our right. Through the arched opening, I could see the plaid couch I'd rescued from my mom's garage sale and a few random pieces we'd kept from our college apartments. Behind the plaid couch were the dark blue front curtains—a leftover from the prior owners. The panels were wide open, pushed as far to the left and right as their gold rod would allow.

We never left them open at night. When they were, the interior was on full display to anyone who drove past. I always felt ashamed of the mishmash of furniture and the dated kitchen just behind it. I looked out the dark window and saw the glow of lights move down the street. A car. If they looked over, if they slowed, if they focused, they'd see me. Illuminated by eighties-style fluorescent lighting, my knees open, Easton's head buried between them. I curved my hips deeper against his mouth. "Don't stop."

"Slut," he whispered. "My gorgeous, delicious fucking slut."

I pulsed my mound against the words, his hands tightening on my thighs, his mouth growing rougher as he ate me out as if he was starving. My clit swelled. My thighs trembled. I knocked the bag of marsh-mallows onto the floor as I struggled not to fall off the counter. Another set of headlights swept down the dark street and I pinched my eyes closed and imagined them slowing. The car would come to an abrupt stop. The man inside would stare, questioning what he was seeing.

I grabbed the bottom of my shirt and pulled it over my head. Easton went to move and I dug my heels into his back, locking him in place. "Don't stop!" I gasped out the words as I stared at our reflection in the front window, the pink cherries of my nipples catching the over-head light, the shadows accentuating my curves. Was there someone out there in the dark? Watching? Wanting? I gripped Easton's head, burying it tighter between my legs.

A knocking sounded against the lower cabinet and I looked down, trying to place it, then realized what it was. Easton, his hand furiously jacking his cock, his elbow rattling against the edge of the cabinet. He lifted his head, and I tightened my legs to prevent the motion. "Don't stop—"

"Move to the couch," he gritted, pushing to his feet. "Put your knees on the cushion, palms on the window."

I pushed off the counter without complaint, my feet slapping against the tile, then silent on the carpet. I crawled onto the couch and it creaked in protest as my knees sunk into the faded plaid cushion. I gripped the back of it and stared out the window. There were no lights on in the living room, but still, we'd be outlines, framed by the kitchen's illumination. I heard the rustle of fabric, then felt the insis-tent press of his dick.

"Hands on the window," he ordered gruffly.

It was a good thing Aaron had moved out. Our house was back to being ours, every surface a potential fuck zone. Then again... I put my hands on the glass, each on a different pane, and closed my eyes, imagining Aaron in the guest room, his head lifting off his pillow, his attention caught by the sound of Easton's voice.

Not that I needed that visual. This was enough. My palms sweated against the glass as Easton thrust in and out of me in short mini strokes. I stared at our reflection, the glow from the kitchen illuminating the swing of my breasts as he pumped into me from behind. "More," I begged. "Deeper."

"Not yet." He tightened his grip on my waist, his left hand sliding around and cupping my breast, squeezing it firmly as he thrust a half-inch deeper. My need grew, ballooned, the sweet jab of his cock taking me closer, his thrusts growing quicker, and one hand slipped off the window as I started to pant.

"Beg me," he demanded.

"Please." I kept one hand on the glass, and gripped the back of the couch with the other, as it began to rattle against the window frame.

"Please what?" he bit out.

"Fuck me harder," I cried, my legs tightening, my back stiffening as I rocked against him, finding a little of the depth I needed as I took it from his cock.

"Deeper," I begged, as his hand journeyed up my chest and wrapped around my neck.

He squeezed just enough and I broke, my nipples aching, my body flexing as pleasure spiraled out from his cock in pounding, beautiful waves. I screamed out from his hand as I stiffened, keeping my body rigid as he finally buried himself inside with a dozen, fifty, a hundred deep and punishing strokes.

I needed every one and once I came down from the orgasm I bucked into each one, riding him back, my hand leaving the window so I could push against the top of the couch and fuck him harder.

I took the second orgasm, pounding my hips against his in a furious rhythm that took me where I needed to go and then pushed him over the edge. He pulled away from me and flipped me over, kneeling before me and pushing back inside, cradling my chest to his as he came, his breath hard against my mouth, our kisses stolen between gasps as he delivered a half-dozen shots of Olympic-worthy cum deep inside of me.

I don't know if anyone was outside watching, and at that moment, I didn't care. I wrapped my legs and arms around him and kissed my husband. I pulled my hips tighter against him, pulled him deeper into me, and tried not to think about the best positions for conception after sex, or the fact that my ovulation window had already passed. Maybe we *were* frantic and desperate for money, and I was hopelessly barren for children, and we had just put on a show for half of the neighborhood. It didn't matter. Together, we were fucking dynamite and I was naive and in love enough to believe *that* trumped everything else.

The wedge of chocolate was gone, as was the box of graham crackers. I hunted them down and found both in Wayland's crate, strips of the crackers' blue box in tatters around him as he feigned the sleep of the innocent. I stood above his crate and watched as he opened one eye, then snapped it shut.

"Bad!" I crouched and crawled into the crate, collecting the trash and putting it under his nose, then smacking the floor of the crate. He licked a layer of graham cracker crust off his nose in response.

Working my way back out, I hefted to my feet, my knees cracking. "Bad!" I said again, in as stern of a voice as possible.

Though, if I had to choose between a box of graham crackers or an uninterrupted sex session—Wayland had made the right choice. The last time we'd gone at it in the living room, he'd sat by the recliner and stared at us, panting loudly from his run through the yard. We'd had to move to the guest bedroom, just for privacy.

In the kitchen, Easton was rummaging through the marshmallow bag.

"So, s'mores are out." I stepped on the garbage lid release and dropped the damage in the can. "Wayland ate the crackers."

"Here." He turned, a chocolate and marshmallow stack in hand. "They're almost better without the cracker."

I popped the combination in my mouth, then chewed, nodding in half-agreement. It felt less healthy, though—when working through the ingredients—losing the carbs and sugar of the graham cracker wasn't a bad edit. Maybe. There was little to no point in trying to make a s'more less nutritionally devastating.

We stood side by side in front of the sink and ate our way through two more in silence. I thought of the pros and cons list I'd made at the open house, the page still buried in my planner. I'd intended to bring it up tonight, but under the influence of sex and sugar, I really just wanted to curl up beside him and go to bed. I washed my hands and rose on my toes, kissing him on the cheek. "I'm gonna go get ready for bed. You coming?"

"Yeah. Let me take out Wayland and clean this up. Don't fall asleep without me."

"I won't."

In the bathroom, I flossed, brushed my teeth, and removed my makeup. Studying my reflection in the mirror, I turned my head to one side, then the other, looking for the wrinkles that the women at today's open house had so joyously removed. None yet though I could see the start of crow's feet. Babies, according to my sister, would hasten the process. She didn't understand my "rush" to get pregnant.

I turned sideways and lifted up my shirt, running my hand over my flat stomach. It didn't feel like we were rushing. Five years of trying felt interminable. The thought sparked a reminder and I crouched before the sink, opening the cabinet, and reached into the back for the yellow zippered pouch that contained my fertility medicine.

I pulled out the foil package and counted off the days, thinking of my last period and ovulation window. I'd stopped taking the pills when my fantasies had bloomed out of control but now... was there any harm in starting again? It wasn't as if the fantasies had stopped. It was as if this medicine had pushed a boulder off the top of a hill. Even without the continual push, the boulder had rolled. Gained speed. Knocked over a friendship and put me flat on my back, between Aaron and E.

Flat on my back, without a baby. I popped an oval pill out of the foil and into my mouth, washing it down before I had time to think about it.

Our relationship, in a small but potentially monumental way, had changed. The fantasies I'd run from were now possibilities. The risk of the medication was worth the reward. The reward of a baby. And, if I was being honest with myself, the reward of pleasure.

I finished the rest of the water glass and flipped off the light, avoiding another look in the mirror.

7

A private messenger, clad in a sparkly purple G-string and matching cowboy hat, rang our doorbell just after ten on Saturday morning. I opened the door and flinched at the sight. Even Wayland shut his trap, both of us caught off guard by the overly tan man who straddled our front mat.

"Mrs. North?" He gave a bright white smile and I fought the urge to ask what brand of toothpaste he used.

"Yes?" I noticed an envelope in his hand, the item tied to a bouquet of black, white, and silver balloons. Even the giant Mylar penis balloons, which bobbed above the others, matched the color scheme. I watched as a giant glittery cock whipped in the wind and decided that this, whatever *this* was, was most definitely tied to Chelsea.

"You are cordially invited to the Funeral of Chelsea Pedicant's Slut-dom. She requests your immediate reply." He extended the card, which brought the mountain of balloons into my personal space. Wayland lunged up in an attempt to get one, and I blocked him with my knee.

I took the card. "Thank you." Pushing back Wayland, I began to close the door, then noticed the man waiting, his hands tucked behind his bare back as if he was a butler, patiently awaiting instructions. "Oh. Like, right *now* you want my reply?"

He nodded, and a line of abs cut across the very tan canvas of his stomach. Wayland's body slammed against me and I heard a balloon snap.

"Wayland!" Easton appeared, a half-eaten breakfast biscuit in hand and pulled on Wayland's collar. "What the fuc—" He battled past the balloons, then flinched at the sight of the purple Magic Mike double. "Hey man. What's up?"

"Good morning." The man took off his hat and bowed forward, revealing a baby bald spot that would be a problem in a few years.

"Chelsea's having a party," I explained to E, ripping open the envelope, which had been sealed with a blob of white wax stamped with Chelsea's monogram. I raised my eyebrows at the extent she was taking this.

"A funeral," the messenger corrected.

Easton looked over my shoulder at the invitation, which carried the somber look of an authentic funeral invitation. It announced that Chelsea Pedicant's Slutdom had died, and a Celebration of Life was being held on Friday night at nine o'clock. Friday... six days away. A tight turnaround for a party, given the magnitude of a typical Chelsea Pedicant event.

"Her slutdom has died?" Easton muttered. "What does that even mean? Did you know about this?"

I shook my head. Knowing Chelsea, she probably came up with the idea over yesterday's breakfast, called her father's marketing team together for lunch, and spent last night getting the invites and stripper delivery squad set up. I glanced past the sequin cowboy and toward his Ford Focus, which was stuffed with more balloons. "How many of these are you delivering?"

"I've got six more. There are about a dozen of us out on delivery." He started to glance down at his wrist, then stopped when he realized he wasn't wearing a watch. "Do you have a response?"

"Oh, we're coming," Easton replied, tearing off a piece of the biscuit and catching Wayland's attention with it. "Come on, bud. Let's go outside."

The man cocked a pierced eyebrow at me, and I nodded.

"Yeah, we'll be there."

He smiled and spun on one white flip-flop, then sauntered along our sidewalk and toward his car. From across the street, Mrs. Vandecamp halted, her white poodle similarly entranced, and stared at the man, who tipped his purple cowboy hat in greeting.

I closed the door with a groan. If our window antics from the night before hadn't already ruined our reputation with the neighbors, this certainly wouldn't help.

I turned toward the kitchen and ran straight into a cluster of inflated penises. Battling through the pile, I found the invitation and ripped it free of the balloon bouquet.

"Well, life is never boring," Easton said wryly, retaking his place at the counter. Hunched over his plate, he took a bite out of the ham and cheese.

"No," I agreed, taking the stool next to him. "It's not." I flipped over the invitation, reading the neatly printed and gold-embossed details. "It says dress code is funeral-appropriate. What the hell is that?"

"Let me call Aaron and see if he knows anything about this." Easton reached for his cell phone and I followed suit, dialing Chelsea's number and listening to it ring. It continued for a half dozen times before her voicemail came on. I hung up and watched as E did the same. "No answer?"

"Nope. Voicemail. It's what—Saturday morning? He's probably at the gym."

"She's probably riding one of the cowboy delivery team," I said, only half in jest. "Who the hell could she be inviting to this thing?"

E didn't respond, his attention back on his food, and I picked up my keto-friendly wrap and took a bite. "I can't believe she didn't tell me about this." The words came out muffled, and I forced myself to chew slowly and completely before I choked. Chelsea didn't have an interesting bowel movement without calling to tell me. Why would she put all this together and keep me out of the loop? Where were the nonstop text messages, wanting opinions on calligraphy font and entertainment? Where was the constant phone calls to discuss the guest list and theme?

"She's a showman. Wants the biggest impact."

A valid idea, and one that didn't calm my irritation at being treated like any other guest. I was her best friend. I was supposed to know things first, be involved in the planning. Enjoy the headaches and excitement that were part of monumental acts.

Though, I *had* just had the most monumental act of my life, save my wedding, and she hadn't been a part of that.

Not that she should have been a part. Still, I felt a little as if I was lying to her by omission. And that guilt was misplaced and unjustified if she was planning a full-out Chelsea Pedicant party without my involvement. I called her again, my hackles rising, but only got voicemail.

I ended the call and ripped off another bite. *What the hell was happening?*

8

Monday came before I was ready for it, and I squandered the first hour of it following royal drama on social media. There was a *lot* of drama, most centered on Meghan Markle, who had managed to piss off an entire army of followers over merching, a Wimbledon box, and something having to do with godparents. It was both disturbing and fascinating, and at ten I closed the browser, conflicted with emotions on the newest royal.

Reluctantly, I picked up the folder Tim had given me with the De Luca's information. Flipping open the top page, I studied the home's scant MLS history. It'd only been on the market once before, back in 2000, when it sold to Brad De Luca for two point four million dollars. I flipped through the listing photos from that time, which I studied without too much enthusiasm. In twenty years, he could have done anything to the house. Still, the bones of it looked good. Airy and open. Some nice architectural features and a huge yard. A rentable guest apartment overlooking the pool, though no one on OLT would rent. Assuming it wasn't a train wreck of decor, Tim's projection of a four-million-dollar sales price had been about right. Maybe even a little low.

I reviewed the rest of the pages, noting that a quitclaim deed several years ago had added Julia De Luca as an owner. They were up to date on their taxes and had filed five permits over the last two decades on various renovation projects, so it couldn't be in too rough of shape. Setting the folder on the desk, I picked up my energy bar and took a bite, crunching through a chocolate and almond bar that contained no sugar, no carbs, and no fillers. I gagged a little on the swallow and washed down the bite with a sip of coffee. Opening a fresh Internet browser, I did a quick search on Brad De Luca.

The attorney had been a very high profile and busy boy. I clicked on a photo result and hummed in appreciation. Okay... not a boy. All man. He'd probably gone through puberty while most boys his age were getting fitted for braces. In his photo, he glowered at the camera with a handsome face that would fit in well between my thighs. I flipped through the photos, surprised to see an image of him and a brunette on a yacht with Hollywood It couple Cole Masten and Summer Jenkins. Zooming in on the brunette that was cozied up to Brad's side, I studied her wide smile, the photo catching her mid-laugh.

This was supposed to be us.

The thought snuck up on me, stabbing me in the sensitive place in my stomach where money worries and insecurities liked to lurk. I closed the photo preview before I caught a glimpse of the jet skis on the roof of the yacht, or the uniformed butler, hovering in the wings.

We'd had that lifestyle in our grasp. Famous friends. Invites to yacht parties and private jets. Weekends spent without a care in the world, our meals prepared by a private chef, our afternoons punctuated with massages and wine tours.

We'd had it and—in the split second it takes for a baseball to connect with a temple—lost it.

I scrolled through the website search results, spotting De Luca office locations in the Bahamas and Miami, as well as a few dozen press mentions pairing him with famous names. He seemed to specialize in divorce, and I remembered Tim's mention that he'd handled Fred's.

I opened a second tab and searched for Julia De Luca, coming up with a short list of results. I frowned, surprised. There were no photo results, and other than the state verification page of her law license and a few charity donation lists, there were no other results. Intrigued, I checked social media. Nothing. I did a marriage license search and pulled her maiden name from the results, then tried again. *Huh*. I leaned back in my chair and picked at the remaining chunk of my chocolate bar. Julia De Luca had to be the only wife in Miami with no social media footprint whatsoever. I picked up the phone and tried the next best thing to Google—a text to Chelsea.

I have a big listing lead for a Brad and Julia De Luca — local attorneys. Do you know anything about them?

While she had ignored my texts wanting details on the funeral invite, she responded to this one immediately. *No but let me dig.*

I dropped the wrapper in the trash can underneath my desk and returned my attention to my computer, closing out the windows before I wasted more time on the search. If there was any helpful information, Chelsea would dig it up. She had the nose of an investigative journalist, which was one of the reasons Easton and I couldn't risk anything else with Aaron. We were lucky to have gotten away with it once, though the jury was still out on whether we had. If we all managed to keep the secret for a month, I'd breathe a hell of a lot easier.

Twenty minutes later I was crouched in front of the copy machine, cursing it to hell, when my phone buzzed against the floor. Scooping it up, I swept my hair out of my face. "Hey Chelsea."

"Okay, I have good news and I have bad news."

I wrenched open the top drawer and verified, for the third time, that there was no paper jam in the tray.

"Which do you want first?"

"I don't care."

"Oh-kay." She huffed in annoyance. "The good news is that Kendra's brother Jake knows a guy at Verizon who has four tickets to Burning Man."

"And that's good news?"

"Elle, don't be like that. It's *great* news."

"We can't afford—"

"It's BURNING MAN. There is literally nothing to pay for. They don't allow money. Remember? We talked about this. It's a gift thing. Like, you're supposed to happily give people stuff."

"So, I'm accepting food from strangers? That sounds like everything my mother always taught me not to do."

"I'm not going to try to explain the dichotomy of the Burning Man economy. It works, Elle. And we'd bring something to offer. I'm not talking about freeloading off strangers for a week."

"Yeah, not interested."

"I'll talk to E about it. Anyway, the bad news is about your listing people. How much do you want this lead?"

I straightened, the jammed copy issue forgotten. "Badly. Why?"

"Well… it's the guy. Brad De Luca."

I thought of Tim's reference of the attorney. What had he said? That Tim's looks were wasted on him but that mine would work? Something like that. "Tim said he likes women."

Chelsea didn't settle on that comment. "It's not exactly him, but his family. Apparently, he's the heir apparent of the Magiano family. We're talking oldest son. Birth name Brad Magiano, Junior—but he changed it to his mother's maiden name."

The hair on the back of my arms stood up. I didn't need to research that name. I knew the Magiano family. Everyone in Miami did. They were the most powerful crime syndicate in South Florida. Mobsters, the sort that drove Rolls Royces and had abandoned drug dealing and prostitution for white-collar crime but still had a forceful finger in every successful industry south of Orlando. A forceful and deadly finger.

Suddenly, the yacht didn't seem so tempting.

Suddenly, Julia De Luca's lack of Internet footprint made perfect sense.

Suddenly, I understood why Tim had been so generous with the lead. *Dick.*

"So, there is a silver lining. Apparently, Brad De Luca is estranged from the family. Spends most of his time in the Bahamas."

"Estranged," I repeated dully as I struggled to keep my breathing and heartbeat level. Closing the side door, I jabbed my finger on the screen, clearing the warning messages and glaring at the new instruction that appeared. CHECK DRAWER 1. "I've checked drawer one," I said loudly.

"Is it the copier? Try unplugging it and plugging it back in. So, yeah. Estranged is good." She sounded cheerful, as if we were discussing a Days of Our Lives plot point and not a new listing that could get me killed. I wasn't sure an estranged member of the Magiano family was any better than a normal member. In fact, it sounded worse. Like, way worse.

I pulled out the power plug and took a deep breath, forcing myself to count to five before I plugged it back in.

"I can talk to my dad tonight," she offered. "I know he's dealt with the Magianos before, when we had permitting issues at the civic center. Maybe he knows something that could help."

"Okay. Thanks." I watched as the machine hummed to life.

"Can you decline the listing? I know he's estranged, but just in case…" her voice trailed off.

"I don't know. I'm going to go and talk to the guy who referred them to me. I think he already set up the appointment." I worked my fingers over my temple and watched as the welcome screen faded, replaced with the all caps notification that the copier was jammed.

"Okay, let me know how it goes."

I ended the call and stared at the blinking copier screen, fighting the urge to slam the phone into the display. Opening the top feed, I pulled out my flyer and tossed it into the trash, abandoning the task.

I needed to find Tim and wring his perfect little tan neck. Then, I had to beat the lunch traffic and head to E's office. I had keys to pick up at the Keller-Williams franchise by his building, and I could use his advice, prior to that errand, on how to handle this new bomb of information.

9

I wandered through the hallways of the wealth management firm and eased into Easton's office, immediately recognizing the sharp accent of Nicole Fagnani. E nodded at me and picked up the receiver, cutting her off speakerphone. I glanced at my watch, irritated at myself for forgetting his call was today. A good wife would have sent him a good luck text, something that would push him to pull up his big boy pants and put down his foot with her. Nicole had jerked his chain around long enough. She needed to make a deposit, and we needed the resulting commission check. Badly.

"Uh-huh." He spun a pen on the desk.

I settled into the chair across from him and pulled out my phone, opening an incoming text from Chelsea.

Two things—when's your big listing appointment?

-- On Friday.

Not enough time to emotionally prepare, but four days was better than nothing.

E's cool with you doing it? Despite the Magiano connection?

I glanced at my husband. I could predictably anticipate his response. A flat denial that I take the listing, one that would waver in strength when I pointed out our dire financial situation. I really didn't want to point that out, or see the tight shift of Easton's features, or feel the weight of his guilt over putting me in what he would see as a dangerous position.

-- I haven't told him yet. At his office now. Maybe I'll just wait until I meet and feel them out for myself.

You know that's not the right move.

For a woman with such a fluid stance on personal morality, she was horrifically accurate on calling me on my shit. I changed the subject. *What was the second thing?*

Oh, my funeral. You need a veil or anything? I got extras.

Of course she did. I swallowed my dozens of unanswered questions about the party and shot back a quick reply. *No, I'm good. Thx*

I locked my phone and returned my attention to E's conversation, picking up bits and pieces of her voice as he spun to face me. I heard the words *video game* and stood, approaching the glass window that separated him from the reception area.

"It's definitely worth a meeting." Easton watched as I adjusted the row of vertical blinds, cutting off his view.

"Next Thursday?" He unlocked his computer screen, then pulled up his calendar. I moved closer and watched his mouse scroll down through dates. He had it wide open.

He hesitated and I wondered what he was debating over. Pushing away from the desk, he leaned back in his chair, his face hardening in determination.

"Nicole, let's be brutally honest with each other for a moment."

My ears perked at the same time that my chest constricted in fear.

"I have to follow the money. At the moment, you're not technically a client of mine. I have to focus my attention on growing the assets of my clients, not chasing possibilities on a California beach. If you're ready to make a commitment to me, then I'll adjust my schedule and invest my time in evaluating this investment. But I can't do that without a serious seven-figure commitment from you."

He paused and I struggled to keep my place at the edge of his desk. On the other end of the phone, all chatter from Nicole had stalled. Easton continued on. "And if you can't make that investment at this time, then I think we should step back from any further communication and let you find an advisor that you trust."

Oh, sweet baby Neptune. I was suddenly on my knees, crawling the few feet toward him, my hands sweeping up his thighs as I headed for his belt. He was risking everything. Potentially scaring away the only real lead he was working. But fuck, it was hot. Hearing the authoritative bite in his tone? Listening to the breezy confidence that didn't hint at our financial troubles?

It was the first moment I had seen him really fit into his shoes in this office—in this new career as Easton North, Wealth Manager. He was a long way from the dugout and I worked his belt open and gave him a proud smile.

He didn't stop me. He watched, his eyes darkening, and we both held our breath as the silence on Nicole's end of the phone lengthened. Fuck me, we needed this. I jerked open his zipper and slid my hand inside. He was soft, the cocoon of his underwear warm, and I rubbed my fingers along his flaccid shaft, waking it up as I massaged his balls from outside his pants.

A single word came from the phone and I tried to decipher it. Easton's expression didn't change, his gaze tight on mine and I stayed quiet. She said something else, the words *transfer* and *million* audible from my spot on the floor, and Easton dropped back his head in relief.

I smiled as his cock stiffened. Had it been my hands or her words? It didn't matter. I freed it and inched forward, tilting it toward me and closing my lips around its head.

"I'll send you the wire instructions now and book a flight once the deposit clears. We can discuss in LA where that initial million should go, but some of the more lucrative opportunities will require a bigger investment than that." The closing line was straight out of his sales scripts, ones we had practiced around the dining room table, a box of pizza between us, and I mentally urged him on as I worked my mouth on and off the tip of his cock, my cheeks suctioning from the effort as my hand stroked his shaft in a matching rhythm.

"I'll send it now." His voice cracked and he wheezed out a breath, the next sentence more labored as he fought the pleasure. "Forward me the materials they sent you on the game and I'll have our attorney take an—an initial look at what they're offering."

The floor was uncomfortable and I readjusted my stance, dropping my butt to my heels to alleviate some of the pressure off my knees. *We can discuss in LA?* Is that what he had said? I'd been so happy over the prospect of income that I'd blocked everything else out.

"Easy," he whispered, his hand covering the phone. "That's going to —" He cursed, his thighs tightening and his feet braced against the floor as his hand bit into my shoulder.

My hand tightened on him as I continued, knowing what he liked and using every trick I knew. Consistent downward jerks against the bottom of his shaft. Heavy suction from my mouth. An occasional bob of my head where I took him all the way, as best I could, into my mouth.

From the next office over, a phone rang and the muffled sound of a male voice carried. Arousal hummed through my body as I focused in on the sounds. A conversation out in the hall. Another phone ringing. Was his door locked? I hadn't thought to flip the latch on my way in.

"A million sounds good. I'll look for it this—this afternoon."

With his one percent management fee it wouldn't be a lot but it was badly needed and would lead to more.

"Goodbye." He almost gasped out the word as he leaned forward and placed the phone in the cradle. The change in position brought him closer to me and he stayed in place, sweeping my hair off my shoulders and back into a makeshift ponytail.

"You're so bad for me," he murmured. "Sucking my cock in the middle of my call. What else would you do? Would you sit back on my desk and show me your pussy? Fuck yourself with your fingers as I checked my email?"

I pulled my mouth off of him, my hand taking up the slack as I stroked his rigid shaft and looked up into his face. "I'd do anything you told me to do." I rose up on my knees, my cleavage close enough that if he came right now, it'd splatter across my breasts.

He groaned, his eyes heavy with arousal. "What if I had an important client? Would you bend over my desk and let him lift up your skirt? Would you let him taste you?" His hand took over the work, relieving the strain on my triceps as he jerked his cock faster, the movements becoming rougher and rougher as he strained beneath me. "Put your mouth back on it," he gritted out. "I'm about to—"

I closed my mouth on his head just before he came, sucking it hard as he trembled, tensed, then broke, his hand gripping the back of my head and pulling it tighter and deeper down on him as he filled my mouth—right in the middle of the loud and busy office floor.

10

As if to laugh at our minor success, eight hours later, we were struggling with crap. Crap that wasn't going away, no matter how many times I held down the handle.

"So *this* is the one we need?" I stared down at the round container that didn't seem nearly big enough. It was also $24, which was alarmingly cheap.

"Maybe?" Easton glanced at the employee to our right, who folded his arms over his orange-aproned chest with a bored sigh. "Is this what we need?"

"As I TOLD you"—he gave us both a warning look—"it depends on the size of the blockage. We got the lightweight, auto-feeding drain cleaner like the Rigid K-30, but if it's a root blockage then you'll need something more powerful, like the Cobra." He nodded toward the shelf and I searched for anything on it that resembled his words.

"The Cobra includes a manual thermal overload protector switch," he added, pointing at a box the size of a refrigerator, with a price tag of over sixteen hundred dollars. I shot him a look, unsure what about the two of us indicated that we had the breadth of plumbing knowledge to even get it out of the box. I pivoted away from the expensive behemoth and referred back to the one in Easton's hand.

"And what's the difference between this and this?" I pointed to an identical-looking snake that was three times as much.

"Well, that's got the bulb augers, C and spade cutters." He scratched at a dark bloody scab on the side of his arm and I think God sent him down just to kill off any lingering handyman fantasies I had left.

"We literally have NO idea what you're talking about." Easton glanced at me for confirmation and I nodded. "We just need our toilet to flush."

"We tried Drano-O already," I added helpfully.

He looked at me as if I was an idiot. "Drano-O's not for toilets. It contains caustic chemicals that'll crack porcelain and soften your pipes."

"Oh." I raised my eyebrows at Easton, who'd come home from Walmart with four jugs of the stuff.

"Have you considered calling a plumber? Most people like you just call someone."

People like us? This guy needed to decide if we were sixteen-hundred-dollar-pump-your-own-septic-system people or call-the-plumber people. I tucked a side piece of hair under the edge of my baseball cap and fought the urge to ask for someone else.

"All we need to know is if *this* is what we should buy." Easton held up the twenty-four-dollar plumber's snake. "Or this one." He lifted the more expensive but still manageable option in the other hand. "Do we need the bulb agers and cutters?"

"Bulb AUGERS," the man corrected, hooking his thumbs in the straps of his apron. "And I'm going to say no, unless you have someone to show you how to use them."

"Okay, thanks!" I smiled brightly and grabbed the more expensive option out of Easton's hand and thrust it back on the shelf. "Have a great night."

The man watched me warily, and if he thought I was going to pen this experience into a yelp review, he was probably right. I looped my arm through E's and pulled him down the aisle, away from the man.

"It just seems cheap," E said dubiously. "And little. Maybe we should call Aaron."

"I don't want to call Aaron and need something. That's like the start of every porno. Calling up the guy next door and asking him to come over and fix something at ten o'clock at night."

"It's our toilet," Easton pointed out, pausing beside a row of power tools, as if he was going to purchase one. "No one is going to try to seduce anyone with a toilet repair. It's the shittiest excuse in the world."

I rolled my eyes at the pun. "Stop."

"He's my best friend. He isn't going to think anything's up."

"I'd still like to have a few weeks of distance before we're begging him for favors." I picked up a baby electric screwdriver that was the size of a hot glue gun. "Look how cute this is."

"I need you to be honest with me. Have you been stuffing tampons down there?"

"Oh my God, can we *not* have this conversation in the middle of the store?" I ducked into the next aisle just in time to avoid a trio of teenage boys. Looking down at our list, I hesitated, then turned back, running into E in the process. "We need floodlights."

"So, you *have* been stuffing tampons." He blocked my exit.

"Stuffing?" I glared. "No. Gradual deposits spread out with plenty of flushing. And I'm weeks out from that sort of activity so this isn't my fault at all. This is you and your man bathroom stuff." I skirted around him and toward the lightbulb aisle.

"Meaning what?"

"You know. Girl poops are smaller than boy poops."

"That's the stupidest thing I've ever heard. This is a tampon issue."

"One that waited three weeks to pop up?" I frowned at him and pulled two boxes of floodlights off the shelf.

"Not those. Get the bright white ones." He pulled two almost identical boxes off the shelf and swapped them with mine.

"So, anyway, back to my listing prospect." I steered the conversation away from tampons and back to the topic I'd tried to broach ten minutes ago, before E had gotten distracted by a dented dishwasher that was deeply discounted to an almost unbelievable price.

"This is the duplex in Miami Shores or the big house on Fig Road?"

"The big house. Not Fig Road. Olive Line Trail." I squinted at him, unsure if he'd been making a joke or was honestly unaware of the prestigious street.

"Okay. The four-million-dollar one that the rich guy's boyfriend referred you." He headed toward the front of the store and I followed, tugging on his arm to slow him down.

"Yes. I asked Chelsea to see what she knew about the sellers and it turns out the husband of the couple is"—I glanced around to make sure no one was in earshot—"a Magiano."

"Really? Like, *the* Magianos?"

"He's apparently estranged but he's the oldest son in the family. Like top tier."

Easton paused, coming to a stop in the middle of the aisle. "How do you know he's estranged?"

"I—I don't know. That's what Chelsea said."

"But he could be involved?"

"I'm not sure if it really matters one way or the other. I'm not sure if it's any safer if he is estranged or if he's chummy with them."

"He's not *with* them, he *is* them. Why is he selling the house?"

I glanced down the aisle. A man was rounding the corner with a large cart. "I don't know. Same reason anyone sells a house?"

He shook his head. "I don't like it. And this is the one where the other realtor is screwing you on the commission, right?"

"Yes. But it'd still be twenty thousand dollars. And a quick sale."

He sighed, scratching the back of his neck as he stared at the ground. "I don't know, Elle. I'll get Nicole's commission this week. That'll tide us through for a little bit. I think you should walk from it."

I couldn't walk away. I couldn't stomach the idea of watching our bank account spiral down when this commission could help to pad our accounts. I could make six mortgage payments with that commission. And maybe, possibly, the De Lucas would buy something else. Roll that money into a different property and use me as their buyer's agent.

E's mouth tightened and my heart broke at the look in his eyes—a war of indecision and frustration at what he wasn't earning. He needed this commission as badly as I did and it was killing him that he couldn't provide it. "I'll get more from Nicole. This trip to Los Angeles—if the deal she's looking at is right, she'll bring over more funds. Don't do it, Elle. You don't know what you could be bringing into our lives."

"With a real estate listing?" I gave my best attempt at a carefree laugh. "Babe, this is nothing. And he isn't even part of the family."

"Then why isn't Tim taking it? I don't buy that bullshit excuse about De Luca liking women. Tim's scared or his boyfriend told him not to, and his boyfriend knows this guy better than any of us or Chelsea does. There's a reason Tim is pawning this off on you, and I'm not putting you in harm's way just because we're tight. Fuck the money."

But it wasn't just the money. It was a prestigious listing. It was a jump in the office ranks. It was proof to myself that I could handle a big client, a big property, one with multiple offers and the sort of address that got mentioned in the weekly deal announcement emails. I needed this and not just for the paycheck. I needed it for myself. Easton felt he was failing at providing for us financially—but I felt I was failing in my ability to give us a family. In lieu of a pregnancy, I needed this, needed *something* for me to be proud of.

He saw it in my eyes and he shook his head, telling me no. I wrapped my arms around his side and rested my head against his chest, ignoring the poke of the lightbulbs against my chest. "It'll be okay," I whispered. "I promise."

That night, at eleven p.m. and ankle-deep in dirty sewage, we called a plumber.

11

If I hadn't known to look for them, I might have missed the signs. The cameras, discreetly hidden in the trees of the driveway. The alarm punch pad that Julia De Luca operated with quick efficiency. The window sensors and motion detectors and twelve-foot wall that surrounded the entire lot. The Olive Line Trail house was a fortress with Julia De Luca as its commander.

She was, by all accounts, a very friendly commander. Also, pushy. Which was why I was eating pancakes ten minutes into our listing appointment.

"Milk or orange juice?" She called out the question from her spot at the fridge, and I noted it was a double door Sub-Zero. I resisted the urge to pull out my notepad and add it to the listing description.

"Ummm... milk please." I looked down at my plate, where a black spotted pancake stared out at me from blue china. *Lots of milk.*

"I'm still mastering the pancake," she announced, pushing the door closed with her butt as she carried a gallon of milk toward me. "Martha's refusing to teach me out of spite."

"You shouldn't be cooking. It ain't natural." The comment came from a woman who sat at the other end of the kitchen table and glared at Julia as if she was sharing enemy secrets. "Some people got the gift. You don't."

"It's true," Julia said cheerfully, pouring me a full glass of milk and pushing it across the counter. "I'm horrific."

"I wouldn't eat that pancake," the woman warned, pointing an unpainted fingernail in my direction. "It's gonna be nasty."

"This, by the way, is Martha. She runs the house but was, apparently, too busy to make breakfast."

"I don't cook on Fridays," Martha said, flipping the Miami Herald before her closed. "You know that so don't pretend you don't. If you're intent on impressing houseguests, you should have put it on some other day and made me put on my uniform and manners."

"She doesn't have a uniform." Julia made a face at the woman, who shuffled toward her and tossed the paper on the counter. "Manners… eh." I watched with cautious interest as the house manager elbowed past her and peered down into the pan, then sniffed in disapproval.

"What?" Julia protested. "Too much oil? Too little?"

Martha waved a dismissive hand in her direction and left the kitchen, heading down a hall and disappearing from view. Julia turned back to me with a sigh. "You don't have to eat them."

"I'm sure they're delicious." I studied the lineup of syrups before me. "Does it matter which one I try first?"

Syrups were the reason I was perched on this stool, fork in hand. This model-thin brunette—who was definitely the girl from the yacht photo —was considering buying into a syrup company and wanted an honest opinion of the product compared to its competitors. I didn't have the heart or guts to tell her that I was keto.

"Doesn't matter." She turned back to the stove and fiddled with a knob. I spread a generous amount of butter across the over-thick, over-cooked pancake and studied her from behind.

She was beautiful. Thin and feminine, with long dark hair and a face that managed to be both mischievous and sensual, all at the same time. Easton would have been all about her, had he met her before me. I was struck with the thought that maybe he had. She had to be close to our age. "Why a syrup company?"

"It's a close friend of mine from college who's starting it. She's looking for start-up capital and I like pancakes." She shrugged. "Seemed like an easy side investment, assuming the product passes my *rigorous* taste tests."

I smiled at her self-deprecating tone. "Where'd you go to school?"

Julia glanced over as she lifted a ladle dripping with batter. "UM for undergrad. FIU for law school. What about you?"

I tried not to visibly sigh in relief that she wasn't a potential Easton ex. Not that his sea of hookups could be considered exes. "FSU." I forcibly sectioned off a piece and dipped it into a glob of Syrup #1. "Did you meet your husband at school?"

She grinned as she poured out three pancakes in a pan that was really only big enough for two. "Brad's a dinosaur. I met him at the law firm I interned at. He was the old guy with the wandering hands."

"Still am." A man six foot something in a suit and with a smile that could disarm a nun walked in and wrapped an arm around her. It caught me so off guard that I missed my mouth. As I managed the first bite, he pulled her tight to his chest and kissed her on the mouth, then turned to me, one brow lifting as he took in the scene.

And that was how I first encountered Brad De Luca. Butter on my cheek, a sticky fork in hand, my mouth full of pancakes.

"Brad De Luca." He extended a hand and I struggled to get off the stool, a wedge of dry yet sticky food stuck somewhere in my gullet.

I swallowed hard. "Elle North, with Blanton & Rutledge Realty." I wiped my hands on a crumpled paper towel and shook his hand, which swallowed mine whole.

The online photo I'd swooned over hadn't done him justice. It hadn't captured the power of his stare or the wave of charisma and masculinity that radiated from him. I tore my gaze away from him and somehow made it back to my chair without whimpering.

Whimpering. Why in all holy hells would I be fighting the urge to *whimper*?

"She's testing the syrups," Julia explained, wiping the back of one wrist across her forehead, a spatula still in hand.

Brad glanced toward the stove. "Oh, no. You cooked these?"

I shifted on the stool and wondered when the house tour would begin. Should I be instigating that? They seemed to have no concept that I was here to list their property.

"Here. Taste." Julia broke off a piece of her latest creation and I winced at the audible snap that the action made. Pancakes had never, in my experience, snapped. She held a piece toward his mouth and he stepped closer, his jaw flexing open as he took it from her. It was an intimate moment and I looked down and sawed off another wedge.

"Wow." He chewed slowly and rigorously. "That's terrible."

The laugh burst out of me, along with a few bits of pancake. I clamped my hand over my mouth in an attempt to contain the damage and saw Julia smack his shirt with a flour-covered hand.

"Don't be mean. It's not terrible!"

"Babe." He glanced around the massive kitchen, which she had somehow managed to cover in flour, syrup samples, and batter. "How many of them have you tried? And where's Martha?"

"I've tried some," she defended. "And you go talk to Martha if you want her to cook. It's Friday."

"Ah, right." He moved past her and I watched as his hand trailed over her ass with easy ownership. Opening the fridge, he pulled out a bottle of water, then turned to me. "So, you're the one who's selling this beast?"

I wiped my mouth and nodded in my most professional manner. "Yes, sir. It's a prime location. Should sell quickly." Quite possibly the most idiotic three sentences anyone had voiced so far today.

"Privacy is a concern for us." He twisted off the bottle's cap and glanced in his wife's direction. "And security. I'd like to limit and control the number of people who have access to the house."

Over breakfast, Easton and I had discussed whether or not I should acknowledge or bring up his family. We had decided against it, and I struggled to keep my features bland and unsuspecting. "It's customary with a house this size for me to be present at any showings, but I'm happy to do anything that makes you feel more comfortable. Was there anything specific you have in mind?"

"Why don't we give her a tour?" Julia suggested, moving to the prep sink and washing her hands. "Then she'll see the control room." She looked at me for agreement and I nodded, as if I knew what a control room was.

"But first," she gestured to my plate. "Eat up."

"Oh yes," Brad intoned. "And if any of those syrups make those pancakes even remotely edible, I'll write a blank check right now because that's bottled magic."

She flung a pancake toward him and he swung the water bottle at the incoming missile. The two connected, and there was a sharp crack as the stiff cake hit the front of a cabinet.

"Go ahead," Julia urged, flashing a breezy smile in my direction. "Try the bacon-flavored one next."

The house was gorgeous. Everything I could have ever wanted in a listing. Vaulted ceilings. Lots of light. Updated bathrooms. A spacious and flowing floor plan. And... a few extras I didn't expect. Deadbolts on bedroom doors. Wired sensors in every window. A panic room with a cluster of monitors that showcased every square inch of the property. I stood at the entrance to the tight space and stared at its interior. There was a wall of guns and ammunition. Three different phones. Nine video screens attached to a laptop. A first-aid kit the size of a mini-fridge.

"We'd like this room's existence to be kept confidential."

"So, you don't want this shown during a property tour? What about in the listing photos?" I consulted my notepad as if it contained instructions on navigating this minefield.

"Just pretend it doesn't exist. We can show it to the buyers after closing." Julia ran a hand over the wall and the light in the panic room dimmed.

"Umm...that might need to be put on the seller's disclosure." I tried to think through the legality of hiding part of the house and then springing it on a new buyer after the close. It sounded illegal, though it wasn't exactly a negative to the property.

"I'll add an amendment to the contract that allows for the home's security features to be kept confidential until after all contingencies are removed." He glanced at his wife. "That work for you?"

"Sure."

"Oh-kay." I made an illegible scribble on the next line of the page, then looked up. "Anything else on this floor?" *Torture chamber? Secret tunnel exit?*

"I don't think so." Julia glanced at Brad. "Should we go ahead and do the paperwork?"

Paperwork? I perked up as his gaze moved to mine, our eye contact holding for a moment before he nodded. "Assuming that Elle is interested in the listing. There are a few other details we need to iron out, but we can cover that in the agreement review."

"I'm interested. It's a gorgeous home and I'll make sure it is properly represented." Properly represented? I pinned my lips shut before I said anything else.

"Then, let's head to the office." Brad turned and held open the door, gesturing for us to go ahead.

I followed Julia's calm and unhurried steps, taking advantage of the journey and double-checking my folder to make sure that I had every piece of the listing agreement ready. It was a standard form, one I had filled out this morning with all their details. I'd held my breath as I'd typed in a six percent commission, hoping that they wouldn't negotiate the amount. I'd left the listing price blank, and thumbed through the left folder pocket to make sure I had the recent comps to help them decide on a number. Four million was the recommendation I would make, though I believed we could ask more. I'd play the figure by ear, depending on their reaction to the recent sales figures I would review with them.

Opening the door to Brad's office, Julia gestured to one of the chairs before his desk. "We prepared a listing agreement but have a few unique items on it to review with you."

I sat down slowly, reminding myself that they were both attorneys.

"Oh, okay. I brought a listing agreement, but I'm happy to use one you've prepared."

Brad circled to the opposite end of the desk and tossed a stack of papers toward me. "We'll give you time to review it but I'm afraid you can't take it with you."

Julia perched on the edge of the desk and gave me a reassuring smile. "We have to be careful."

Careful of what? I slid the contract closer, reassured only slightly by the LISTING AGREEMENT title across its top.

"I've included all of your broker's standard language and only added the non-legal details and instructions we need followed for our particular listing."

"What kind of instructions?" I pulled the pages closer to me.

"We'll have security present at all showings, both uniformed and plainclothes. In order to accomplish that, we need forty-eight hours advance notice." Brad settled back in his chair and smoothed his blue tie down the front of his white dress shirt. "Ideally, we'd like you to coordinate all of the showings to be in one four-hour window. Like an open house, but where every visitor has been properly vetted and approved."

"Approved by who?"

"Brad or myself." Julia spoke up. "As I stated before, security is a concern."

"And that's all in here?" I scanned the first page, then the second. They already had an asking price decided upon—$4.25 million—and a listing term of three months. I frowned at the short window, though it was peanuts compared to the fact that they wanted security at any showings. I paused. "Am *I* in *danger?*"

Brad and Julia exchanged a glance, which was not reassuring in the least. Brad leaned forward, and it was incredible how he managed to instill reassurance with just eye contact. You didn't just look into his eyes. You sank into them. I tried to pull my gaze away and failed. "Are you already aware of my family?"

My family. I tried to imagine being part of a family like that. The Miami Herald had run an exposé piece on the Magiano family last year and put their net worth at one point four billion and their annual estimated death count at twelve, though the Miami-Dade Police Department had never been able to get a Magiano conviction.

I nodded.

"And I'm assuming that the reason that Fred Mount referred us to you, instead of his boyfriend, is because of my family." Brad didn't wait for a response, which I was grateful for. "I am not responsible for my family, but I can control my environment and the things that do and don't spur them into action. If I thought that selling this house would anger them, then I would sell it myself and not involve you. It's a popular street, it should sell quickly. Our concern isn't that you will be in danger, but that someone might pose as a buyer to try and gain access to the house. Plant a listening device, or leave something incriminating. Take something of value. That's the reason for the security."

I thought of my missing iPad, and the reason I use cameras on my open houses. Was this any different? I tried to convince myself that it wasn't.

Brad met my eyes. "Trust me when I say that it's better to be safe rather than worry about impressions. Besides, it won't hurt the sales potential. People love a good story, and buying a 'mobster's' house is intriguing. This will play into that image and give them something to brag about during their housewarming party."

He had a good point. I'd be disappointed if I visited Steven Spielberg's house and didn't see any movie memorabilia. Maybe I should play up the angle. If we did a full security sweep, maybe even a pat-down for weapons... I'd been worried that the Magiano connection would scare off buyers, but maybe it would have the opposite effect.

"We understand it's more work on your part, which is why we added a listing bonus." Julia leaned forward and flipped the page, running a pale pink fingernail down the paper and stopping beside the final paragraph.

I scanned it quickly. A listing bonus of twenty-five thousand dollars. Payable directly to the primary listing agent at closing.

"I can put that in a separate addendum to the listing and purchase contract," Brad said quietly. "Something you can keep private. We'll pay you that directly, outside of the title company's and brokerage's books."

I understood exactly what they were offering. Twenty-five thousand dollars that wouldn't be taxable. Twenty-five thousand dollars that Blanton & Rutledge or Tim wouldn't get a piece of. It would have to be in a separate and very confidential addendum.

I turned the page as if it was no big deal and reviewed the next, my hands beginning to sweat. I moved one into my lap and wiped it on my pants.

"We'll leave you alone to review the rest and confirm the legalities mirror your broker's listing form. Please do not take photos of any pages or take anything with you." Brad De Luca stood and Julia followed suit, flashing me a reassuring smile before she headed for the office's double doors.

And then I was alone. Me, my sweaty palms, and twenty-two more pages to review. I pulled myself closer to the mammoth desk and forced myself to focus. It was a struggle, the excitement at the bonus competing with the realization I hadn't really earned the listing at all. It seemed they'd decided, before I even walked in the door, to list the home with me—the evidence of that right here, in the pre-completed listing agreement with my name across the top. Was it just from Fred Mount's recommendation, or had they already vetted me? And honestly, did it matter? Why was I questioning it?

I'd been hesitant to take the listing before, Easton's concerns and opinion lingering in the recesses of my mind—but the listing bonus had sealed the deal.

I could handle some risk. I had to. I needed the reward far too badly.

12

I found the funeral party invitation and studied the start time, then glanced at the clock, doing the math for traffic. Setting down the invitation, I unzipped my makeup bag and continued my recap of the listing appointment.

Beside me, Easton squirted a dollop of shaving cream into his palm and raised his brows when I got to the bonus. "That's a pleasant surprise. A twenty-five thousand dollar bonus?"

"Yep. With the commission, it'll be almost fifty grand. Plus, the deposit you just got, plus maybe more from the LA trip..." I put a fresh layer of concealer underneath my eyes. "I feel really good about everything." Finally.

"And he didn't hit on you at all?" A question that had already been asked and answered, but I let it slide.

"I told you. His wife is stunning. And they're super cute together. They even throw food at each other. Just like us." I gave him a sweet smile.

"Yeah, that's not a good thing."

"It often turns into a good thing."

"Unless it's something that I was enjoying eating. Like those—"

"AHH—I won't ever throw brownies at you again." I stuck the cap on my concealer. "I'm SORRY. It was three years ago. You've got to move on."

He spread the cream across his jaw. "I'm still not happy about this listing, Elle."

"I know, but you have to trust me. There's going to be security there and any potential buyers are going to be vetted through them first. This is the safest open house I will ever do."

He didn't say anything, but I could feel the grumble in his aura as he tapped his razor on the edge of the sink.

Leaning closer to the mirror, I swept the mascara wand over my top lashes and aimed for a subject change. "My mom called this afternoon. She's already wanting to claim us for Christmas."

He groaned. "I already told my mom we'd do dinner with her."

"So, we do both. We go to my parents' for a Christmas brunch, then make it to Tampa in time for dinner with your mom."

"Or do Christmas Eve at your parents', then we aren't in a rush to make it to my mom's."

"We did that to them last year and it hurt my mom's feelings. She is insisting she sees us *on* Christmas Day. Plus, Steph will be there with Bryant and Mark and you know how much Bryant loves you." I uncapped my lipstick and grinned at him in the mirror. My brother-in-law had a creepy one-sided bromance for Easton, which we all attempted to ignore but it was impossible to miss.

Easton made a face and switched strategies. "What if we hit Tampa first, give my mom Christmas Eve and your parents' Christmas Day?"

I rubbed my lips together and eyed him. "Sounds great."

"But then we'll need to do Thanksgiving at my mom's."

I groaned. "Have I told you lately how much I hate the holidays?"

"No, but it's early in the year." He scraped a razor over the line of his jaw and a swell of affection rose in my chest. I remember the first time I ever saw him shaving, his cheeks covered in white foam, his face close to the mirror. It had felt like such a personal glimpse at him and I remember dreaming of a day when I would be married to him and get to see that view every morning for the rest of my life.

I moved behind him and slid my arms around his chest, hugging his back. He straightened and I felt his chest muscles move as he lifted the razor and dabbed it along his neck. "What are you thinking?" he asked, his voice muffled from the task.

"I'm thinking about how much I love you, and how much I appreciate you, giving me feedback and advice while still supporting whatever decision I make. And… I'm thinking that's rare and that I'm extremely lucky."

"Decisions like holiday plans with our families?"

"I was thinking more about my listing, but sure. I'll give you credit for holiday plans also."

He smiled at me. "Elle, you're one of the smartest women I know. It's me who's the lucky bastard."

"I don't know." I ran my hands down the front of his abs, then worked them underneath the waist of his dress pants. "There are a few other things I'm grateful for."

"Easy." He glanced at the battery-operated clock we kept on the counter. "Don't start something you don't have time to finish."

I raised on my toes and gently nipped the back of his neck. "We could be late."

He rinsed the razor under the water and left it by the sink. Grabbing the hand towel off the ring, he challenged my gaze in the mirror. "How late?"

I undid the tie of my robe in response.

Turning, he removed his shirt from the hanger and peered down at me with an amused look. "Grab my tie."

"*Please* grab my tie," I amended.

He worked his arms through the sleeves and buttoned up the front, a cocky challenge in his eyes. "Get my tie or I'll make you do it on your knees."

I got his damn tie, wrapping the black silk fabric around my fist. Glancing back to find him waiting beside the sink, a dark and amused look on his face, I dropped to my knees just for the hell of it, but crawled in the opposite direction, from the closet to the bed, my back arched, hips swinging as I took my time.

I heard his steps sound across the bathroom tile, then the wood floors. Just before I reached the bed, his hand closed around my ankle and pulled.

"Stay," he ordered. "And bite down on that tie, because you're about to start screaming."

I lowered the sun visor and adjusted my black veil, the mesh net looking deadly with the smoky eye I had applied. "This thing is going to drive me crazy."

"Just take it off until we get there." His hand found my knee and closed on it, his thumb rubbing along the top of it. "And do me a favor, don't dress like this at my funeral. Every guy there will be too busy staring at you to properly rave about my contributions to society."

I smiled, my hand covering his as I closed the visor and settled back in the seat. We'd finally gotten the Range Rover's air conditioner fixed, our first big purchase after getting Nicole's commission check. It'd cost eleven hundred dollars, but was worth every penny. I tilted the vent toward me and let out a happy sigh.

"I—uh, got an email from that website." Easton pressed his foot on the gas, speeding through a yellow light.

"Which one?"

"You know." His hand tightened a little on my knee, then released. "The one from the club. The one by the airport."

"Oh." I shifted in the seat. "The sex club."

"Yeah. Remember that I told you about their member website where you can chat with other people? It was an email about that. My membership ends pretty soon."

"I told you I didn't want to go to that club." I moved my knee away, irritated by the conversation.

"I know. But what do you think about doing it again?" He rested his wrist on the steering wheel. Immediately, I missed his touch. "Elle?" he prodded.

"It? You mean, hooking up with Aaron? I thought we agreed not to do anything with him again. We can't, E. It's too—"

He wrapped a hand around my wrist and I fell silent as he pulled it to his mouth. As he kissed the back of my hand, I curled toward him, desperate for more. "Not with Aaron. Would you want to do something with someone else?"

I laced my fingers through his as I thought over the question. "Why? I mean... I don't *need* that." But I craved it. I wanted that look back in E's eyes. That raw possession. The dominant way he had fucked me in front of Aaron. Maybe I did need it. Right now, my hips twisting into the seat, my body humming back to life... we had *just* had sex. Hot, filthy, scream-out-his-name-at-the-top-of-my-lungs sex. Yet I was already ready for more. Dirtier. Kinkier sex.

"*I* might need it." Easton said the words so calmly I almost missed them. "I've been thinking about it, a lot. A lot more than I should be."

"What part of it?"

"All of it. The visuals..." He ran a rough hand through his hair. "Fuck. You were so hot, Elle. So fucking hot. So wet and willing and horny. Which, you always are—but having someone else see that part of you and be blown away by that... I was so proud of you. So proud of us. So turned on to see how badly he wanted you. And I agree, we can't meet with Aaron again. But, I do think we should find someone else. Someone new."

Wow. I settled back in the seat and pulled at the belt, giving myself more breathing room. Maybe I *didn't* need the real estate success. Maybe my contribution to our marriage could be my voracious sexual appetite. I smiled at the thought. "Where would we find someone? In that membership group?" I was part of nineteen Facebook groups, most focused on makeup, used item sales, and real estate marketing. I tried to imagine an online group centered around fucking, and envisioned it containing every creepy Instagram stalker I'd ever had.

"I don't know. But I don't want to do anything you don't want to do. Or push you into anything. When I said I need it, I just meant that it's been stuck in my head. Constantly."

I liked the idea of him thinking about it. Liked the idea of his dick growing hard, his visualization of the act, the way he'd described me.

"Finding a stranger on an internet site... I don't know. I'm worried we'll become *that* couple."

"What couple?"

"You know. Those creepy couples. Like cuckolds and stuff. And I'll be that wife. Like, a swinger wife." I had a horrific thought. "I guess I already am that wife."

He chuckled. "We had one threesome, Elle. I don't think it's branded you into a category."

"Well, I feel differently," I shot back. "And I'm worried you'll look at me differently. It's like that cocksucker joke."

He shot me a glance as he made a turn. "Which one?"

"You know, the one about the old couple."

"I don't know that one."

I sighed. "Yes, you do. Aaron's mom told it to us at his rehearsal dinner. Right before she did that ridiculous toast."

"That was years ago, and I have no idea what you're talking about. Tell it to me."

There was road construction ahead, a group of men bent over a brightly-lit hole in the ground. Easton put on his blinker and slowed. I cleared my throat and started the joke. "This old couple was celebrating their fiftieth wedding anniversary. The wife asked the husband what he wanted as a gift. And the man said he wanted a blowjob, that he'd never had one."

"The guy was married fifty years and had never had a blowjob?"

"I think it's a generational thing. I don't think they gave blowjobs back in the fifties. That was when they slept in separate beds. Look, the guy wants you to turn right."

"If I turn right, I have to go all the way around on Fulton. It's a one-way."

"Well, it's blocked off."

He turned with an irritated scowl and I grabbed the dash as the Range Rover bounced over a huge pothole.

"Okay, so what did she say?"

"She told him that she'd always been afraid to give him a blowjob because she thought he wouldn't look at her the same way. When the man heard this, he gathered her in his arms and told her that they had been married for fifty years." I warmed to the story, drawing out the vowels as I painted the picture of the joke. "She was the mother of his children. She'd nursed him through *cancer* treatments. There was nothing she could do to cause him to lose respect for her."

I paused to point at the detour sign. "So she immediately moves one of their paisley-print couch pillows onto the floor and gives him a blowjob."

"Oh, this is the Goodwill Hunting joke. The one she tells in the bar."

"Would you shut up and let me finish? It's not the Goodwill Hunting joke." I glared at him. "Anyway, she finishes the blowjob and wipes off her mouth, and he says, 'Thank you, honey. That was amazing.' She settles back in her recliner and they continue to watch the news."

"Hilarious joke."

"A half-hour later the phone rings and the old man picks up the receiver and says hello. After a beat of time, he pulls the phone away from his ear and hangs it back up. His wife waits for an explanation. After several minutes pass, she asks him who it was." I paused for effect. "Her husband shrugs and says 'How would I know, cocksucker? It was for you.'"

Easton took a moment, then laughed. "Funny."

"It *is* funny," I protested, a little miffed he hadn't found it more so.

"Aaron's mom told that joke?"

"Oh my God, in front of the entire wedding party. Becca turned white with embarrassment."

He paused. "So, uh, you're the cocksucker in this scenario?"

"I'm the cocksucker."

"Literally *and* figuratively."

I laughed and he braked at a stop sign, then leaned toward me, cupping the back of my neck and pulling me toward him. Navigating around the veil, he kissed my lips. "I love you and I will always respect you."

"Thank you." I kissed him back, then settled into the seat, thinking over everything he'd said. "So, if I wanted to, you'd be okay with doing something like that again?"

"Yeah. And if you don't like the idea of the club's website, we can try something else."

I chewed on the inside edge of my cheek. "Okay. I'll think about it."

Easton was right. We had to go all the way around on Fulton, then back north, and twenty minutes passed before we pulled up to the guard shack of Chelsea's neighborhood. A security guard waved us forward, then approached the car. E rolled down the window.

His gaze flitted from Easton to me and zeroed in on my veil. His face hardened. "I take it you're here for the Pedicant event?"

"Yep."

"Name?"

"Easton and Elle North."

"Do you have any animals, weapons, or noise-creating items?"

"Uh... no?"

The man peered at him. "It doesn't sound like you're certain about that."

I leaned across the armrest. "I don't understand why it's any of your business if we have any of that stuff. You've never asked me that before."

"We've had multiple complaints from our residents about Miss Pedicant's... event. We are keeping order best we can."

"Oh my God." I sat back into place.

"We don't have anything like that," Easton said.

"Please give our regards to Miss Pedicant, along with a reminder that the association noise ordinance goes into effect at ten p.m. In fifteen minutes." He held out a pass, which Easton tossed onto the front dash.

The iron gate before us began to move, a slow and arduous process that seemed to take even longer than usual. I waited until E's window was up before I spoke. "What was up with that? Asking if we had animals? What if we'd brought Wayland?"

"Or your can of pepper spray." He grinned.

"I wonder how many people she invited, if they're already getting complaints."

"Well, you know what this neighborhood is like. They've had it out for her ever since she moved in."

"Yeah. I told her she should have bought the house on our street. Half our neighbors are too deaf to hear anything."

"Shit." E came to a stop at the intersection before her street. "Look."

He pointed to a row of cars parked on the side of the street.

"What? You think those are for *her*?" I craned my neck forward, trying to see the end of the line of vehicles. "No way." We were a quarter-mile from her house, if not more. There was no chance the parking was backed this far up.

"Does that answer your question about how many people she invited?"

Ahead of us, a car was stopped in the middle of the street. As we watched, partygoers in skimpy black outfits crawled into the back.

"I think it's a shuttle." He spun the wheel to the left and pulled out, going around the vehicle, which ended up being a hearse.

"She's really sticking to the funeral theme, huh?" I glanced in the side mirror, watching as the long car began to follow us.

"Looks like it." He turned down Chelsea's street, where the parked cars clogged both sides of the road. "I'll drop you off out front."

"I have her garage opener. She said we can park there." I bent forward and opened my purse, looking for the small fob.

"Yeah, I'm not sure that will work." He nodded toward Chelsea's driveway, which was a parking lot of cars. "Just hop out here. I'll park, and then come and find you."

I leaned over and brushed a kiss on his lips. "See you inside."

I opened the door and was hit with loud music and the smell of fire-works. As I stepped out, a fissure of blue and gold shot into the sky behind her house, illuminating the palm trees in color before exploding overhead with a deafening pop. From behind the majestic home, a crowd cheered and the music resumed. I adjusted my veil and closed the door, stepping across the golf-course quality lawn and onto the driveway, following the sounds of the party and steeling myself for what might be inside.

13

Amid belly dancers and a naked Brad Pitt ice statue with excessive genitalia, someone called my name. I turned, looking over the sea of black-clad bodies, and searched for a familiar face.

I didn't see anyone I knew, the group a mix of late twenty and thirty-somethings, half of who were wearing the same veil I was and all who were a lot drunker than me.

"Elle!"

It was Aaron. I felt a wave of relief at the familiar face and worked my way through the crowd toward him. He crushed me against his chest in a hug. "Elle Bell."

I pulled away enough to look up at him. "Who are all these people?"

He shrugged. "You know Chelsea."

Yeah. The girl had never met a stranger she didn't befriend, and managed to effortlessly maintain her connections for years after creation. "Where's she at?"

He said something, but I couldn't hear it over the band, who kicked into a Katy Perry song on the other side of the pool. "What?" I leaned closer to him.

He placed his hand on my hip and spoke into my ear. "She's the only one wearing white. You'll see her."

"Hey, HEY!" Chelsea collided into us with the grace of a bowling ball. She flung her arms around both our necks, kissing Aaron on the cheek before doing the same to me. "You're late," she accused.

I shrugged. "Traffic."

"Yeah, whatever." She began to jump in place. "Let's dance!"

Aaron held up his hands and stepped back. "Unless it's a two-step, I'm useless. You guys have fun."

She shimmied up to me and I laughed, looping an arm around her shoulders. "Fine. But I need a drink first."

"I can help with that," Aaron offered. "Chels, you want another Malibu and pineapple?"

"No, I'm good." She grinned up at him. "Find us by the stage?"

"Sure." He held her gaze and my blood chilled at the warm smile that tugged at the corner of his mouth. This couldn't be what it looked like. They were roommates. Maybe the last two weeks had brought them closer as friends, but this couldn't be sparks between them. Not after a decade of friendship. Not after what had happened in my bedroom between Easton and Aaron and me.

He stepped back and was quickly swallowed by the crowd, who swelled across the pool deck in dangerous proximity to the glowing red depths.

"Did you see the trapeze artists? And just wait—at midnight is when all of the excitement will really start." She high-fived a passerby.

"Oh yeah. The guys at the gate wanted me to remind you of the neighborhood noise ordinance which is starting, like, now."

She waved her hand dismissively as she climbed the stairs down to the pool deck. "They came by once already. There's nothing they can do, short of fining me. If someone calls the cops, I'll turn it down a smidge, but for now..." She shrugged.

I needed her attitude toward things. That laissez-faire approach would probably kill half the knots in my back. Oh, our cell phone bill is overdue? Fuck them in a forest of unicorns. It's all good. But that sort of attitude only worked for people like Chelsea. Fun, happy, fat allowance and salary from daddy, Chelsea. I'd managed to control my envy over her money during the course of our friendship but it still stung at times.

"Are you hungry? We have steak kabobs on the grill and finger food platters out."

"I'm good."

"Oh! Your listing appointment with the mafia! How'd it go?" She zeroed in on me, and I hesitated, struggling with what to share in this noisy and crowded place.

"It went well. They signed the paperwork—or rather, I signed their paperwork..." At her confused look, I waved off the story. "Nevermind. It's good. I got the listing!"

"And that's... good? Right? We're happy?"

"Yes, very happy," I assured her.

"You have to tell me everything. Play hooky one day this week and let's do a pool day. This outfit has made me realize how pasty I've gotten." She swung her hips to the beat, and I focused on her outfit, noticing the all-white getup that was way too conservative for Chelsea to ever wear anywhere, much less a party.

"Yeah, what's going on with all of this?" I twirled a finger over her outfit. "The death of your slutdom?"

"I'm turning over a new leaf. Celibacy."

"Celibacy?" I repeated, unsure if the loud music was screwing with my hearing.

"Yep. The Chelsea that you know and love is growing up." She beamed at someone across the party and gave an enthusiastic wave.

"Why?" I folded my arms across my chest, unnerved by the sudden tilt of this very reliable axis.

"Stop being so SERIOUS, Elle. This is a party!" She sang along with a line in the song and grabbed my hand, pulling me deeper into the crowd.

I followed, unsure of what to say. I danced with her and when Aaron handed me a drink, I guzzled it and tried to ignore the way his gaze moved to her face and lingered there. I had seven years of history that proved Aaron and Chelsea were miles deep into the friendship zone. There was no way that right now, that would be changing. It couldn't be. Because if it were... then Easton and I had made a monumental fuck-up.

Police lights bounced against the white brick of Chelsea's house. I cupped a drink against my chest and watched as a trio of Chippendale dancers gave their information to a female cop who couldn't stop smiling.

Apparently, Monroe County had a noise ordinance as well as Chelsea's neighborhood association, so she'd been in violation of both jurisdictions. The neighborhood president had shown up a half-hour ago in golf shorts and house slippers, a thick stack of papers in hand, just in time to see the conclusion of the vibrator race. He had dressed down Chelsea as if she was a child, then vowed to have her kicked out of the neighborhood by Monday—a proclamation that had triggered a low "oooooooo" from the crowd, as if we were in high school and someone had been called to the principal's office. Then the police cars had pulled in, and all of the crowd had scattered.

"Well, that was fun," Easton said, lifting a beer to his lips. "Can't say I'm too surprised."

Me either. I wasn't sure if it was the noise, or the fireworks, or the boatful of male strippers that pulled up to Chelsea's dock, but the cops had come in full force, their sirens barely audible over the beat of the band's bass.

"Think she's going to jail?" Easton glanced at me.

I shook my head. "Nah. I think this is minor stuff. Code violations and noise issues. Plus, Aaron said she had two attorneys in his guest house, waiting on call."

"Wow." He chuckled, then finished off the final sip of the beer. He wrapped an arm around my waist and pulled me against him. "Chelsea is insane."

"This party is insane. The death of her slutdom? How long do you think this celibacy kick will last?"

"You know her better than anyone. You tell me."

Yeah, I knew Chelsea as well as I knew myself. Which is why this party—one she organized without a single call to me for help—was a giant red flag. Something was horribly wrong, and I was afraid I knew exactly what it was.

14

I squirted makeup remover on a cotton ball, then dabbed it across my face. From outside, I heard Easton call Wayland's name, then yell it with a fierce level of severity that would most likely be ignored. I yawned as I slid the cotton ball over my eyelashes, then my lids, tossing the black and blue ball into the trash before moving to the next eye.

Easton yelled again and I glanced at the clock, extra mindful of the noise after tonight's mild brush with the law.

In all of the excitement, I'd never gotten another moment alone with Chelsea, and I felt unease at the pivot that she was taking. Maybe it was nothing. Maybe this "funeral" was just like the wedding dress she'd worn to Vegas, or the veganism diet she'd attempted and abandoned. Maybe this celibacy was an excuse to throw a party and would be tossed aside within the week.

The back door slammed shut and I turned to see Easton approaching the bedroom, Wayland cupped against his chest like a baby. Only... this baby was one hundred and forty pounds and licking the side of his face as if it were coated in peanut butter. Easton made it through the door of the bedroom before setting him on the floor. Wayland immediately bounded onto the bed.

"You need to get your son in line."

"E—" I protested. "Get him off the bed."

Wayland rolled on his back, then thrashed at the sheets. Easton bent over him and gave a low warning growl.

"STOP," I warned him. "You're going to get him all riled up."

"I think it's too late for that." He snapped his fingers and pointed to the floor. "Wayland, down."

Wayland rolled to the opposite side and beat his tail against the headboard. I returned my attention to the mirror and heard a loud thump as Wayland was pushed to the floor.

"There." Easton leaned against the bathroom's door frame. "Order restored."

I worked at my right eye. "How much did you talk to Aaron tonight?"

"Not much. Chelsea had him running around a lot. Why?"

I chucked the cotton ball and ran the sink, pulling a washcloth off the top of the stack and holding it under the water. "I feel like there's something going on between him and Chelsea."

He pulled at the knot of his tie. "Like what? You think they're hooking up?" He said it as if it was no big deal, as if that wouldn't be a monumental event that would change everything about our joint friendship.

I hesitated. "Do *you* think they're hooking up?"

"No." He pulled the tie loose from his neck. "Are you still wearing those thongs?" He cocked one brow and ran his hand underneath the hem of my dress. "Damn, you are."

"Babe, focus." I squirted a dollop of face wash onto the cloth. "This is serious."

"Okay, I seriously don't think they're hooking up. Aaron would tell me. And Chelsea?" He tossed his tie toward the closet. "Don't you think she'd rent out billboard space to announce that to you?"

He had a point. I rubbed the soapy rag over my face, scrubbing at the areas where my blackheads liked to hide. Chelsea would definitely tell me if she did anything with Aaron. Just like, I'm sure, she assumes that I would definitely tell her if I did anything with Aaron.

But I hadn't. I'd kept it a secret from her.

Maybe she was keeping this a secret from me. But why? At least I'd had a reason.

I bent over the sink and splashed water on my face. Easton's watch clunked against the counter, followed by his wedding ring. I turned off the faucet and reached for a towel. "I just felt like there was something between them. Something new. A chemistry."

"You worried he's going to tell her about us?"

"I'm worried that I should tell her about it. What if they started dating? She would need to know that." I got busy with my toothbrush.

"Why?" He moved behind me and undid the clasp at the back of my dress, pulling down the zipper.

I tried to conjure a parallel situation. "If Aaron wanted to ask out a girl, and you had had sex with her, wouldn't you tell him that?"

"Aaron wouldn't care." He watched as I scrubbed at my teeth. "He wouldn't. Seriously. Guys don't care about stuff like that, especially if it's just sex."

"Well, women care. A lot. Especially in this situation, where we're all friends. This is a secret that three out of the four of us knows about, and she's going to be pissed when she finds out." I know I would be royally pissed. Anxiety rose in my stomach and I leaned forward and spit into the sink.

"Okay, so tell her." He unclipped my bra and I wiped my mouth.

"You aren't focusing."

"I can't focus when your gorgeous breasts are right here in hands' reach." He ran his hands around my side and up the front of my body, cupping them in each hand. "There," he whispered reverently, squeezing them gently. "Now you have my full attention."

"It's teeth whitening night."

He sagged in place. "Nooooo."

"Don't give me that. We had sex earlier. You can cup my gorgeous breasts while I put them on, if that helps."

"It doesn't help." He dropped his hands. "Nothing helps the agony of teeth whitening strips."

I laughed. "Shut up and brush yours. Use the stiff toothbrush."

He moved to the other sink, his steps slow and posture heavy, as if I was subjecting him to hours of manual labor and not thirty minutes with a WhiteStrip. He lifted the toothbrush and stared at it for a long moment. "This was not in our vows."

"Yeah, well. A lot of what we do wasn't in our vows."

"Speaking of which... did you think about what we talked about? Doing something else?"

I huffed out a laugh, and passed him the tube of toothpaste. "You mean, since the ride to Chelsea's? No. I haven't thought about it." But I had. One of the male strippers had eye-fucked me so hard I had considered pointing him out to Easton. Maybe introducing him to Easton. Leaving the two of them to discuss possibilities while I found an empty bedroom and waited for them on my knees.

Then I remembered that I was at a party with two hundred witnesses. Chelsea. Aaron. Tina from my office. I remembered that I was a semi-respectable member of society, trying to grow a business and reputation in this cutthroat town. I remembered how quickly rumors spread and how harmful they could be. I had turned away from the man and sipped on my cranberry and vodka and pushed the thought out of my head.

Now, I considered sharing the fantasy with Easton. Meeting his gaze in his mirror, I held my tongue and smiled instead. "I'll think about it."

"It's fine if you don't want to."

No, I want to. I really want to. I nodded. "I know."

"We never went down your pros and cons list." He put a line of paste on the bristles and stuck it in his mouth.

I crouched before the sink and opened up the bottom cabinet, sorting through the contents until I found the blue box of whitening strips. Cracking open the lid, I pulled out two sets. "Well... the pros were that it was hot."

I paused. There had been more pros, hadn't there? I peeled the top sticker off the strip and pressed it along my teeth, buying some time as I tried to remember the other reasons.

Easton brushed his teeth and there was a moment of companionable silence that he did nothing to fill. I finished my top teeth.

"And, I liked thinking about it before and after. Like when we role-played about it."

He leaned forward and spit into the sink. "Right. What else?"

"I liked that I felt different afterward. Like, sexually empowered." I looked down and thumbed open the bottom strip. "What did you like about it?"

He wiped off his mouth and faced me, crossing his arms over his chest. "It turned me on seeing how into it you got. But also... it felt like game day again. That competitive anticipation. It was shooting through me when he walked over to you. When he touched you. It was like this enormous rush of testosterone hitting me straight in the dick. I felt"—he lifted his hands and looked around the bathroom as if there was a thesaurus handy—"I don't know. Like a caveman. Like I was down to my most basic instincts to kill, claim, and fuck. And you were there with me in the middle of it, with your skin glowing, and your body offered up to us, and you were *so* fucking hot, Elle. So fucking hot and willing and eager. It was insane and addictive, and I couldn't believe that I was married to you. That you were mine." He looked at me and that was it.

I yanked seven dollars' worth of Crest Whitestrips off my teeth and snatched up the hand towel, scrubbing it across my teeth. "Come on." Grabbing his hand, I led him to the bed and said fuck it to Whitestrips night.

"We didn't cover the cons." I curled around his back, my fingers tracing our initials along the tan expanse of skin.

Easton sighed. "What are the cons?"

"What happens if people find out?"

He rolled onto his back and stretched his arm out, cradling me into his side. "No one will find out."

I readjusted, moving in closer and resting my cheek on his shoulder. "You don't know that."

"If someone found out, we'd deal with it together." He kissed the top of my head and I let out a soft grumble. *Deal with it together.* A romantic notion that didn't touch on the massive disaster that would mean. "What was the next con?"

"Umm... STDs? Pregnancies? A massively stretched out vagina?" I smiled.

"Condoms cover the first two. Also, I've been slowly stretching out your vagina for some time now. It's practically a cavern by now."

I poked him with my longest and sharpest nail and he jerked away from me. "Please take this seriously."

"Okay, you have my full and serious attention. What else?"

"What if we start to need it? What if we get bored with sex with just each other?"

He rolled onto his side, so he was facing me. "I'm figuring this out, just like you are. But what we did has only made me *more* attracted and aroused by you. I can't imagine a scenario where I'd ever need anything more than just you." He frowned and a cute new wrinkle appeared in between his brows. "Has it made you less interested in sex with me? Or bored with our—"

I shook my head. "No. Not at all." He was right. It had only poured gasoline on the chemistry between us. Still, a tense coil of nerves flexed in my stomach at the idea of doing it again. It had been three weeks. Was it too early to be discussing it again? Were we being greedy to consider diving back into it already?

He kissed me. "I think we should try it again."

"You do?"

"Yeah." He studied me. "And see how we like it—if you enjoy it as much."

I nodded without daring to speak, my heart beating faster at the thought of what I was agreeing to.

"While I'm in LA, why don't you look into it? See if there's a website or process that *you* feel comfortable with."

I inhaled. "Okay."

Our gaze met in the dim bedroom light and he smiled. "Stop stressing."

"I'm not stressing," I sighed and settled deeper into the pillow. "But now I'm thinking about my cavernous vagina."

He chuckled and pulled me closer. "You know I was joking."

"Maybe," I amended. "Or maybe you weren't."

He gathered me against his chest and I tried not to think about three-somes or Chelsea and Aaron or my vagina or the sticky residue of the un-brushed-off WhiteStrips. I closed my eyes and focused on his heartbeat and, after a few minutes, didn't think about anything at all.

15

Another Monday loomed, and brought with it my period. I normally got emotional when it arrived, the initial bloodstain a giant F on my pregnancy report card. This month, given my extra sexual activity with Aaron, I almost welcomed it. It retaliated, coming at me with fists that hammered my stomach and twisted my ovaries into painful knots.

I made it through fourteen emails and a half-hearted series of cold calls before I took two Midols and started slacking off, focusing my attention off real estate and onto research on how to have a three-some. I was engrossed in a Buzzfeed article about a woman who was banging her boss and his wife when someone gently rapped on my office door.

I hissed out a curse and began minimizing browser windows. I was still busy, closing pop-up ads for penis enlargement and horny local MILFs when Maria Bott stuck her head in. I closed the lid of my laptop and spun to face her. "Hey. What's up?"

Her eyes darted over the tight office, one that was barely larger than the supply closet at the end of the hall. She stepped inside. "Not much. You busy?"

"I've got a minute."

"I saw that OLT listing hit the board." She raised her brows. "Sweet score."

I shrugged as if it was nothing. "I got lucky."

"No joke. I interned at Clarke, De Luca & Broward in college. Brad De Luca is fucking cake to look at. And alpha male as hell. It was super scandalous when he started banging Julia."

I snapped my gaze up from her pale pink Tieks. "You knew Mrs. De Luca?"

"Well, she wasn't Mrs. De Luca then." She leaned against the doorframe and giggled. "She was like the rest of us. A broke college student."

I could see a little of it still in her. Even in the big house, leaning on the arm of the powerful attorney, she still had an innocence about her. An easy relatability that had put me at ease, despite all the reasons I should have been intimidated.

"But yeah," she continued. "I knew Julia. Wish I'd kept up with her after school. That'd be my name on the board next to their address." She grinned at me, but I could feel the competitive barb behind her words.

She could keep dreaming of the listing. It was mine, a fact that still surprised and thrilled me. "I'm actually setting up showing appointments now for it. I better get back to them."

"Sure." She straightened and turned back to the hall. "Tell Julia I said hi."

"Absolutely. And if you have any buyers that might be interested, let me know."

She flashed me a thumbs up. "I'll let you get back to work. There are donuts in the break room."

I waited until she pulled the door tight, then reopened up the laptop. I finished the Buzzfeed article, then switched tabs, returning to an in-process profile application. The site I'd chosen held a database of kinky participants I could filter by race, gender, age, and kink. It seemed like the cleanest and most respectful of the sites I had found. It also had a lengthy profile questionnaire, which had been entertaining at the beginning but now, eighteen questions down, was starting to get tedious. Maybe tedious was a good thing—something to weed out the crowd.

I took a sip of water and tabbed down to question 19.

> Please use the following scale to indicate the level that best matches your sexuality levels.

There was a twin set of scales, one for me and one for Easton. The scales went from straight to bi-curious to bisexual to gay, with halfway points between each classification. For my scale, I initially clicked on straight and then hesitated, moving the pointer a little to the right, in a pale yellow area that would qualify as mildly bi-curious.

I scrolled down to Easton's scale and stared at the screen. On first impulse, I'd say Easton was straight with a capital S. But what if he wasn't? I'd had a thousand conversations with my husband but had never thought to ask him his sexual orientation, not when he spent his first three years at Florida State wading through a sexual pool of women.

I called him. He didn't answer, and I tapped out a quick text instead of leaving a voicemail.

I'm filling this out for a website. How should I answer for you?

I took a picture of the screen, careful not to include my own selection, and sent it.

I skipped on to the next question.

> **What are you looking for?**
>
> - *A single man*
>
> - *A single female*
>
> - *A couple*
>
> - *A group of men*
>
> - *A group of women*

I clicked on the checkbox next to a single man. I paused before continuing on, studying each of the other options. Prior to meeting with Aaron, I would have said that I was vehemently against doing anything with Easton and another woman. But I had a different view of it now. I wouldn't say that I was ready for it yet, but I was more accepting of a threesome with a girl as an *eventual* possibility. For now, I skipped over the single female option and scanned over the rest of the bullet points, dismissing them all as something too advanced for us at this point.

My phone rang, Easton's name on the display. "Hey."

"Straight," he said without preamble. "One hundred percent."

"You don't have to say that," I offered. "I mean, there are a lot of steps on that scale. In case—"

"I'm not anywhere else on that scale. And if I ever thought I was, that was diminished when I saw Aaron pull out his dick. I can say with absolute certainty that I had no interest in touching anything in that bedroom other than you."

"Okayyy," I drawled. "I'm clicking on extremely straight. Happy?"

He paused. "What did you click for you?"

"Ummm..." I was suddenly embarrassed with my choice. "The pale yellow area in between straight and bi-curious."

"Really? Have you ever done anything with a girl?"

"No."

"No drunk kisses in a bar?"

I laughed. "No."

"Boring Elle." He clicked his tongue in disapproval and I was instantly transported back to high school English, and the ravenous crush I'd had on Mr. Boles.

"You can't really talk," I countered. "I'm a bar and a half more adventurous than you."

"Good point. And speaking of my boring self, I've got to get on a call. Keep filling out your sex questionnaire and I'll try to concentrate on quarterly projections without thinking about you scrolling through cock profiles."

"I know you're joking, but for real, there are a *lot* of penis pictures," I informed him. "Like everywhere. For like, ninety-five percent of guys, it's their main profile pic."

He laughed. "Just don't get too impressed. The angle can make a huge difference in how big it looks."

"Thanks for the tip," I said dryly. "Now, get to your call. I love you."

He returned the sentiment and I ended the connection, scrolling down to the bottom of the application, where there was a large MAKE PROFILE ACTIVE green button.

Taking a deep breath, I clicked on the button.

Done. Submitted into cyberspace without a profile pic and with a fairly scant description that wouldn't stand out for any reason whatsoever. We might not get a single message, but the act still felt powerful. What might this trigger? Who might we find, and how would they affect our relationship?

I closed the browser window and stood, stretching my back until it popped. Tomorrow, I could start to search through profiles. I'd look through my camera roll and see if I could find a profile pic for us, something that would give a hint as to our looks without exposing our identity.

For now, this baby step felt massive enough. I drained the rest of my water and chucked the bottle into the trash. Glancing at the clock, I grabbed my laptop and hurriedly stuck it in my bag. Donuts didn't last long in the break room and with my shiny new OLT listing, I actually had something to shut up any teasing from the senior agents. Opening the door, I paused as a painful cramp rolled through my midsection, then pushed on.

Donuts. Donuts could solve anything and I deserved a keto-cheat day.

16

As Easton settled into a first-class seat next to Nicole Fagnani, my email inbox filled with notifications from the sex site. Our non-photo profile generated over fifty messages by the time I got home from work the following day. I changed into pajamas and settled into Easton's recliner, clicking through the messages with increasing frequency. Fifty-odd messages, but all surprisingly similar. It appeared that online sex partners fell into one of three categories.

The first was an overly sweet, drown you in compliments, unattractive older man. *Pass.*

The second, an I'll bang you till your tits fall off misogynistic who liked to attach dick pics like it was an Olympic sport. *Gag me now.* Not literally, of course.

The third was more bearable, but still unsettling. A cautiously friendly and respectful intro that had clearly been cut and pasted who knew how many times. *Thanks, but no thanks.*

I lasted a half-hour of reading messages and then logged out of the site, prepared to never ever have a threesome again. As if to combat the move, my phone dinged.

I clicked on the email notification on my way to the fridge. It was another message, this one from OrlandoC11.

> *I saw that you're new to the site, so you're probably being hounded by messages. If you ever have any questions for someone who's been around the block a few times—I'm here. It can be a sketchy place, especially for couples.*
>
> *Welcome to the lifestyle.*
>
> *Kurt*

The lifestyle. Was that the term for it? I clicked on the link to his profile and clicked through his photos. Mid-thirties and clean-cut. Not bad looking. A nice smile. He had a picture of himself at the beach, a dog leash in hand. A nice body. I looked for a dick pic and was surprised and pleased when he didn't have one.

I set my phone on the counter and took a bottle of wine from the fridge, twisting off the lid and pouring the cheap moscato into a glass.

I could respond. Out of the fifty-four messages I'd received so far, I hadn't responded to any. But this one I could handle. He was offering his help and I did have a *lot* of questions. I picked my phone back up and leaned against the counter.

> *Hey Kurt. This is*

I paused. We hadn't put any names in our profile, and using Elle... though common enough to hide my identity, just seemed wrong. I settled on my middle name.

> *Hey Kurt. This is Rachel. I'm the wife. Thank you for the warm*

welcome. We are still feeling out the site and figuring out if it is
something we want to get into.

I sent the message and watched the indicator change to delivered.
While it wasn't going to win any Pulitzers, I was happy with it. Simple
and non-committal. Which was good, since the chances were high that
he'd turn into one of the three types soon enough.

I took a sip of wine and wondered what Easton was doing in Los
Angeles. It'd been forty-five minutes since his last text message, when
he'd checked in and told me that they were headed out for drinks with
Nicole's agent.

My stomach knotted and I took another sip, pushing away the bit of
doubt that liked to creep into my head when he was out of town. I'd
met Nicole and gotten a strong lesbian vibe. Still... the last time he'd
been out of town alone was Phoenix, and he'd confessed of a flirtation
at the bar, one he had enjoyed a little too much. I knew that he would
never do anything, that he was fiercely loyal but...the uneasy feeling
persisted. My phone chimed and I returned my attention to it, opening
the newest message from OrlandoC11.

Take your time. It can be intimidating at first. Have you guys tried
anything already or are you complete newbies?

I set down the wine glass.

Not complete newbies. We had a threesome with a friend of ours. We
don't want to mess up that friendship, so are hoping to find a
replacement for him.

I pinpointed the root of my concern at the exact moment that I sent
the reply. My nerves weren't about Easton, they were about *me*. It felt
like *I* was being sketchy. Looking at men. Reading messages from
them. And now—chatting with one. Even if my communication with

Kurt was innocent, I understood what he was doing. Easing me in. Making me feel comfortable. At some point, maybe later tonight, after three more glasses of wine and a dozen more emails... our conversation would change. Twist. Deepen. Maybe he'd send that dick pic I was suddenly curious for. Maybe he'd ask for a nude pic of me.

A volley of messages passed between us, and with each one, my comfort with Kurt, and my unease with the situation, grew. I finished off the glass and texted Easton.

I've been going through our messages on the site. Lots of crude and creepy ones. Found one guy who seems nice. We've messaged back and forth a few times.

I watched as it was delivered and then read. A minute passed before Easton replied.

Give me a minute to step outside.

I refilled my glass and took it into the living room. Wayland was lying on the couch and I eyed him, then let the forbidden location slide. Settling back into the recliner, I pulled a blanket over my legs. My phone rang. "Hey."

"I'm getting jealous."

I winced. "To be honest, it feels sketchy, chatting with guys without you here."

"Oh, there's multiple guys?"

"Well, I've only responded to one. An accountant out of Orlando. He's nice. It's been a G-rated conversation so far. Maybe PG."

"An accountant? Sexy."

"I know. At least he's being honest. I don't think anyone would lie about being an accountant." I picked up the remote and flipped through the guide.

"What's his dick like?"

I laughed. "I don't know. He doesn't have it on his profile."

"Good. It's probably small. Miniscule."

"You know, you sound a little insecure," I teased.

"I'm three thousand miles away from my sexy wife. I'm hella insecure."

"Oh please. I'm at home in pajamas while you're out in an LA bar."

"Elle, there's not a woman in California that can hold a candle to you. You could walk into this place in a potato sack, and you'd break every single one of these assholes' hearts."

I brought my knees to my chest and smiled, feeling better about the distance. "How's it going with Nicole?"

"Pretty good so far. I think this game could be great for her. We've got meetings all day tomorrow with the designers and marketing team for it."

The game he was referring to was a video game, one where you picked a tennis player and competed in various tournaments. Unlike the other existing games, there was also a reality component where you could make life and financial decisions for your player and then deal with the positive and negative consequences as that player. I hadn't yet decided if the idea sounded stupid or brilliant. MGM Entertainment, who was creating the game, wanted the rights to Nicole's name and image—plus wanted her to invest in exchange for putting her on the cover. Ten million dollars was the number that had been thrown out. She'd pay ten million for a sixteen percent stake in the game and her image on the cover and all promotional material.

It was new territory for Easton, and the pressure was on to give her intelligent advice that wouldn't come back and blow up in his face. The game could release in as quickly as eighteen months, and depending on its success or failure, Easton would be judged. He had to make the right decision, and I willed him to see the correct path for her to take.

"Go back to them," I urged. "I just wanted to check in with you. Do you want me to wait and chat with this guy when you get home?"

"It's all through the online messages?"

"Yeah, on the site."

"Then, no. Keep going. I can read through them later." His voice dropped. "Are you flirting with him?"

"No. Not yet. But I'm worried it's going to head in that direction."

"Just do as much as you feel comfortable with. I'll read through it tomorrow. I trust you."

Did he need to trust me if he was going to read through the transcript of our conversation? I clamped down my irritation and reminded myself of how I'd feel if I were in his shoes. "Okay. Good luck."

"Thanks, baby. I love you."

I ended the call and felt the phone buzz with another new message from Kurt.

> *I've got to run. Hit me up if you have any questions. Also, if you guys need a guinea pig to practice on. Your husband is a very lucky man, and I think you'll enjoy this lifestyle, if you do it the right way.*

My fears had been unfounded, and I felt a little disappointed that Kurt hadn't pushed the envelope with flirtation. His abrupt departure only increased my interest in him as a potential candidate. I replied back with a quick final question.

> *What's the right way?*

He responded almost immediately.

> *With full honesty between the two of you. Don't ever do anything sexually—or let him do anything sexually—that you aren't comfortable with. And stop if it stops being fun.*

From beside me, Wayland let out a snore. I glanced at him and composed back my best attempt at a casual yet door-opening end.

> *We may take you up on that guinea pig offer. Enjoy your friends—chat soon.*
>
> *Xoxo Rachel*

As soon as I sent the message, I regretted the x's and o's. Was I twelve? Smitten? A pathetic horny housewife? I kicked my feet free of the blanket and turned up the volume on the television, watching as a solemn narrator recounted a brutal crime scene and the forensic clues that had been left behind.

Gathering up my blanket, I heaved out of the recliner and moved to the couch. Lying beside Wayland, I put one arm around the big dog and laid my head on his shoulder. He wasn't Easton, but in a pinch, he worked pretty well.

I tried to focus on the show, but had lost some critical elements of the crime during my messaging. I changed the channel to a QVC tutorial on eye shadow and thought through everything Kurt had shared. He was divorced. Came to Miami frequently on business. Had been a member of the site for a year. Got into the lifestyle with his ex-wife. Preferred to be the third with married couples. Less drama, he said, assuming the husband wasn't an asshole.

All in all, he seemed really nice. Safe. I tucked my feet under Wayland and stared at the screen until I fell asleep.

17

The next morning, my period had retreated to a barely present and entirely manageable second-thought. Checking my phone, I saw a late-night text from Easton along with a new message from Kurt.

I opened Easton's text first.

Can't sleep. I tried to call you but it went straight to voicemail. I just wanted to say that I love and miss you.

I texted him back, letting him know that I was awake and missed him too. It was strange, waking up in our bed alone. In five years of marriage, we'd only been apart a handful of times, and the bedroom felt strangely vacant without his presence. On the upside, I didn't need to worry about the remaining hot water for my shower, and hadn't woken up six times during each one of Easton's snooze cycles.

I rolled onto my left side, then remembered the message from Kurt. It had come at 7:19am.

I'll be in Miami next Sunday if you guys are free. No pressure. We can just meet for drinks.

Drinks sounded incredibly awkward. Casual messages between me and him were one thing, but the three of us, perched at a high top in a bar? I flopped on my back and stifled a groan.

Next Sunday. No pressure. Just drinks. 10 days away.

He seemed like a nice guy. The right mix of playful and respectful. Good looking enough, though he wouldn't win any beauty pageants. Maybe, shockingly enough, we had found our new third. And it hadn't even been that hard.

I would have patted myself on the back, but I was too achy to move. The thought of getting dressed up and going into the office was cringe-worthy, which was good, since today was my date to play hooky at Chelsea's pool.

I hid my bloated stomach in a muumuu, one that had looked amazing on the Instagram ad (and only $13!) but ballooned out from me like a purple circus tent. I staggered through Chelsea's pool deck and collapsed on the closest cushioned chaise lounge that was in the shade. "I'm claiming this one," I announced, and lowered my sunglasses into place. "Hey, Aaron."

Aaron nodded from his spot beside the pool pump, his toolbox open beside him. "Hey. How's E's trip going? He a movie star yet?"

"Not quite, but I'm sure it isn't for lack of trying. Chelsea, stop putting Aaron to work."

"It's his fault. I told him to let me call the guy." She followed me to the chair and peered down at my toes, a glass of iced lemon water in hand. "Good lord, woman. How long has it been since you had a pedicure?"

I curled my toes against the cushion in an attempt to hide the picked-apart pink nails. "Leave me alone. I've been busy."

"At least take the polish off and let your nails breathe. I'll go get some remover. Want some water?" She offered the glass, which I took. From her pocket, Katy Perry started playing and she pulled out her phone and answered it.

"Got any Midol?" I whispered hopefully.

She gave me a thumbs up on her way up the steps, her freshly high-lighted hair bouncing as she went. I watched the flex of her calves and noticed, for the first time, that she had lost a little weight.

"Aaron." He glanced up and I patted the lounger beside me. "Come sit."

"Oh, no." He stood, a rueful expression crossing his face. "Now I know how E feels when you summon him. What'd I do?"

"Nothing." I tugged at the cushion and glanced toward the house, which had swallowed Chelsea up. "I'm just wanting to catch up. How's everything going?"

"Fine," he said warily, taking a seat and pulling off his baseball cap. Underneath, his hair was sweaty and messy, the damage enhanced as he scratched at the back of his head. "I got a new contract. Restaurant remodel. You know that Chipotle over on—"

"Yeah," I interrupted. "Congrats. That's great. How's it going living here?"

He grinned. "Good." His grin widened, almost shyly. "Really good. I mean—not that I don't miss staying with you guys."

"Right," I said dryly, watching as a uniformed maid carried a set of towels toward us. "I'm sure you miss doing your own laundry and picking Wayland's hair out of your toothbrush." I smiled at the woman, who set the towels down and then picked up an empty coffee cup and half-eaten muffin, wiping down the side table's surface before quickly walking off.

"Not going to lie, the maid service and setup is pretty swanky." He pulled his hat back onto his head.

"And what about with Chelsea? Are you guys getting along?"

"You know Chels. She's super chill. It's been good. We've gotten to know each other more."

"As friends?" I clarified.

He glanced at me and hesitated. "What—"

"SWINGERS!" Chelsea screamed the word from her upper balcony and down at us. I tensed as I watched her whirl around and into the bedroom, the door slamming shut behind her.

"What the fuckkkk...." Aaron drawled out under his breath. "Did you—"

"No," I hissed. "I didn't."

The back slider ripped open and Chelsea all but fell out, her pink coverup billowing around her as she scurried down the steps and toward our spot in the shade. She didn't look pissed. If anything, she looked gleeful. "Swingers!" she panted out, pausing before us, her large chest rising and falling in dramatic fashion as she caught her breath.

Aaron and I didn't respond. I felt frozen in place, my heart rapidly pounding as I tried to figure out how to handle this.

"That she-wrench-from-hell told me."

"Your stepmom knows?" That didn't make any sense. Of all possible leaks, for the news to get all the way to Regina Pedicant... everyone must know. *Everyone.*

"She heard from some snuffy nose who used to work at the law firm. Apparently, rumors have been swirling around them for years. But it's like, legit. One hundred percent true." She beamed at me. Beside me, Aaron let out a slow and grateful breath, processing the clues before I did that she was not accusing or talking about us.

"I'm sorry," I said carefully. "Who are we talking about?"

"Your new listing!" She tucked the hot pink wrap tight around her waist and carefully lowered herself to the chair. "The mobster-attorney-guy."

"Wait—Brad and Julia De Luca are swingers?" That couldn't be right. They had seemed so... normal. Well, not normal. Annoyingly perfect. Madly in love. Uncreepy in every way. I glanced at Aaron and found him watching me, his face guarded, and I realized the hypocrisy of my thoughts.

It was as if I was putting Easton and me in a separate category from the rest of the people in this...what had Kurt called it? Lifestyle. Not that we were *in* the lifestyle. We were just... I frowned, trying to think of what it was we were actually doing. Testing the waters. Yes, that was it. We'd had one quick dip to see the temperature. That was all. One quick dip and a few harmless and fact-finding messages. *I'll be in Miami next Sunday if you guys are free.*

"I know," she said gleefully, settling back in her chair and closing her eyes. "*So* fucking crazy."

Irritation bloomed in my belly. "Oh, I'm sorry. You're a born again virgin and you're suddenly judgmental of others?"

She cracked one eye open and squinted at me. "Who put your granny panties in a bunch? I wasn't judging. I just said it was crazy. It *is* crazy, Elle. Being single and cock jumping is one thing. It's a lot different when you have a wedding ring on your finger."

I struggled to process a response. I opened my mouth, then clamped it shut. I couldn't. *Shouldn't.* Aaron shot me a warning look and stood. "I'm gonna run up to Ace and get another connector bib for this pool pump. If you need me to pick up anything while I'm out, just text me."

"Thanks, I think I'm good." She smiled sweetly up at him and I fought a sudden and intense wave of dislike toward her. Just as quickly as it came, the emotion was replaced with panic. Was it jealousy about Aaron? Shame and insecurity over my actions? Rightful indignation over her comments?

"Did you grab me some Midol?" I asked tersely and God, I was being a bitch. Maybe it was my period. Day 3 hormones pushing on my hot points as well as my cervix.

"Oh, no. I forgot in the juicy gossip. Aaron, can you—"

"I'll just get it," I grumbled, gathering up the muumuu and pushing to my feet. "Where it is?"

"In the medicine cabinet in my bathroom. I mean, I can go and get it..."

I didn't respond, already striding toward the house and up the steps that led to the back deck. It was nice to know that Chelsea considered married threesome participants open targets for ridicule and scorn. My stomach flipped, and it wasn't the cramps. I thought of Brad's hand, settling on Julia's butt. Their kiss in front of me, in the kitchen. There was no way my new clients—my first big clients—were into this kink. No freaking way.

"Elle!" Aaron called out my name just before I reached the back stair-case that led to Chelsea's master suite. I paused and turned to watch him gently close the slider door.

"Talk to me for a minute." He approached warily, the way Easton did when he needed to capture a skink. Coming to a stop before me, he peered down at me. "What's wrong?"

"What's going on between you two?" The question exploded out, as if it had been bottled up and pressurized for days. And maybe, possibly, it had. "Are you dating? Fucking? Giving each other goo-goo eyes over dinner each night? Does Becca know what we did?"

"Whoa." He raised his hands and gave a half-step back. "I'm not doing anything with Chelsea, and I'm not sure it's any of your damn business if I am." The country boy came out a little in his voice and I'm sure Chelsea just *swooned* over that too.

"Something is going on with you and Chelsea, and if you don't see it —then you need to be a helluva lot more careful with my best friend, because she is falling for you and I'm watching it happen."

"Chelsea doesn't fall for anyone. You're talking about a heart of fucking steel over there." He pointed toward the pool and his forearms flexed in a way that—a month ago, I might have noticed.

"Yeah, well, Chelsea also doesn't swear off sex. Or lose weight. Or stay home at night and play fucking Scrabble."

"It was one game of Scrabble, and it was my idea," he argued. "Would it make you feel better if I told you that she was terrible at it?"

"Not particularly," I said. My stomach let out a low groan of indigestion. "Did you see her reaction to that news about my clients? She's going to freak out if she finds out what happened between us."

He stepped closer, so close I could smell the faint scent of grass and chlorine that rose off his clothes. He lowered his voice. "*If* she finds out what happened. Do you think we should tell her?"

I stumbled. "I—I don't know. What do you think?"

He put one hand on the counter, shielding me from the back door, and studied the floor, thinking. "I don't know. I would have thought that she'd be cool about it—but that reaction..." He lifted his chin and met my eyes. "I don't know."

Something clattered behind us. I jumped, he spun and we both gawked at the maid who stood at the entrance to the washroom, a basket of laundry in hand. She hesitated. "Mr. Aaron, do you have any dirty clothes for me?"

"No, thank you." He eased another step away from me and I realized how bad this must look. "Thanks though." He tossed a look in my direction. "I'm headed out. See ya, Elle."

"See ya," I said dully. Turning away from the woman's judgmental eyes, I cupped my aching midsection and ran up the back stairs to Chelsea's bedroom.

18

"I'm just worried that..." I stuffed a celery stick in my mouth and spoke around the crispy stalk. "I don't know. That they'll be able to tell."

Easton's voice crackled through my BMW's speakers, the noise of a crowd in his background. "That they'll be able to tell what?"

"You know." I swallowed the bite. "That I've done stuff too."

He chuckled. "It's not a stamp that gets branded on your forehead. They've already met you. Did it seem like they could tell?"

"No," I said dully.

"And could you tell that they were swingers? Or were you too busy shoveling pancakes into your mouth?"

"Very funny, asshole." I made a face. "I paid for every one of those later. But pancakes aside—I was too busy trying to keep myself together to notice anything like that." But now that I'd had ample time to look back... no. There hadn't been anything in my meeting with the De Lucas that would have made me think that they were anything other than a normal couple. Well, as normal as a wealthy, painfully good-looking couple with reluctant ties to organized crime could be.

"Are they both going to be at the house tomorrow?"

"I don't know. The photographer will be there, so at least we won't be staring at each other the entire time. I can fluff pillows and hide picture frames and stuff." My phone chimed and a reminder about my appointment flashed across the BMW's navigation screen. "Crap. I've got to go. I've got a showing appointment at three and I'm still in the parking lot at work."

We said our goodbyes and I told him to call me when he finished for the day. Stuffing another stalk of celery in my mouth, I shifted my car into reverse.

The following afternoon, at three p.m. sharp, I pull down the De Luca's well-kept street. Floyd was already in front of their house, his van emblazoned with the logo of his real estate photography business. I parked behind his car and walked up to the window, knocking gently on it to catch his attention. He rolled down the window and a grin broke through his thick red beard. "Big house."

"I know. I'm moving up in the world. Let's pretend like it's normal for me."

"I'm good at pretending." He reached in the passenger seat and patted his bag. "You ready to roll?"

"Yeah. Let me buzz in through the gate, then I'll help you carry in your stuff."

Floyd's stuff included three tripods and four bags worth of gear. I lugged the lighter of the two tote bags and struggled up the drive behind him. Julia met us at the door with a friendly smile. I waved, unsure if a handshake or hug was in order. I decided on neither and gestured to Floyd, introducing him. She shook his hand and I wondered if she was comparing him to the driver's license that he'd been required to send over, prior to his arrival.

Floyd hadn't flinched at the request, shrugging it off without asking why it was needed. "I'm poking around their house," he'd said. "I get it."

I followed the pair of them inside, surprised to see that the house had been wiped clean of all personal items. No more photos hanging in the hall. No bag hung on the hook by the door, or keys in the basket, or dog toy by the—even the dog bed was gone.

Julia followed my gaze and stepped forward. "We had everything but the bare essentials moved into storage."

"Wow." I folded my arms across my chest, just to have something to do. "You've been busy."

"Well, our house manager has." She grinned, and I tried to picture her at an orgy. It didn't fit. She was casually classy. Nude lips, a dimple in one cheek, with glossy dark hair and a mischievous smile. No tattoos, small natural breasts... she barely looked old enough to drink. I would have assumed that she spent her weekends with a good book, not elbow deep in sexcapades. "We'd like the main living and exterior areas photographed, and the master suite. None of the other rooms."

Floyd glanced at me for approval and I nodded, the details lined out in the listing agreement. "All right," he drawled. "Let's go look at the light."

"Looking at the light" entailed him walking around and opening blinds, peering at the position of the sun and weighing his options on what to photograph first and from which direction. Julia soon grew bored of the process and opened a bottle of wine, which I quickly agreed to and then immediately regretted. What if she got the wrong idea? What if she propositioned me?

"Let's go into my office so we're out of his hair." She glanced at their house manager, who gave a wary nod of disapproval.

"I'll stay here and watch him." Martha sniffed. I'd offered my hand in an attempt to re-introduce myself earlier, but she'd marched off, yelling at Floyd for his tripod placement on a certain rug.

Julia led the way down the main hall of the home, the wine bottle swinging from one hand, and I fought to calm the anxiety that crawled up my chest. I could sip a glass of wine with another woman while photos of her house were taken. It was something I had done countless times before. No big deal.

"I brought the seller's disclosure form with me. If you could go ahead and fill it out, that'd be great." I tried to pull the form out of my new Betsy Johnson purse—a TJ Maxx special. The zipper snagged on the edge, and I almost ripped the pages before getting them clear. Letting out a ragged breath, I passed it to her.

Julia perched at one end of a sleek leather couch and twisted her long dark hair into a messy bun. Picking up the wine bottle, she poured us each a glass, then got down to business. Pulling a pair of glasses off the bookshelf beside her, she placed them on and peered at the form.

"Here's a pen." I held out a cheap orange pen emblazoned with the Johnny's Filling Station logo on it. She probably already had pens. Monogrammed gold Cross ones that wrote beautifully and didn't have an indent in the top half that looked suspiciously like a tooth mark.

"Thanks." She placed it and the form to the side, picking up her glass of wine. Like a well-trained monkey, I followed suit, tilting back my glass and taking a generous sip.

"If it sucks, I'm sorry." She grinned at me over her glass. "I'm a wine idiot. This is literally the only label I enjoy. And Brad's more of a champagne guy. We're useless at society events."

"You're in good company, then." I smiled. "I like cheap moscato. It's sweet like this. If you had pulled out a bottle of red, I would have declined. Actually..." I tilted my head to one side. "I probably would have taken you up on the offer, but secretly hated every sip of it."

This seemed to please her, and I felt a warm blush move over me at her resulting laugh. "Okay, so we're both lost at wine tastings." She nodded in approval. "What else? How long have you lived in Miami?"

"About four years. I met my husband at Florida State and we moved down here after we graduated. He was playing for the Marlins." I don't know why I added that in, except that I *always* felt the need to add that in. We had been *someone*. We had been *something*. Really, honestly. Admire us even though you are so much better.

"What position?"

"Pitcher."

"You said he was playing for the Marlins. What does he do now?"

"Financial advising. Wealth management, mostly for professional and ex-athletes, but his clients come from everywhere."

"Wow." She nodded, impressed. "Good for him."

"Well, it's *okay* for him. He's still building a business. It's been..." I faltered, not sure of why I felt the need to dent her approval with the truth. "Hard. Not hard, just..." *Hard.* Hard was the right word.

I took another sip of wine.

"Hard isn't a bad thing," she said quietly. "Marriage, in itself, is hard. Figuring out our lives is hard."

"Yeah," I said. "But you seem to have it all figured out."

She coughed mid-sip, her hand clamping over her mouth as she struggled to contain her wine. I watched in concern as she gasped for air, then coughed, the glass trembling in her free hand.

"I'm sorry," I said as soon as she stopped hacking, her eyes watering from the effort. "I didn't mean—"

"No." She let out a final small cough. "It's just funny. For anyone to think that I have things figured out. Oh my God, Elle. If you only knew the things that Brad and I have been through." She cleared her throat and swallowed, wiping at her eyes. "But you know. Things you wouldn't think, even bad things—they can bring you closer as a couple." She stared off into the corner of the office and I wondered if she was talking about something with Brad's family or their sex life.

Probably Brad's family. In fact, the longer I sat there, the more I was questioning Chelsea's intel. Had it been legitimate? In my alarm at my misunderstanding her excitement for accusation, I had barely gotten any details before making an excuse and running away. It'd barely been twenty-four hours since that revelation, not enough time for us to properly follow that conversation up.

My phone hummed in my purse and I reached down and hit the side button, silencing it. It immediately hummed again, and I glanced at the screen. Speaking of the devil... Chelsea. Why was she power calling me? I hit the button again, then dropped it into my purse, the now-familiar sense of paranoia sneaking back up on me. She knew about Aaron and us. Or suspected. Maybe her maid had told her what she'd overheard. Or, worse, she was calling to tell me that she and Aaron were hooking up. Was that worse? Probably not. I went to take another sip of wine and realized that my glass was already empty.

"Here." She held out the bottle. I lifted my glass and watched the rim of it tremble. I tightened my grip but it only became worse. What was wrong with me?

"Let me take that from you." She carefully tugged it away and set it on the low coffee table before the couch. Lifting the bottle of wine, she glanced at me with concern. I knotted my hands into fists as my phone hummed *again* in my purse. Fucking Chelsea. I felt the insane urge to drop-kick my new purse into the open hall.

"If you have to get that—"

"No."

"I know you have other properties," she offered. "It's fine if you—"

"It's not work. It's my best friend. I'm not sure why she's power calling me."

"Maybe something is wrong."

"No, I think it's probably about a guy. A friend of ours. My husband's best friend. I'm worried she likes him." Oh my God, I needed to seriously SHUT THE HELL UP.

She gave me a curious look. "He's a bad guy?"

"Oh, no. He's a great guy. A really great guy. And I used to want them to get together. They had years to get together in college and it never happened and so I thought it was safe…" My voice trailed off. Not that I'd been thinking of Chelsea at all during that decision process. Why would I have? But should I have?

"What was safe?"

I lifted my gaze to find her watching me, her expression calm and open. What if Chelsea was right and they were swingers? She might be the only woman in Miami who could give me confidential and judgment-free advice. I made a split-second decision that could prove fatal. "My… uh… husband and I. We got drunk one night. Things happened with him. Him and me."

"The guy best friend and you?"

"Yeah. My husband was there. It wasn't… cheating." I took a deep breath and stared into my lap, barely noticing when she held out my glass of wine. I closed my hands around it numbly.

"And you haven't told her."

I shook my head.

"Elle." She tapped my leg and I looked up. "Listen to me. Stop feeling guilty."

"I—"

"Stop feeling guilty," she repeated, her eyes clear and understanding. "You haven't done anything wrong. You are three consenting adults who had some fun one night." She lifted one tan shoulder. "Forget it."

"Three consenting adults who are now keeping that secret from her," I pointed out. "We're all close. It's like this giant thing in the room with us when we hang out."

"Was it a one-time thing, what happened?"

"With him, yes." I hesitated, unsure if I should jump off this cliff. "But I liked it. A lot."

The corner of her mouth lifted. "Yeah, I get it." Then, as suddenly as her grin came, it left. "But here's the thing, Elle. You can't put this secret back in the box once it's out. Right now, it's only between the three of you, right?"

I nodded.

"Once you tell one person, just one... it's a loose thread. A delicious bit of gossip that someone *has* to share. They just can't help themselves. And it's not something that a 'normal' woman or wife or couple understand. And when they don't understand, they judge. They judge and make decisions and tell more people and it becomes a wildfire that you are trying to put out with a damp washcloth." She leaned back and took her own sip of wine. "And at that point, you have to decide if you are going to say fuck it to society's expectations or if you're going to hide behind lies and denial." She lifted her arms and gestured to the house around her. "Maybe you're in a position of power and wealth where you *can* say fuck it." Her face softened and I knew she was thinking of earlier and my emotional stumble over Easton's job. "Or maybe you're not."

"And all of that"—she circled her fingers around an imaginary pile of gossip—"doesn't take into account how this information will affect your friendship with her, or her future relationship with him. And then there is the moral question of if it's even your secret to share. This is a secret that involves all three of you."

She sat back on the couch. "If you tell her, it will, at some point come out. And then it will follow you and your husband. You'll have complete strangers judging you before they meet you and people you've known forever who suddenly go out of their way to avoid you." Her eyes met mine and she cocked one brow. "Think about it. How did you find out about us?"

I hadn't expected the question, my mind too full of what-if scenarios and this horrific future that she was spelling out in such clear and devastating detail. "I—what?"

"How did you find out about Brad and me?"

I could pretend that I didn't know what she was talking about, but that would be a little weak given the honesty that she was displaying. "Umm... a friend. The one who's calling me, actually. Her stepmother knows someone who used to work at your husband's law firm."

And in that one moment, it all clicked into place. Julia De Luca was right. The zigzag of gossip about her that had jumped through four people to get to me. Chelsea's sprint out to the pool, pure glee on her face about sharing the news. My own holier-than-thou judgment and irrational sexual opinions of the De Lucas. I was a baby version of them, and I was judging them. What would five-months-ago Elle have thought?

"Shit." I leaned back against the cushion and cupped the wine glass as if it were a security blanket. "What was I thinking?"

"You were thinking that it was hot and you wanted it. There's nothing wrong with that. But here's a tip. Don't do it with any close friends. Especially virgins to that sort of thing. Emotions can get involved, and things can get complicated."

"Ugh." I let out a low groan.

"It's okay."

No, it really wasn't okay. I was hyper-paranoid, drinking as if I had a problem, and talking off the rails about my sex life with the first big client I'd ever had. "I swear this is not how a home photo session normally goes."

She burst out laughing, and I couldn't help but join in. Maybe it was the wine or the relief of finally having someone to talk to, but suddenly—in that big house on Olive Line Trail—it all didn't seem so bad.

19

Brad De Luca found us in the media room, stretched out on dark leather Restoration Hardware sofas that I was already plotting to steal. I'd ignored six more calls from Chelsea, drank two bottles of wine with Julia, and had been chewed out by her house manager for putting my shoes on the ottoman. Floyd had left at some point, giving me a wry smile as I gave him an over-enthusiastic and fairly sloppy hug.

"Wow." The man stood before Julia, his hands on his hips and looked down at his wife, an affectionate smile breaking the stern lines of his face. He was *really* handsome when he smiled. "How drunk are you?"

"A wee bit," she informed him, holding her thumb and index finger an inch apart.

"Oh damn." He bent over and kissed her. "Been corrupting our realtor?"

"No corruption," I interrupted. I attempted to sit up and somehow swayed to the other side. "We were just about to do the seller's disclosure." Seller's somehow turned into weller's and Julia giggled.

"Yeah, let's wait on that." Brad sat down on the end of the couch by Julia's head, carefully repositioning so that her head was on his lap. He ran his hand over her forehead and she closed her eyes, letting out a low hum of approval.

"How did the photos go?"

"Good," Julia said. "Martha kept him in the areas we talked about while Elle and I held down the couch in my office."

He grinned at me, and it really wasn't fair for a man to be that attractive. "You'll have to excuse my wife. She's a naughty thing." His hand, which had been resting on her stomach, slid over her breasts.

I looked away. I should go. They probably had stuff to talk about. Mob defense strategies to coordinate. Hot people sex to initiate. I groped along the floor for my phone. "Do you know what time it is?"

There was a pause, while Brad checked his watch. "Almost six-thirty."

"Crap." I half fell off the couch as I dug through my purse. "My husband's flight is landing any minute. I need to get home."

"Why don't you have him swing by here?" Brad ran his fingers along the top of Julia's hair. "We can put steaks on. I hate to be a prick, but you can't drive home. We can take you if he can't come here."

"Oh, no." I found my phone and hefted upright, aware that my butt had been stuck in the air like a burnt offering. "That's fine. I can get a ride." Yep. I was officially the worst Realtor ever. They'd probably email me the minute I left. *Sorry, Elle. Things aren't working out. It turns out you're an emotional train wreck who drooled all over our couch.*

As if on cue, my cell vibrated. I glanced down, expecting to see Chelsea's number again, but it was E. I hesitated. "This is my husband now. He must have landed." So much for my plan to have started dinner.

"Give me the phone," Brad ordered. "I'll talk to him." He looked at me, really *looked* at me—and I don't know how anyone ever refused him anything. I tossed the phone toward him and he caught it with one hand, swiping across the screen and lifting it to his ear. Our eyes held as he said hello, and he winked at me. In between my legs, I clenched.

"He's really bossy," Julia apologized in a whisper loud enough to be heard in the kitchen. "But it's sexy, right?" She laughed, and I laughed, and I'm glad she didn't want a response, because she was right. It was sexy. My overeager fantasies began to churn and I killed that mental detour before it had a chance to take flight. Even drunk I could recognize that being this attracted to my biggest client was a bad thing. *A very bad thing.*

Easton showed up just after seven, his tie tight, concern etched on his handsome features. I launched myself into his arms and felt him stiffen, his arm circling my waist protectively. "Thank you for calling me." He stuck out his hand to Brad and there was a minor skirmish of alpha male egos in the middle of the foyer. "I'll get her home. Have a good night."

"Wait, Easton." Julia appeared in the doorway, and I felt him straighten a bit at the sight of her. Sober, I would have been jealous, but I was in the sort of love-everybody mood that was impossible to crack. "We just put some steaks on. You've got to be hungry. You're on LA time, right? Please, stay for dinner."

"She's right. Come on." Brad turned away and waved over his shoulder, eliminating the option to decline. "We can't waste this meat. Besides, I've got a box of Cubans I need an excuse to smoke."

"Are you okay?" Easton asked quietly, keeping me in place beside him.

"I'm fine. Slightly drunk." I laughed. "Relax, babe. I promise, it's all good." Dipping out of his arms, I tugged at his hand and he reluctantly followed me through the great room and toward the outdoor kitchen.

Dinner was paired with drinks, and after two Scotches, Easton's tension had mellowed and his bromance with Brad was in full force. As it turned out, Brad was familiar with his failed baseball career and had played himself, in college—not pro. Their conversation turned in the general and boring direction of sports, while Julia and I bonded over peppermint schnapps and books. It was almost ten before we found ourselves back in our respective couples, tongues loose and limbs languid, clustered across from each other on the circular seating that framed the dark fire pit.

Around eleven, the conversation turned sexual, and we laughed over Brad and Julia's stories about sex resorts and awkward misunderstandings. They spoke freely and without shame, and I found myself less and less embarrassed of our own minor experience that seemed like a fairly tame drop in the bucket compared to their hedonistic adventures.

Brad blew a stream of cigar smoke into the dark night air. "Julia." He patted his leg and she rose, stepping before him with confidence. I expected her to sit sideways on his leg but instead she straddled it, the hem of her skirt riding up to expose a toned and tan thigh. She bent her head and kissed—or maybe bit—the side of his neck. "How do you feel when I fuck other women?"

She grinned and slid her hand down the middle of his dress shirt. "It drives me crazy. I come alive with this raw and insane possessive instinct."

"So, you don't like it?" I asked, curious.

She glanced at me. "I hate it, but it also turns me on so much. Like, more than I've ever been turned on by anything."

"I'm just not sure I could do it. The idea of it turns me on, but I'm worried I wouldn't be able to get that image out of my head." I looped my fingers through Easton's. "What if I hated him for it afterward? And what if the girl became a problem?"

"Single girls don't work," Brad interrupted. "They're either prostitutes or problems. And prostitutes can work, but there isn't as much of a feel of authenticity there. That's why couples swap—or you borrow a wife for a night."

I could see Easton weighing the idea and I hurried to cut his thought process off at the pass. "If we *wanted* to do that. But a lot of couples just do threesomes with a guy, right? We could just hook up with single men, and not do anything else?"

"You can do anything you want. Anything you both are comfortable and happy with."

"But you said the thought of seeing Easton with a girl turns you on." Julia turned to me. "Is fear the only thing holding you back?"

"Maybe?" I struggled to find the right words to describe the mix of panic and arousal that I felt when I thought of Easton with another woman. But what was I afraid of? No one knew E's body and needs better than me. *No one.* I knew that more than I knew anything else in this world.

"Elle." I turned to look at Easton and found strength in his quiet smile. The firm hand that he cupped against my waist. The confidence in his eyes when he looked at me. "You know, I was terrified that night with Aaron."

"You were? Why?"

"Why wouldn't I be? My wife—you—were about to be touched by

him. Pleased by him. I didn't know how you'd react to that, and I didn't know how I'd react to it. I knew him, and I knew you, and I trusted both of you enough to push through that fear and try it out."

"For me," I said quietly.

"Yeah..." He grinned. "But it was good for me too. I figured that out the minute he walked into the room. I thought I'd hate it, but I didn't. I saw the way you responded and I fucking loved it."

I lifted my glass of wine and took a small sip. "Do you think I'd love it?"

"I don't know," he admitted.

"Let's try an experiment," Julia proposed from her spot on Brad's lap. She spun forward and met my gaze. "How would you feel, right now, if I sucked your husband's cock?"

She threw it out so casually, as if we were deciding who was going to drive to dinner, or whether we should brew a pot of coffee. *Do you prefer decaf? A blowjob for Easton?* Brad said nothing, his features calm and unaffected, though I watched his hand slide possessively up the front of her shirt, almost high enough to cup her breast.

From beside me, Easton inhaled in surprise, his grip on me tightening. Did he want it? Normally, I'd be alive with jealousy and territorialism, but instead... arousal was licking up from between my legs, tingling and growing as it skated up my belly and coiled around my nipples. She wouldn't do it. Not right here. Not right in front of her husband. These were all hypothetical questions. Right?

Everything boiled down to that question, and my focus tightened on her. Her sharp and intelligent eyes, holding to my face. Her hand, still gripping Brad's. Her posture, curved toward us. The excitement that radiated from her. She *wanted* to do it.

I gave an awkward laugh. "Is that a hypothetical question?"

"It's a serious question. How does the thought of it make you feel? If it pisses you off, or turns you off, then you guys should probably stick to just you and a guy. But if it turns you on... then let's try it right now and see how you feel. If you, at any point, hate it—then I'll stop."

"I'm sorry," Easton interrupted. "I'm not trying to look a gift horse in the mouth, but you're talking about giving me a blowjob, right here? Like, right now?"

Brad thumbed the end of the cigar. "If Elle and you are comfortable with it."

I didn't have to look at E to know what he was thinking. I could feel him stiffening against my leg. I had picked up on the vibration in his voice, the husky catch in his question. He wanted it. Of course he wanted it. It had been six years since another woman had seen his dick. Six years since anyone, other than me and a medical professional, had touched his dick.

He started to speak, to politely protest, and I stopped him. Inside, I was on fire. Hot, panicked arousal. It was roaring through my head and out of my ears. It was chasing my heart around my chest and drumming a beat of pleasure between my legs. I was already wet. I was terrified. And if I was ever going to do it, this was the time. My eyes met Brad's and he nodded as if to command me to speak. "Let's try it and see."

Julia turned to Brad and kissed him deeply, her fingers skating across his chest and wrapping around his tie, tugging it toward her as she deepened the contact, then broke from him and turned toward us.

I looked at Easton and wondered if I should kiss him too. He studied me warily, his hand tightening on mine when I went to stand up. "Stay," he said gruffly. "And kiss me."

I kissed him swiftly, almost desperately. His hand curved around my head and he pulled me tighter, pinning me against him. I pulled away from his mouth and watched as Julia took a seat on the other side of him, her leg close enough to brush his. I expected her to comment on his erection, which was now tenting the front of his pants, but she didn't. Instead, she relaxed against the back of the white cushion and picked up Easton's Scotch, bringing it to her lips. "Will you show me how he likes it?"

"Jesus," Easton swore under his breath as he stretched out his legs and tried to adjust his dick to a less painful angle. I glanced at Brad, who watched his wife with dark eyes. How much had this couple done together? What boundaries did they have?

"I—ah…" I swallowed hard and watched as Julia sat up, then reached forward and gripped the leather end of Easton's belt.

"You don't have to," she said softly, just loud enough for me to hear. "But it might help. We can do it together."

"I really fucking like that idea." Easton lifted his arm up and around me, urging me forward and closer. "Show her. Please." The beg tore out of him, the word rough and jagged, as if he was choking on the single syllable.

Could I? If it wasn't for Brad, I'd already be on my knees, his dick out and pushing down my throat. But knowing he was watching… I… Fuck. *Could I do this?*

As if he could read my mind, Brad pushed to his feet and reached forward to stub the cigar out on the tray. "I'm going to go get a refill on my drink." He walked behind the sofa and bent over the back of it, his hand sliding down Julia's chest and squeezing her breast. "Behave, wife."

She laughed and tugged on the ring finger of his hand, looking up at him in adoration. "Take your time."

He released her, then turned and headed up the series of steps that led to their back deck. I watched him move up the first set of stairs, his steps confident and relaxed, then focused on Easton. Dragging down his zipper, my hand brushed hers and I let out a shaky breath at the twist of anticipation that unfurled in my gut.

"On your knees," Easton breathed, his bossy dominance coming out to play now that Brad had gone. I pulled a pillow from the couch and put it on the ground, kneeling onto it and working him out of the opening of his pants. Julia fully undid the belt and button, helping me to peel back his slacks and underwear until his cock popped free.

She grinned in approval. "Wow." Reaching out, she brushed her fingertip along the bulb of his head, then all the way down his rigid shaft. It twitched, and I felt a flare of jealousy that her touch had caused the reaction. She turned to me, her grin dropping and a studious concentration came over her features. "Show me how you suck it, what he likes."

I scooted forward, my hands settling on his thighs, and opened my mouth, running my tongue along the underside of his shaft and flicking it along the ridge of his head. I relaxed my throat and took him as far as I could, then worked him in and out of my mouth. He let out a groan of approval and leaned forward, gathering my hair in his hand and securing it away from my face.

She knelt next to me, sharing the tight area between his open knees, and I flinched in surprise when her hand ran up my side. I pulled my mouth off his cock and worked it with my hand, watching as she undid the top button of my blouse, and then the second.

She opened up the material, exposing the top of my cleavage to the warm night air. "Is this okay?"

I nodded, curving into her delicate and cool touch, the sensation so foreign compared to Easton and Aaron's firm and masculine hands. "You're beautiful," she said, pulling apart the final buttons, her hands skating over my lace bra and undoing its front clasp.

If it was possible for Easton to get harder, he did, his foreskin stretching drum-tight as he watched Julia lift my aching breasts in her hands. My hand, which had grown lazy, worked back into action as I tried to pull my attention off my tender nipples and toward his cock. She brushed her lips over one of my nipples and I inhaled at the soft touch of her mouth. "Here," I said quickly. "Take it." I needed to see her put that mouth on him. I needed to get the focus off me and onto him before I ripped all of my clothes off and begged someone to fuck me.

She lifted her mouth from my breast and moved toward his cock. I needed her to do it quickly, before my wave of arousal crested, or turned into insecurity, or some other card in this towering stack fell out of place. The fire in my head roared and when she wrapped her hand around him and lowered her head to take him in, I expected it to burst. She slid her mouth down on his shaft, her lips gliding over the thick rod, and I braced for impact.

Nothing. Nothing but the slow and mounting need to be fucked six ways to Sunday. Nothing but the love burning through me for my husband, who gripped her ponytail in his fist and stared into my eyes. He short thrusted up into her mouth—Julia De Luca's mouth—and worshipped me with his stare. I lowered my face until it was beside hers, my nails skimming along his thigh, and flicked my tongue out and along the base of his cock. She tilted her head to one side and together we licked up along his thick shaft. I took in the swollen head, then she did, and when I looked back at him, his features were almost delirious with pleasure and arousal.

"You're so fucking beautiful," he groaned. Pulling at my arm, he lifted his chin. "Sit on my face. I have to taste you."

I sat back on my heels and pushed to my feet. Unbuttoning my slacks, I pushed my underwear and pants down, then ripped my shirt and bra off, stripping down to nothing in the middle of their backyard. From above me, I heard the slide of the door and realized Brad was return-

ing. Empowered, I stepped onto the cushion and over Easton, straddling his shoulders and fisting his blond tufts as he kissed my hips
and fought for access to my pussy. Slow footsteps sounded as Brad
came down the steps.

"Kneel on the back cushions," Easton gasped and I heard Julia
gagging, looked down to see her face buried in his lap, his thick dick
fully down her throat. I held on to his head for balance and knelt on
the cushions on either side of his face, struggling to stay upright as I
pitched dangerously over the back of the sectional.

"Here." Brad's voice came out of the darkness, his hands gripping
mine, supporting me as I balanced over Easton's face. My husband's
mouth settled between my legs, right where I was hot and aching, and
I moaned aloud as his face buried in and focused on the most intense
spot of my need.

"Does that feel good?" Brad's voice was gruff and close.

I kept my eyes closed as my back arched in pleasure. "So good," I
panted.

He moved my hands to either side of his neck. "Keep your hands on
my shoulders." He leaned forward and his breath tickled my hair.
"Can I touch you?"

"Yes," I gasped without thinking, my nails digging into the thick fabric
of his shirt.

He chuckled. "Forgive me for being careful, but this is a litigious era.
I'm going to need to hear you ask for it. Better yet..." I flinched in
surprise when his thumb grazed over my mouth. "Beg."

"Please touch me," I whispered.

"Where?"

I could feel his breath, the question uttered somewhere around my
collarbone.

"Everywhere."

His hands were hot and thick, hitting the sides of my body and sliding down, then back up, his fingers flexing and gently curling around me. They rose, up from my ribcage and came forward, cupping my breasts and lifting them up. So different from her touch. So much stronger. Less tentative. More possessive and confident. "Ask your husband if I can touch you."

Easton's mouth, which had been pulsing against my clit slowed and he lifted his head back against the cushions and looked up at me. I found him in the dark, his features raw with arousal, his eyes hungry with need. "Can he touch me?" I asked, and it wasn't a question. It was a plea. A *beg*. A wanton request from a woman so far over the edge that I'm not sure I would have been able to stop if he had denied it.

"He can do anything you want," Easton rasped out, and then Julia did something between his legs, something that made his eyes dull and his body stiffen. I knew that look. I'd given him that look countless times, in countless situations, doing countless things, but knowing that she had delivered it... I lowered myself back onto his mouth. I pulled Brad De Luca closer to me and shivered as his hands settled on my ass, squeezing and pulling apart my cheeks as his mouth settled onto my neck, kissing and teasing over the flesh. My nipples rubbed against the stiff cotton of his dress shirt and I scraped my hands through his hair, listening as my husband gasped against my clit, his tongue slowing, then quickening as she sucked his cock.

I had worried that this would ruin us. I had worried that I would see this sight, hear those noises, and freak the F out—but that wasn't what happened at all. Instead, there was only more.

More arousal.

More need.

More emotion.

More love.

More trust.

More risk.

More reward.

Brad's finger pushed into the tight and needy bundle of my ass and it was the push that sent me over the edge. I came hard, my fingers digging into Brad's muscles, my mouth needy on his neck, his voice thick and commanding in my ear. Easton's mouth tightened, his tongue focusing, and he delivered the orgasm perfectly, stretching out the pleasure until a point that was almost painful, then relaxing his jaw and letting me sink into his mouth. I sagged in Brad's arms and didn't resist when he lifted me up, carried me around the long end of the sectional couch and gently set me next to Easton.

"Julia," he commanded, and his wife immediately pulled off E's cock. "Let her finish him. I need you right the fuck now."

I didn't move, couldn't. I heard Easton, the creak of the couch, the clink of his belt. His knees sank into the cushion, moving apart my legs, his wet and rigid cock pushing in between my legs. "We can't—" I protested, and from the dark, I heard a feminine gasp, one of plea-sure, then a moan, as Brad did something to Julia that sounded posi-tively sinful.

"We can," Easton whispered, settling on top of me, his shirt brushing against my bare breasts, his thighs heavy against mine. He thrust his hips and he was inside me, my core aching from days of neglect, my body flexing as my arms stole around his neck, my mouth finding his, my hips moving of their own accord as he started to drag that thick beautiful cock in and out of me. Beside us, close enough that I could feel the shake of the sectional, they fucked. I could hear them, the slapping of connecting bodies, the labor of breath, the quiet huffs and moans out of Julia's mouth.

Easton pulled away from our kiss and lowered his mouth to my ear. "Look at them," he whispered, then kissed my ear. "Watch them."

"I can't," I gasped, his thrusts quickening, an urgent pulse of intrusion. Had he ever been this big? This hard? This turned on?

That night. That night, with Aaron beside him. But this... this was different. This was a sea of sounds and the cool night air, and the taboo realization that I was in someone else's backyard, beside them. Fucking beside them. I turned my head and forced myself to look. My eyes widened.

Brad, on his knees behind her. Her bare breasts rubbing against the cushion, her hands pulling her ass cheeks apart. She was looking back at him, her cheek against the couch, and urging him on, quiet words of filth that were floating over to us.

"Harder. Harder. Yes. Oh my..." her head lifted as she came, and I could see it take over her body, her hands tightening, her pleasure blooming, the tight pinch of her eyes, the gap of her mouth. He consumed her with his stare, his hands gripping her at the wrist, keeping them in place as he maintained his rhythm, maintained the collide of his thighs against her hamstrings as he drilled his—"

Oh. I stared at the juncture of his body, questioning the view as I saw peeks of it, illuminated by the fire. He was so thick, and from the length of his strokes, the distance that parted their bodies with each withdrawal—long.

"You like that?" Easton whispered in my ear. "I can feel you, getting tighter. Wetter. You're fucking quaking around me."

"I like it," I moaned, returning my attention to him. I gripped the back of his neck and stared into his eyes. "Did you like her mouth on your cock?"

"I loved her mouth on my cock." He let out a grunt, and I could see he was close, his chest tightening, his thrusts quickening. "I almost came in her tight little throat."

That was it. My breaking point. I let out a sharp cry of pleasure, louder than I'd intended, my voice keening as my body tightened, the orgasm racking up in intensity at the wild look on Easton's face. He devoured me with his eyes, his hand fisting my hair as his breath came out in short, hard puffs. I pinched my eyes closed, unable to handle the surge of pleasure as it peaked in one huge, wild sweep of emotion and sensation.

Beside me, I faintly registered the sounds of Julia, her own cries heightening, Brad's voice soft and urgent, pushing her on. What was he saying? Was he watching us? Did he—

I lost my focus as Easton pulled me up, his dick coming out, and pushed me to my knees.

"Open up," he said tersely. "I'm about to come like a fucking virgin."

20

"Seriously, what the *fuck* was that?" Easton ran his hand over his mouth and merged onto the interstate in a speed that would get him pulled over.

I leaned back in the seat and propped my feet on the dash. "I don't know. I swear, it was all G-rated before you got there."

"I'm curious to what exactly led to you getting drunk."

I sighed. "I don't know. Peer pressure. I was nervous, she had wine and... yada yada yada." The Seinfeld quote fell flat and he said nothing, his blinker clicking loudly in the silence.

"I'm sorry," I added. "Do you think I lost the listing?"

He glanced at me. "I don't know. Ask your broker what he thinks." E spoke in a wry tone, but there was tension in the way he gripped the steering wheel, my stress level rising with the hum of the engine.

"Slow down." I glanced in the rearview mirror, concerned about cops. He had three Scotches, maybe four? Though they had been stretched over... I checked my watch. "Shit, it's past midnight."

"What time did you let Wayland out?"

"About one." It was official, I was a horrible everything. Mother. Wife. Realtor. I twisted my watch on my wrist. Earlier, before we'd moved to the backyard, Brad and Julia had offered for us to stay the night, and I almost, *almost* took them up on the offer before E reminded me of Wayland. Which was good, because while we had parted with smiles, if we had stayed the night, the morning would have been super awkward. Similar to how the interior of this car now felt.

"I'm not sure if you're mad at me," I ventured. "You're acting really weird."

"*I'm* acting weird," he mused, nodding his head in an annoyingly slow fashion, as if he had massive intellectual processes going on. "Interesting."

"So, you think I'm acting weird? You could have said no. When she offered to suck your dick, you could have said no."

"I can't believe we're even having this conversation. Are you *listening* to yourself? When she offered to suck my dick. Next time warn me before I get on a plane that I'm going to be headed straight to a fucking Penthouse Forum scene the minute I land."

"Umm... okay." I frowned. "It wasn't a Penthouse Forum scene when you got there. I was sobering up. We were cooking dinner. It's not my fault that we stayed for four more hours and that came up."

"It's completely your fault that that came up. You *brought* it up."

"Well—" I really didn't have a defense for that. I had brought it up. Chelsea had called again, and Julia had asked me about it, and then I'd told E that I'd asked her advice about it, which had led to Julia explaining to Brad what we were talking about, which had steamrolled into a conversation about the airport swinger club, which Julia had a hilarious story about, which had led to a drunk toast by E, and then...

somehow... hours later... orgasms. Really, *really* strong orgasms. I changed tactics. "So, you are mad at me."

He sighed. "I'm not mad. I'm worried. I feel like we're moving too fast. It's been, what? A month since Aaron?"

"Yeah." Almost exactly.

"A month, and we've gone from an isolated instance with someone we were both very comfortable with to orgasming with complete strangers."

They didn't feel like complete strangers to me. Julia felt like a friend. And— "Wait, a few days ago you were pushing me to find a complete stranger on that site. How are Brad and Julia different from that?"

"Maybe it's not." He came to a stop at the red light of Flagler and took a deep breath. "I'm just worried."

"I know. You said that. What are you worried about?"

"I'm worried that..." He closed his eyes and dropped his head back against the quilted leather headrest, letting out a heavy breath. "I'm worried I'm losing you. Losing us. We aren't like them, Elle." The light on his face changed as the signal turned green. He sat upright and pressed on the gas. "We don't have our shit together. To them, what just happened was no big deal. That guy walked inside and left his wife alone with us, and it was nothing to him. It didn't matter if I had a big dick, or what she did to me—he trusted her enough to just leave. And when he came back and he put his hands on you... it scared the hell out of me. I was trying to focus on her blowjob, but all I could think about was that he was going to fuck you the minute you came off my mouth."

I shook my head. "That wasn't—he didn't even try that."

"I thought he would. And he's not Aaron, Elle." He looked over at me. "That guy... that guy makes me look like a chump. And of course he has a big dick. I'm fucked sideways if he knows how to use it."

Which it certainly seemed he had. "No one has ever made you look like a chump."

He shook his head with a hard laugh. "Elle. Come on. Brad's watch is worth more than what we have in the bank, my 401k included. That's the kind of guy you should be with. That's what you deserve."

"Fuck that," I said fiercely. "You're my husband. I chose you."

"You chose me when you thought I was something that I ended up not being."

"I chose you because I love *you*. Not the uniform, not the signing bonus, not the big dick."

He said nothing, and the Range Rover bounced over the dip in our driveway before coming to a stop in front of our garage. Unclipping my belt, I waited for him to get out, but he didn't move.

"E." I touched his arm.

"Let's go inside." He pulled at the door handle. "Wayland's got to be dying to piss."

I watched as he stepped out of the SUV and opened the back door to grab his bag.

"You coming?" he asked tersely, and I nodded, my still-drunk brain struggling to process where all of this had gone wrong.

He had certainly seemed into it, and we'd been all smiles and stolen touches as we'd gathered our clothes and giggled goodbye to Brad and Julia, who had still been mid-sex on the dark end of the couch. But somewhere between their street and Flagler, his mood had flipped. Maybe in the morning, with my buzz worn off and my hangover kicking, I'd change too. Maybe I'd freak out over him getting head from her. Maybe I'd panic over the listing, and at the incomplete seller's disclosure, and at the sexual actions that could lose me the listing, and my license.

Not that I could lose my real estate license. My mouth grew dry at that thought, one my logic tried to quickly dismiss. It wasn't like I was their doctor, or their boss. I was in that idiotic profession that counted bedrooms and tied balloons to mailboxes and preached on decluttering and locking up pets during a showing.

I managed to make it over the driveway's crack and through the front door. Kicking off my shoes, I left them beside the mat and flipped the deadbolt. Moving through the house, I watched as Easton followed Wayland into the backyard, pausing beside him as the dog lifted one leg.

By the time they made it back inside, I was in bed, my makeup still on, teeth unbrushed, in socks and a baggy T-shirt, a pillow in between my legs. I heard him walk into the master suite and closed my eyes, deepening my breathing and feigning sleep. He paused beside our bed, and then there was the click of the bathroom door and the sound of the shower.

I should have stayed up. I should have discussed it with him and figured out the root of the problem, and fought through the issue and faced up to whatever I did wrong, though I didn't feel as if I did anything at all. If either of us was going to be freaking out right now, it should be me. He was the one who had been with another woman, and I was supposed to be the insecure party who was being held and petted and told that I was sexier and more amazing, in every single way.

But I hadn't flipped out, and I wasn't feeling insecure about what had happened. And I didn't feel like apologizing when he had asked for it and wanted it as much as I did.

I closed my eyes, and when he got into bed, I didn't say a word.

21

"Okay, *what* is wrong with your phone?" Chelsea barged into the kitchen, a donut box in hand. "I tried to call you like ten times yesterday."

I tilted back my mug of coffee slowly, taking a deep sip of the rich blend. I'd splurged this week, getting the local roaster's beans, my credit card more easily swiped after E's commission check. Setting down my cup, I met Chelsea's expectant stare. "I had a photoshoot at the Olive Line Trail listing. I left my phone in the car."

"For seven hours?" She shook her head in disbelief. "I even came by here last night. Took Wayland out, by the way. You're welcome. Where was E?"

"Los Angeles. His flight got in late."

"Well, so did you. I came by around nine. What were you doing?"

I paused, annoyed that she suddenly seemed to have so much time for me. Where had she been for the last month? What had been the emergency that had required ten calls but not a single voicemail or text? "I stayed for dinner with the clients. We had some paperwork to fill out."

Her eyes bugged out. "With the De Lakeys? The mobster sex couple?"

"De Lucas," Easton corrected, coming in the kitchen and opening the lid to the box. "Thanks for the donuts."

"You're welcome," she said pointedly, looking at me as if needing a second pat on the back for eleven dollars' worth of sugar.

"I'm keto," I reminded her. "No carbs." *Or sugar.*

She took the other stool and opened the lid, peering in. "I can't believe you went to their house alone. E, you can't let her do these things. Did she tell you about them? Did she tell you that they are SWINGERS?"

"Yes, she mentioned that." E avoided my gaze as he lifted a chocolate glazed out of the box and bit into it.

"I'm telling you, Elle. You're lucky they didn't rape you." She dangled one foot from the stool and I watch as her flip-flop fell off. "E, back me up."

He lifted the mug and poured himself a cup. "I made my feelings clear on the De Lucas last night. Elle's a big girl. She knows what she is getting into."

I glared at him and Chelsea suddenly stiffened. "Are you two fighting?"

I ignored the question and unlocked my phone, swiping away the long list of Chelsea notifications and opening my inbox.

"Well, this is awkward," she remarked tartly, as if our fight was inconvenient to her pop-in schedule. "Easton, how was your trip?"

"Fine. It was worth the trip. I told Nicole she should invest in the game."

"You did?" I looked up from my phone, my email forgotten. "When?"

"On the flight home. We reviewed the contract and the timetable and the numbers and I told her she should do it." He swung his foot toward Wayland, who had started to scratch at the baseboard. "Wayland, stop."

"Do you think she's going to?" I stared at him, doing the math. Ten million, at his one percent fee—*a hundred thousand dollar commission.* My heart soared at the possibility.

"She agreed last night and wired the money this morning into the account. It's done." He stood and carried his cup to the sink, turning his back to me.

"What? And you didn't tell me?" All last night, he had known. He could have whispered it in my ear as we ate dinner, side by side at the table at Brad and Julia's. Could have shared it when we kissed as I passed him on the way to the bathroom. Could certainly have brought it up during the long ride home. He'd known that our money problems were over and he hadn't said a thing about this payday. "Why not?"

"You didn't ask." He rinsed his cup out and picked up the sponge, suddenly progressive enough to wash his own dishes.

"Okay dokey, I'm going to take my carb- and sugar-loaded donuts and skedaddle before it starts to rain." Chelsea scooped the box up against her chest and edged toward the door. "Great chatting with you both. Once you exit the war zone, call me and we can grab lunch."

I stared at E's back, noting the rigid line of his shoulders as he scrubbed the coffee mug hard enough to remove the paint. "Congratulations," I managed. "That's huge. Does Don know?"

"Yeah. I forwarded the deal memo to him last night."

"And she already wired the money?"

He paused. "I said she did."

"Okay." I tapped my fingers slowly along the counter and waited for him to turn. This was stupid. We shouldn't be fighting. We should be celebrating. Fucking. Flipping open the Frontgate catalog stuffed in my office trash and ordering a new patio set.

I set my mug down and stood, moving to stand behind him. Leaning my chest against his back, I wrapped my arms around him. "I'm proud of you," I whispered.

"I'm not getting paid on it." He set the coffee cup down on the counter and I watched as water drops splattered onto the granite. "I referred her to Don. She'll be working with him now, unless she decides to return to Morgan Stanley."

"What?" My relief evaporated and I stepped back, stunned. "Why?"

He turned to face me. "On the flight back, she hit on me. I took a Xanax and fell asleep. I woke up with a blanket across my lap, my pants unzipped and her hand on me. I was hard and she was jacking me off. I pushed her away and she said..." He shrugged, pulling the dishtowel off the counter and wiping his hands dry. "A lot of things. Things she wanted to do to me. To us."

"But—but she's gay."

"Apparently, she's bisexual. I told her I couldn't continue advising her, that it would be inappropriate. She got pissed. But the investment is still a good one for her. I told her to take it, and I waived the commission so she'd understand that I wasn't motivated by that. It *is* a good opportunity for her. She should take it."

I didn't know why he was even talking about the investment, or trying to convince me of its validity. "She touched you? Pulled out your dick in the middle of the plane?"

"Under a blanket, but yes." He rubbed his forehead with the heel of one hand. "I swear, when I woke up, it was already hard. I don't know how the fuck that happened, but—"

"Is this why you got mad last night?" This was too much. The roller-coaster of emotions. The financial highs and lows. I took a deep breath and reminded myself that he'd just gotten paid. I would sell Olive Line. I'd get the selling bonus that Brad and Julia had offered and we'd be flush for at least six months. Long enough for him to find another client, or another deal, or convince his current portfolio to make fresh deposits. We didn't *need* this, but I was also struggling to wrap my head around the fact that Easton had just walked away from a six-figure paycheck. "And it's done? You're definitely not getting paid? She was okay with that?"

His chin lifted stubbornly, his eyes arrestingly blue. "Is that what you care about?"

"I care about *everything*. I care that you're mad at me, for a reason that I can't figure out. I care about putting us back together, in a way that gets us past whatever has gotten us off track. I care about the fact that you got assaulted on a plane last night. And YES, I care about the fact that the woman who hand-raped you saved a hundred thousand dollars in the process."

"You're being overdramatic."

"No, I'M NOT. If that was a guy who fingered a sleeping girl on a plane, he'd be in jail right now. She sexually assaulted you. That's what she did, and you could sue her or threaten her but what you shouldn't have done was do her any favors. And *she* got pissed? What the fuck was *SHE* PISSED ABOUT?" I inhaled sharply, trying to catch my breath.

"I'm not talking to you when you're like this. I'm going to work." He tried to move past me and I grabbed him, clawing at his arms and chest when he tried to shove me away.

"TALK TO ME," I screamed as he got away and stomped toward the front door. I picked up his wet coffee cup and flung it at him, the heavy mug hitting the door just as he slammed it closed.

I ran through the entry and out the door, pausing for a moment at the rain, which was starting to fall, the drops dotting across the white driveway. I ran forward, my bare feet scraping on the stepping stones, and I caught him halfway down the walkway. He came to a stop, his white dress shirt already dotted with rain, the drops staining my Ann Taylor sheath.

"I was mad last night because I felt like I fucked up." He spoke quietly but the words carried over the rain, the sound of defeat heavy in the tones. "I fucked up by not getting the commission. I fucked up by putting myself in a situation with another woman where that happened. And I felt the weight of all that when I saw you last night, in that big fucking house, coming alive under his hands. I'm not good enough for you, and it scares the ever-living shit out of me."

"You are good enough for me. You are made for me." He had to know that. He had to know that my life would be nothing without him, without our love. I circled him carefully, worried he would move, and wrapped my arms around his waist, hugging my cheek against his damp back, shielding my face against the increasing downpour. "Listen to me. Things are crazy right now, but I need you here beside me. I can't have us cracked. I need you."

He turned and I stayed in place, retightening my grip and burying my cheek against the wet front of his shirt. He lifted his hand, almost hesitantly, and gently brushed the sodden strands back off my forehead. "I know how much we needed that money."

"No. Not that badly. What we need is us. What she did to you..." I knotted my fists in the bottom of his shirt and moved in closer to him, almost yelling to be heard over the rain. "It was criminal. But you chose us when you walked away from that deal. And that's one of the reasons why I love you so much." He dipped his head and our wet lips met, just a brush of cold contact, then a pause.

"I love you, Elle. I'm so—"

"I know." I lifted on my toes and met his mouth, my hand stealing up his shirt, my kiss greedy for more. He pulled me closer, his hands roughly moving down and gripping my ass, pulling me tight as he kissed along the open neck of my dress.

When he lifted me up, I wrapped my legs around his waist. When he carried me into the house, I deepened our kiss. When he laid me down on our bed, I peeled the wet shirt over his head and struggled out of my soaked dress.

When he tenderly made love, I inhaled each touch, each thrust, each kiss. And afterward, I didn't talk, or ask questions, or bring up anything. I curled into his arms and stayed silent and weathered this swell of the storm.

But inside, I burned with anger over that bitch.

22

Hey Rachel. How's everything going so far? Don't be shy—if you have any questions or need any advice, I'm here for you both. If your husband needs to talk through the shitstorm of emotions that this stuff brings, have him call me. 407-214-2001.

I took a screenshot of the message and texted it to E.

Any questions for him?

Exiting from the messages, I locked my phone and placed it on the desk, returning my attention to my laptop. One email from my mom. I scanned it quickly.

Cruise to Jamaica...

Don't forget your sister's anniversary next week...

Pet food from China is contaminated...

I clicked on the next email and scrolled through the sales stats for last week, pleased to see the De Luca listing in the top tier of new listings.

"So...tell me everything." Tim swung into my office in a cloud of Aqua De Gio and pastel colors. He perched on my desk and picked up the listing flyer for Olive Line. "And don't leave any of the good stuff out."

"Tell you everything about what?" I deleted a mortgage rates email, then a Pottery Barn promo about linens.

"The De Luca photoshoot! It was Thursday, right? Did you see Brad De Luca there? The photos look gorgeous, by the way. *Love* this." He held up the rough draft of my flyer, the page pinched between two recently buffed nails.

I minimized my email and leaned back in my desk chair, considering and quickly discarding the possibility of telling Tim *everything*. "Brad was there and it went fine. Floyd sent me the reel over the weekend, and I emailed them a link to the photos and the flyer this morning. I'm waiting for their approval before I send it out."

I had spent the better part of the weekend working on the listing description and flyer, grateful for the distraction from Easton's quiet brooding. We hadn't really discussed Nicole—or Brad and Julia—and between the two hot topics, I hadn't really known what to say. I needed Chelsea's advice, but had gotten her voicemail all weekend. Apparently, her urgent desire to chat had faded, along with her ability to return a phone call.

"You're smart to get their approval." He nodded. "Especially given their, you know, privacy issues." He glanced out into the hall, then toed my door closed with the tip of one brown and black saddle shoe. "So, Fred says he's gorgeous. Is it true?"

"Gorgeous?" I shrugged. "I don't know. That's not exactly the adjective I'd use." Manly. Devastatingly intimidating. Pure fucking temptation. "He's very muscular." That was a safe term—one no one could argue about, given Brad's large frame, but also one that wouldn't raise any red flags.

"Maybe it's just the danger element Fred liked. He's into all that stuff. Action movies. Kick-ass guys." He shrugged. "You know. The exact opposite of all of this." He pointed to his reed-thin torso which was wrapped in a skintight pink polo shirt.

"Well, he's married. And straight," I offered. "So I don't think you have to worry about Fred."

"Oh, sweetie." He laughed. "I don't ever worry about Fred. Plus, I've heard De Luca doesn't mind adding more to the party, if you know what I mean."

I frowned in confusion, as if I didn't know what he meant. Did *everyone* know about their sex life? Was that the potential future for E and me? Casual innuendos tossed out like party favors whenever either one of us was discussed? I thought of what Julia had said. That if I told Chelsea, that it would, at some point, come out. And that it would follow Easton and me.

"Also... I heard you have seven showings set up. Which I'm *really* happy about." He smiled thinly, and I could see, in the rigid way he set down the flyer, how unhappy he really was.

"It's a hot street, you know that."

"Oh, I know. Like I said, I'm happy for you. I didn't have time for this listing anyway, with everything else I have going on. That's why I gave it to you."

Right. Funny how quickly his story was changing. A week ago, when I'd found out about the Magiano connection and confronted him over his avocado and blueberry salad, he'd all but begged me to stay on the listing. He'd blamed Fred, said that he'd wanted to tell me about the Magianos but Fred was worried I wouldn't take it. Now, he was suddenly doing me a favor? I spun back in the chair toward my computer. "I've got to get this email drafted before the contracts workshop. Save me a seat in it?"

"Of course." He rose and placed the flyer on the edge of my desk. "I'll see you there. Don't forget, Tahoma is the new eblast font choice according to Tracy."

"Right." I double-clicked on our lead management software, aware of his gaze lingering on my screen. "Thanks for the reminder."

As soon as he left, I pulled the door closed and flipped the cheap lock. Opening my email back up, I refreshed the inbox, flinching as a new arrival from Julia De Luca appeared.

> *Photos look great! Please go ahead with the flyer distribution. The house can be ready for a showing as early as Wednesday. I'm assuming this means you guys got home safely on Thursday night? We are flying back to the Bahamas right now, but will be back on Sunday—if you're free for lunch next week, let me know. I'm dying to try that new sushi place on Lincoln.*
>
> *Julia*

I reread it twice, surprised to find that it was so... normal. No mention of my husband's dick, or our same-backyard sex, or of the taste of Easton's dick or... any of it. Had that been a normal Thursday night for them? Or was this the appropriate response? To act as if nothing had happened?

I leaned back in my chair, stretching out the tight knot in my back and staring up at the dingy popcorn ceiling. I knew the restaurant she was talking about. Chelsea had sent me a link to it, along with a long line of gagging emoticons, because it was rumored that Charlie Sheen owned it. Which was highly unlikely, but enough of a reason for her to cross it off with a hot-pink Sharpie.

I loved sushi. And she was my biggest ever listing client. I wasn't even sure I could turn a lunch invite down. If there wasn't any awkwardness now, there would be if I got all stiff and distant from her. I scrolled down the page to my prior email, which had been addressed to both of them.

> *Mr. and Mrs. De Luca,*
>
> *Here is a link to view the photos of your home, along with a draft flyer I would like to distribute to prospective buyers. Please let me know if you approve of the flyers, and if you'd like any of the photos to be omitted from the listing.*
>
> *Thank you,*
>
> *Elle R. North, Licensed Real Estate Agent*

It was so stiff it smelled of starch. Why had I used my middle initial? I stifled a wince and tried to read it again, in a better light. I'd been trying to set a professional tone, something to make up for the fact that I'd drunk all their wine, blabbed about my threesome, then stripped down in their backyard and moaned loud enough to wake up the neighbors.

My phone dinged and I jumped on the distraction, opening a text from Chelsea.

Everything okay with you and E? I'm catching up on voicemails, yours sound stressed.

Of course she'd wait until now, when I was ten minutes away from a workshop. And texting me? Why had she still not returned my calls? *Things are fine. I'm about to walk into something, but I want to catch up with you.*

She texted back before I even had a chance to set down the phone.

Wahoo on E's new deal! Don't forget—I'm the one who referred Nicole to him. You guys can thank me with cupcakes or fudge-covered Oreos. Your pick.

—Don't pat your back too hard. I'll tell you why later.

I didn't have the energy to discuss the Nicole debacle through text. Plus, Chelsea was an expressive reactor. The only upside of this entire situation would be seeing the volcano of emotion that would spew out of her at the news. I hit reply on Julia's email, then was distracted by another Chelsea text.

Lunch? I'm on day 12 of No Dick and literally no one has congratulated me yet. I can buy you tacos and protest that it's no big deal as you heap me with well-earned praise.

I smiled, realizing how much I missed her. Ever since Aaron moved out of our place and in with her, we'd barely seen each other. In part, because I'd been avoiding her, heavy with guilt over what happened with Aaron and terrified of the new (and probably completely imagined) possibility that she was into him. But I hadn't been the only MIA member of our friendship. She'd been notably absent these last three weeks, and leaving me out of the funeral party preparations was just one example of that.

We had to get back to normal. I needed my best friend back, and I had to assume that she was missing some of me as well.

—I'd love lunch. I've got a workshop, so can it be late? Taco Taquito at two?

Works for me. I have a wax appointment at one. 😣 😨

—Sounds good. See you then.

I added a thumbs up and sent the text. Placing the phone on the desk, I moved the laptop closer and squared my shoulders, staring at the blank email before me. While lunch with Chelsea was easy to accept, the idea of having one with Julia triggered an alarming amount of stress. But... I could do this. It'd be good too, like drinking a glass of water in between tequila shots. I flipped open my planner and thumbed to next week's grid. It was wide open, like my legs on their couch. I winced.

I clicked on the REPLY button and forced a breezy and happy tone to come through in the response.

> *Julia,*
>
> *Great! I'll get these online and set up the showings for Thursday. I'd love to meet you at Dante's for lunch. Are you free next Tuesday? I'm open any time after 11:30.*
>
> *Elle*

There. I hadn't spent four years in a sorority house without mastering the art of a flippant yet friendly response. I arrowed back and removed the exclamation point after *Great*, replacing it with a comma. Better. Less desperate.

I was uploading the twenty-second image into MLS when I stopped, thinking back to Chelsea's text message. Why was she getting waxed? She was in day whatever of her dick drought. She should be growing underarm hair and embracing self-love, or whatever this was about.

On a whim, I opened Instagram, pulling up her feed. Scrolling through her photos, my heart sank with each one.

23

The contracts workshop ran long, putting me in an irritable mood that traffic wasn't helping. I leaned on my horn, exasperated by the bleach-blonde who was paused in the middle of the crosswalk, smiling for a selfie. Her smile remained fixed as her phone swung left, then right, angling for the best shot. I honked again and she kept the smile in place as she raised her middle finger in my direction. "Tourist bitch," I muttered.

I tried Easton's cell for the third time, cursing when it went to voice-mail. The girl moved and I hit the gas, my tires squeaking on the pavement as I made it a good quarter of a mile, then hit traffic. I scrolled down to Aaron's number and considered calling him. A private conversation with him suddenly felt taboo after our three-way, but I was desperate for some inside intel before I walked into lunch with a freshly waxed, dick-deprived Chelsea. I placed the call.

"Hey, Elle."

"Hey. Look, I'm about to meet Chelsea for lunch."

"All right."

I picked at a loose thread on my steering wheel. "Have, you...uh, seen her Instagram?"

"I'm not on Instagram."

Right. Of course he wasn't. Up until last year, he'd still had a flip phone because he "didn't need all that garbage." Garbage like the Internet and the ability to type a letter without hitting the 5 button multiple times. "Well, there are a lot of photos of you on her feed."

"You know Chelsea. She likes to take photos."

This was like talking to a child. A dense, stubborn child. "Yes, but her entire feed is basically you. You've topped idiotic memes and inspirational quotes."

"Okay."

I sighed. "Has anything happened between you two?"

"Nope."

"Nothing?" I stressed. "Not a kiss, a grope, a flirt?"

"Flirting is a loose concept. It's hard for me to say if we've flirted."

I eased my car up a half-length and hit the brakes, then switched tactics. "Have you told her anything about what we did?"

"You mean, that night at your house?"

I sighed in exasperation. "Yes."

"I told E I wouldn't. He made me swear to it on my baby niece."

I sank against the car seat in relief and sent a mental *I love you* over to E. Aaron was romantically dense and technologically inept, but he was loyal and he kept his promises as if he had a death pact behind them. "Okay. I'm on my way to lunch with her now. I just needed to know."

I was preparing to hang up when he spoke.

"Elle."

"Yeah?"

"I just got divorced. I'm not emotionally ready to move into anything right now. Especially with all of the games Becca's trying to play."

Games? I suddenly realized that, ever since he had moved out of our house, I'd pretty much abandoned him as a friend. If Becca had been playing games with him, I wasn't aware of them. My innate instinct to protect him reared its head.

"But there *is* something with Chelsea. Something I don't want to mess up."

"Uh-huh." I opened a text to Chelsea. *Just heard that Becca is screwing with Aaron? Tell me everything at lunch.*

She immediately replied. *Ugh. I hate that bitch so much. I'm ten minutes away. Are you close?*

"And I don't know how she'd react, if she did find out what happened."

"Fuck her," I snapped. "It's not her business what you're doing." I couldn't believe Becca had the gall to say shit to Aaron—to even have an opinion with Aaron—after everything she's put him through.

"It just feels wrong, keeping it from her."

Oh my God. "LISTEN TO ME, Aaron." I slammed on my brakes to avoid a car that pulled out on the left. Blowing the horn again, I swerved around him and increased my speed, trying to find an opening in the right-hand lane. "You don't need to feel guilty for shit. You're a grown man and she's a total slut. I hate to say it, Aaron, but she is."

"She's not a slut." His voice gained an edge of steel, and I couldn't believe he was defending Becca, who left him for her supervisor, like this.

"Are you kidding me? You're jaded by love. We all think she's a slut. Look at what she's done."

"I didn't say I was in love with her. There's just... something there. Something I haven't felt before. A connection."

Like I said, romantically dense. This was what happened when I abandoned him. He's over there, pining away for Becca like a lost fucking puppy. And I had been worried about him and Chelsea? At least that concern could be squashed. "Aaron," I said quietly. "Listen to me very carefully. You are the only one feeling a connection. She doesn't love you, and I don't think she ever did. I don't even think she likes you, despite how she might act."

"What? Did she tell you that?"

"She doesn't have to tell me. Look at her actions. Look at what she's done to you."

"She hasn't done anything to me."

Chelsea's Mercedes shot past me, her convertible top down, her hair whipping in the wind. She darted into the right lane as if it were easy, then whipped into the strip center and slid into a front spot. I flipped on my blinker, forced to come to a complete stop in the middle lane as I begged the cars on the right to let me in. "Fucking Chelsea," I muttered. "Aaron, I have to go. If Becca calls or texts you, ignore her."

"Whatever." He sounded pissed, and I still couldn't wrap my head around why he was defending *Becca's* honor.

Yo bitch, I'm here. Getting a table.

Chelsea's text pinged through just as an elderly man in a Ford truck waved me over. Giving him a dozen thank-you waves, I inched through the opening he provided and into the parking lot, finding a spot a hundred yards away from Chelsea's.

I peeled myself off the seat and grabbed my bag, running a quick hand through my hair as I got out of the car. Rolling back my shoulders, I strolled toward the restaurant and forced a smile.

Fucking Becca.

24

I found Chelsea at the back of the restaurant, embroiled in a heated conversation with a Cuban woman. Sinking into the seat across from her, I gave a friendly smile to the stranger, who ignored me.

"Tell your father the ads need to go. I know the man. He wouldn't support this. Tell him Julian Pozo said so."

"I'll tell him," Chelsea promised, then half-rose out of the booth, accepting the fierce hug that the woman offered.

I pulled the menu off the side display and flipped it over, waiting for the woman to leave before speaking. "Trouble in advertising?"

"Meh. Display ads on entertainment pages. Nothing major." She pushed a blue cup of sweet tea toward me. "They didn't have Splenda so this has got Equal in it."

"Thanks."

"What's with the curiosity with Becca?"

"Aaron said she was playing games. I didn't know what he was talking about."

She perked up. "Oh, you talked to him? Did he say anything?"

"About what?"

"I don't know. Anything."

"Yeah, we talked about Becca." I swallowed the comments he had made—the obvious protectiveness and affection he still felt toward her. "But I didn't get details. I figured you'd tell me what was going on."

"Just bullshit." She pulled her necklace free of her shirt and drug the diamond pendant on it to the left and right. "She's calling him in the middle of the night. Saying she made a mistake, then giving him the cold shoulder the next day. Posting pictures of her and the new guy on social media. Trying to make him jealous, then freaking out on him if he says anything. You know." She shrugged. "Girl bullshit."

I thought of Aaron's defensive tone. What had he said they had? That they had a connection? I hesitated, unsure of whether to share that part with Chelsea. I decided not to, anxious to get to Nicole and what had happened on their trip. "So, on Easton's trip back from Los Angeles—"

"Yeah, yeah, yeah, tell me about your dinner with the swingers." She leaned forward and lowered her voice. "*Please* tell me they have sex shit all over their house."

I studied the menu. "Sorry to disappoint you. No sex shit anywhere."

"Ugh." She slumped in the booth. "They probably got rid of it before they listed the house. Regina says their main home is in the Bahamas. Maybe they shipped it all there." She grinned at me and I set down the menu.

"It seems a little hypocritical for you to judge them for their sex lives, given the fact that you've always been sexually... free."

She stiffened. "You say free like it's a bad thing."

"You're calling them swingers like it's a bad thing. Why are you allowed to sleep around and they aren't?"

"Ummm... because they're MARRIED?" She cocked one brow at me as if I was dense. "Monogamy, Elle. It's what is supposed to happen when two people agree to spend their lives together. And besides, didn't you hear? I'm celibate."

I swallowed my response to that, saved by the waitress, who took my order for fajitas and Chelsea's for tacos. As soon as she left, Chelsea dove back in.

"But seriously, how would you react if Easton wanted to start banging side pussy?"

"If he wanted to start banging side pussy"—I said carefully, watching the volume of my words—"I would not be okay with that. But is that what Brad's doing? I thought you said they were swingers. That's different than being in an open marriage."

And let me just say that in this arena, thanks to lengthy Internet research and soul-searching, I knew my shit. Open marriages were when married individuals were given permission to date and/or have sex with people other than their spouse. It allows them to live a separate life, often under a different persona, with the full permission of their spouse. And some open marriages were one-sided. The wife, for instance, was allowed to do her own thing, while the husband remained faithful.

Easton and I had discussed open marriage and agreed, with *complete* certainty, that it was something neither of us was interested in.

On the flip side, swinging was swapping or sharing that was done together. The premise was that of a shared and honest experience, which I was one hundred percent on board with.

"They're the same thing," Chelsea bulldozed on. "And who knows the lines they do or don't cross. I don't know why you're arguing with me on this. You just said you wouldn't be okay with it."

"I wouldn't be okay with Easton fucking another girl on the side. I didn't say I wouldn't be okay with something that I was a part of."

She gawked at me in the sort of overblown manner of someone attempting to make a point, then laughed loudly and hysterically. I sipped my tea and waited for her idiotic show to be over.

"A threesome?" she sputtered. "Please. You're the biggest prude I know. You could never have a threesome."

"Okay." I unrolled the napkin and placed it on my lap, then lined up the silverware on either side.

"Oh, you think you could? Elle, I've *had* a threesome. You don't understand what it entails. Just, trust me on this." She got a look on her face, as if she knew everything and I knew nothing, and I struggled not to reach across the table and slap her.

"You've had a threesome?" I confirmed. At her nod, I raised my brow, not certain I believed her. "When?"

"At Florida State. A Pike party. With that hot guy. Hunter whatshis-face. A bitch from KD and I gave him head. No biggie." She shrugged.

"I'm not sure that I'd consider that a threesome." Though, two months ago, I would have. Two months ago, I would have been slack-jawed and shocked at the thought. Also, slightly turned on, the arousal taken care of in the shower, right before I had pleasing and mostly vanilla sex with my husband.

"Oh please... it was a threesome." She rolled her eyes and pulled her giant Dior sunglasses off the top of her head. "And trust me, you would never ever, *ever* do it."

It was the second ever that got me, looping its four letters around my tongue and yanking it into action. "I've already done it. So don't never ever, ever this shit with me."

She let out a strangled laugh. "No, you didn't."

I held her gaze, my face stiff, my lips beginning to pinch in the way that always clued E in that I was about to lose my shit. "I did."

"With who? E?"

"Yeah." Beneath the table, my fingers began to drum insistently at my thigh.

"When?"

Careful... "In the past."

"At Florida State?"

"No. After that."

"After you got married?"

"Yes. It's called ethical non-monogamy, so please don't pull out your soapbox and spout shit at me."

Chelsea's eyes widened and I tried to remember the last time I had spoken to her like that. Or the last time we'd had a fight of any kind. Sophomore year. Someone had been stealing items from the sorority house, and I saw Kelly Snyder pick a pair of forgotten Manolo Blahniks up from the foot of the staircase and stick them in her bag. Kelly, who could never afford a pair of Manolo's and was in on scholarship. Kelly, who was kicked out of the sorority after I told Chelsea and Chelsea told Brandi Hodgkins, even though I had sworn her to secrecy. Kelly, who had found me a week later and screamed at me in the middle of the library, and called me a bitch, and made me feel like absolute shit, all because Chelsea made the executive decision that the secret I told her wasn't worth keeping.

"Let's take a big step back." She held up her palms as if to prove they were empty. "I was talking about your clients. If you and Easton did something back in the day, that's your business. I'm not trying to judge you."

My nails scraped against my linen-covered thighs.

"Okay?" she asked. "Are we okay?"

"We're fine," I said stiffly, regretting meeting her for lunch at all. It didn't matter if I missed her or if I needed her advice on Nicole. With her newfound celibacy and judgmental opinions, it wasn't a good time for our friendship. I needed to focus on Easton and me. I needed to focus on my new listing. I didn't have time to stuff my face with food and listen to Chelsea bitch over whatever wrinkle was currently occurring in her diamond-studded life.

"Okay," she said again, picking up her glass and taking a long sip of it. Over the rim of the glass, she studied me. "I must say," she said carefully. "It surprises me. I just never thought you were open to being with Easton and another girl."

How stereotypical. Was that always the assumption? That everything was about the man? That we pushed aside our own needs and took care of his fantasies first? The distaste must have shown on my face, because her thick eyebrows pinched together. "It was a girl, right? I mean, you didn't…"

I didn't say anything and her eyes widened, her cleavage squishing on the linoleum edge of the table as she leaned forward. "Nooooo," she crowed in hushed disbelief. "A guy? No way. No fucking way." She let out a giggle. "I have seriously underestimated you this entire time. Elle!"

Despite myself, I felt a bubble of pride forming at the admiration in her tone. In her astonished and gleeful reaction, I felt the swell of desire to tell her everything. How it had felt. How nervous I had been. The fear that, after these hits, I was addicted.

"Where did you find him? Was he one of E's teammates? Oh my God." She stiffened. "Do I *know* him?"

Every bubble of goodness stilled and congealed, all at once, like hot-glue batter hitting the air, seizing my ability to talk. Her eyes sharpened and she leaned even farther forward, the edge of the table cutting into her midsection. "I *do*. Wait, don't tell me. I can figure this out."

No. No. No. Nonononononono. "You don't know him," I said quickly.

"Shut up, I do. I can see it in your face." She closed her eyes and put the forefingers of each hand on her temples, as if she was telepathically pulling it from my head. "Easton's boss at work—Don? Is that his name? The hot redheaded one?"

I didn't respond, looking over my shoulder for our waitress, desperate for our food to hurry up and get here.

"No." She rejected the idea. "Too risky. Oh! That shortstop grooms-man. The one who brought the girl with the back tattoo?" She opened one eye and sneaked a peek at me, then shook her head. "Never mind. This has to be someone closer. Someone you are as comfortable with as E is. Someone who won't fuck up your jobs. The problem is that you guys don't know like anyone. Other than me and Aaron, you're basically loners. And he's been with Becca up until—"

"Chelsea," I said urgently. "Listen. I think—"

"Oh my God." She stilled, the smile dropping from her face, her eyes snapping open and catching me flush-faced and panicked. "It was Aaron. That's why he moved out. That's why you've been acting so strange around him."

"It wasn't…" I paused, not fully able to complete the lie. "It's not important who it was with."

If she could have taken a step back from me, she would have. Instead, she leaned back against the black plastic booth, her hands pushing at the table, which was affixed to the floor. "Tell me it wasn't Aaron."

"It wasn't Aaron," I whispered, not trusting my voice at full volume. I had to lie. I had to. I looked in her face and saw the plummet of emotion and there was no other option.

"You're lying."

"Alrighty, we've got an order of chicken fajitas with an extra side of cheese!" From somewhere to the right, a steaming platter waved through the air. I lifted my hand numbly, holding Chelsea's eye contact as the giant frying pan was set before me. Steam curdled the air, dotting my face with perspiration as the loud crackle of sizzling meat sounded.

"And three steak tacos with extra sour cream!"

Chelsea didn't move and the man set the plate down in front of her.

"Anything you guys are missing? Hot sauce?"

"We're fine," I said quietly.

"You're LYING," she said, louder this time, her eyes burning into me. "Don't fucking lie to me."

The man took that as his cue and left.

"Okay," I moved the fajitas to the side so I could see her clearly. "Okay. It was with Aaron." This was fine. This would be fine. This mini-eruption of emotion would pass and we would be back to having lunch, laughing over the insanity of it all.

"When?"

"Ummm," I place a tortilla on my plate in an attempt to buy time. "After his divorce."

"After the divorce that *just* happened?" She spoke in very precise tones, like a trial attorney who was laying a trap.

I looked through the words for any bombshells, then answered truthfully. "Yes."

"After that, but before he moved in with me," she confirmed, her tone growing even colder.

"Yes."

She shook her head slowly, her face turning grey. "Elle, this is not okay."

"Not okay?" I stared at her, still not quite understanding her reaction. "What do you mean?"

"You and E had a threesome with *Aaron?*" Her voice grew shrill. "How do you not understand that that is not okay?"

"Because…" I searched for the true source of her anger. "Because it's fine? Because we're three consenting adults? It wasn't cheating. His divorce was final."

"Right. After his divorce but before he moved out ten days later. So, what? Did you start to hump him on the way home from the courthouse?" Her face reached a new level of red, one I hadn't seen before. "That's swell. That's just SWELL."

My dread over revealing Aaron's involvement turned a fresh corner and I hoped, I really, really hoped, that this emotion wasn't coming from where I thought it was. "What are you so mad about?" I glanced around to see who was in earshot of this meltdown. "We—"

"Because I LIKE him, Elle."

And… there it was. Made even worse now that I knew he was still hung up on Becca. Chelsea liked Aaron.

That's why she was swearing off men.

That's why she was losing weight.

That's why, right now, her eyes were welling with tears.

How did I not see this? And why... why hadn't she told me? She could have told me in Vegas, or when we found out about Becca's cheating, or at any time in the last six years and I would have known. If I'd known, I wouldn't have gone near him. I never would have told Easton that I liked him watching us fuck, and I *never* would have put myself in a situation where I knew what his dick *tasted and fucked like*. I closed my eyes and searched for a way out of this.

"I liked him—I like him—and you took him. It wasn't enough that you had E. Perfect fuckin' E. The guy that God handcrafted to check every single checkbox." She jabbed her finger on the table with each strike against me. "You had to have Aaron too?"

"I—" I didn't know what to say. And it didn't seem like an appropriate time to mention that she had screwed Easton too. I glanced toward the exit and noticed every eye in the surrounding four tables, locked on us. "I didn't *take* Aaron. You can have Aaron. You could have had Aaron."

"I couldn't have had Aaron because he was married, Elle." She stated the fact as if I was stupid, and maybe I was, because I'd been elbow deep in this dynamic for eight years now and it felt like I'd just been hit in the face with a shovel. "And the minute, the actual *nanosecond* that he becomes single and lifts his head from Becca's ass, you're there. Naked. And it was probably hot. Full of sparks and chemistry and orgasms. How am I supposed to compete with that?"

I swallowed, fighting an overwhelming bubble of guilt and dread. How would I fix this? There was no way to fix this. Initially, I'd been worried that our threesome would dismantle E and me, but this was a new and horrifyingly opposite side effect, one that was almost as bad. "I—"

"Just fucking go. Seriously." She pointed in the direction of the door and I watched the pale pink tip of her index finger as it trembled in the air.

"You want me to leave?"

Her finger remained suspended. "Yeah. I'm not fucking with you. Go."

It was sixth grade all over again, when the cool kids told me I couldn't sit at their table again because they found out I hadn't started my period yet, and *babies had to eat somewhere else*. I slid my phone off the table and into my bag, working my way down the tight plastic booth. My fingers bumped against the still-sizzling iron skillet and I bit back a cry of pain. Lifting my hand, I sucked at the burnt flesh and stood.

Around us, there was pure silence.

"GO." Chelsea pulled her glass closer to her and waved her hand in the air, dismissing me as if I was an annoying child. "Jesus. Stop staring at me."

I turned, tears pricking at the corners of my eyes, and left, my bag bumping against someone on the way, my eyes pinned to the floor. When I made it to the door, I paused, hoping to hear her call my name, or stand from the table. But there was only the loud jangle of the bell, and I swung the glass door out and stepped into the parking lot, hurrying toward the sanctity of my car.

Driving away, I realized that I'd stuck her with the bill.

Coming down the 195 bridge, my phone sang with Easton's ringtone. I made it across and pulled into a gas station and dug frantically through my bag, finding the iPhone and answering it.

He said hello, and I tried to speak but hiccupped out a cry instead. Then, the sobs started and didn't stop until he was beside me at the station, pulling my phone from my hand and wrapping me in his arms.

25

I pulled the blanket higher up to my chest, and Wayland pawed at the material. "No." I pointed toward the back of the house. "Crate."

His ears fell and he turned, his tail pinned in between his back legs. I felt a stab of guilt but said nothing, listening as his nails clicked along the hardwood floors toward the laundry room.

"Here." Easton came into the room with a box of Thin Mints and a Dr Pepper. "Bringing out the big guns."

My eyes widened at the non-diet soda. "Where'd you get that?"

"I have a few hidden in the back of a case of beer in the garage fridge." He winked at me. "Don't tell my wife."

"I won't," I grumbled, pulling open the box and stealing one hand inside. "She'd tell everyone because she can't keep a secret."

"Don't be like that." He sat down on the couch next to me and leaned over, pushing my hair away from my forehead. "You were feeling guilty before because you were keeping it from her. Don't feel guilty now because you told her."

"I'm not guilty because I told her." I pulled a couch pillow from underneath my shoulder and hugged it to my chest, studiously avoiding his gaze. "I'm guilty because I did it to begin with."

"Screw that," he said sharply. "You didn't know how she felt. None of us knew how she felt."

"I don't know... now that I think back, there were some signs." Her inappropriate comments about his looks—though, to be fair, she made inappropriate comments about everyone's looks. Her offer to let him live with her, though she had done the same for me at multiple times in our friendship.

The problem was, Chelsea flirted with everyone. She was nice to everyone. She was crude to everyone. She helped out and fawned over everyone. I had dismissed any clues that *had* occurred, chalking it up as standard behavior. The only non-standard behavior was that she hadn't tried to sleep with Aaron, and maybe *that* was the giant red flag I should have noticed.

"This wasn't your fault," Easton said again, his fingers working past mine to get a cookie out of the box.

I passed the entire thing to him. "She hasn't called me yet. She always calls me by now."

"Give her time and let her cool off."

I lay down, putting my head in his lap, and stared at the dark television screen. Maybe I didn't need to feel guilty about telling her, and maybe it wasn't my fault that I had sex with Aaron, but all that aside, we were now in this situation and had to figure a way out of it.

From behind us, the front door slammed against its frame.

"Damn, you guys know how to fuck something up." Aaron's drawl echoed from the entry hall as his heavy steps moved closer.

"Did you talk to her?" I craned my neck up, trying to see over the back of the couch.

"Yeah." He took off his baseball cap and smoothed his hair down. "She's pissed off." He looked at me. "Next time you plan on throwing me under the bus, give me a heads-up."

"I didn't plan on telling her. It just came out that I had done something, and then she figured out that it was you, and I couldn't lie to her when she outright asked." I watched as he leaned against the support column, wondering how much she had told him. The chances were high that she'd kept her feelings for him secret and only bitched and ranted about the threesome.

He gave E a hard look. "You fucked me by making me promise not to tell her. Now I look like a piece of shit for keeping it from her."

"Is she mad at you?" I shifted to the edge of the couch.

"I don't know. She was too mad at you to talk about anything else, and I probably didn't help your case any."

"Thanks," I said tartly.

His eyes narrowed. "Let's just be upfront for a minute, Elle. We can do that, right? Set aside all the bullshit and be honest?"

"When am I not honest with you?" I looked to E for help, but he seemed as confused as I was by Aaron's sudden coldness.

"I told you I was developing feelings for her and you wanted to sabotage it." He crossed his arms over his chest, his jaw flexing. "Well, congratulations. She's looking at me as if I'm a fucking—"

"Whoa." I held up my hand. "What are you talking about? You never told me you were developing feelings for her."

He looked me square in the eye and sighed in exasperation. "Elle. Don't play this shit."

"I'm not playing any shit." I pushed to my feet. "I don't know what you're talking about. Maybe you told E, but you didn't tell me."

"I did." He glanced at his watch. "Two, maybe three hours ago. When you were on your way to meet her for lunch. Right before you fucked us both to hell."

I searched through the conversation. "You told me that you'd never done anything with her. No kisses, no sex. Just maybe flirting. You want me to jump from 'maybe flirting' to knowing that you're developing feelings for her?"

"I told you that something was there. A connection."

"No." I shook my head. "We moved from that to talking about Becca. And see!" I straightened, strengthened in my resolve. "How was I supposed to understand that you liked Chelsea when you were going on and on, defending and blabbing about Becca?"

"I barely even mentioned Becca." He peered at me. "Wait. You thought we were talking about Becca that entire time? When you called Chelsea a slut and told me that she wasn't interested in me?"

"I didn't call Chelsea a slut," I said indigently. "I wouldn't call her that." Though maybe, at some point, I had—but in loving terms.

He groaned as he linked his fingers and set them on top of his head. "This is so fucked up."

I was still trying to backtrack through the conversation and figure out whatever it was that he had just put together.

"You thought I was talking about Becca, but I was talking about Chelsea," he explained. "I told you that I was developing feelings for her and you told me to give it up—that she wasn't interested in me."

"Oh." I sat on the couch, trying to remember everything I had said. Not good stuff. I'd been on my high horse about Becca and preaching on all of the reasons they shouldn't be together. Bitch. Had I called her a bitch? Probably. Probably a lying slutty bitch. "You didn't tell her anything I said, did you?"

"No. Did you tell her anything I said? Or what you thought I said about Becca?"

"No." I'd been trying to spare Chelsea's feelings, to dilute her anger over the threesome. Thank *God* I hadn't attempted to soften that blow by telling her my false impression of Aaron being hung up on Becca. That was one bright spot in this torrential downpour.

"So..." Easton spoke up from the other end of the couch. "You like Chelsea?"

"Yeah," Aaron answered. "Not that my brilliant plan to seduce her has been working, or has any legs left. She fucking hates me right now." He sat in the recliner and picked his baseball cap off the floor, working the brim into a curve.

The truth about Chelsea's feelings sat like an egg under me, shuddering with the need to crack. Should I tell him? Fan the romance flame? Or should I keep her secret? I'd already screwed up this situation in ten different ways. I couldn't tip the scales further. I had to be very, very careful about what I did, or didn't do, next.

I eyed Aaron, who pulled the baseball cap low over his eyes, and warred over which path to take.

26

"You really don't have to be here." I straightened a row of water bottles on a glass tray and smiled at the house manager, who glared back in response. She still hadn't warmed to me, but maybe snarls were just her love language. She'd spat the same attitude to Brad and Julia, who had responded with warm affection.

"Are you kidding me?" Tim sipped on an iced latte and peered around the room. "There's more eye candy in this room than in Azucar on a Saturday night."

"Oh, so you're here to pick up a day. Good to know." I glanced at my watch, anxious for the first showing to arrive. I needed this to go smoothly, and not just for the boost in my reputation and business. With Chelsea ignoring my calls, Aaron sulking at me and Easton refusing to let me claw Nicole's eyes out—I needed something to go right.

"Don't be like that," Tim chided, and I couldn't even remember what we were talking about. "I'm here to help keep an eye on things. You know, in addition to the gazillion cameras and delicious security detail."

"Uh-huh." I noticed a light switch hidden by the sink and hurried to flip it on. A row of lights illuminated underneath the counters.

"Mrs. North?"

I turned, spotting the wiry black man who was in charge of the security detail. "Yes?"

"If you could follow me, I just want to go over a few things in the control room, before we begin."

"Certainly." I glanced at Tim. "I'll be right back."

He waved me on, and I followed the man closely, visually sweeping each room we passed. Pillows fluffed. Counters empty. House sparkling. Martha may be lacking in the hospitality department, but she had presentation down to a science.

Pausing in the hall, he glanced around for others, then pressed on the hidden panel and ushered me into the room. He closed the door behind us, and I found myself in very close quarters with the man. I moved further in and bumped into the opposite wall.

"Okay, I'll be in here for the four-hour window, and will be communicating with the team the entire time. He held out a small earpiece. "I'd like to fit you with a mic also, so I can alert you to any problems."

"Sure. Do I just—"

"Just stay right there. I'll hide it in your hair."

And Easton had thought my blow out was unnecessary. As he loops a plastic wire over my ear, I watched the grid of monitors, my attention caught and focusing on the backyard cameras.

Brad's finger pushed into the tight and needy bundle of my ass and it was the push that sent me over the edge. I came hard, my fingers digging into Brad's muscles, my mouth needy on his neck, his voice thick and commanding in my ear.

I hadn't even thought about the cameras. I tapped on the screen. "Are these the only angles we have on the backyard?"

He left my earpiece and moved to the laptop, typing a string of commands. The grid changed, every single screen filled with different pieces of the backyard. The cabana. Outdoor kitchen. Chaise lounges beside the pool. The stairs leading to Martha's apartment. The perimeter of the property wall.

I looked through the angles twice but didn't see what I was looking for. "Where's the fire pit and outdoor sectional?" My heart, which had begun to beat in double-time, slowed at the slim possibility that maybe our sexual exploitations hadn't been caught by a high-definition camera.

"That area isn't covered. There are a few spots in the house that the De Lucas wanted to be avoided by cameras. While I don't encourage that, I do understand a need for some semblance of personal privacy. My team is aware of those areas and removed any valuables. We'll also sweep those areas thoroughly, after the showing is concluded."

"Oh." I nodded as if I didn't care. Inside, my chest collapsed in relief.

"This needs to be clipped to you somewhere. We suggest the small of your back. May I attach it to the top of your slacks?"

"Sure." I turned, fidgeting in place as he clipped the small box to my belt, then smoothed my shirt over it. He tested the mic, and I gave him a thumbs up when his voice came, low and clear, over the tiny bud in my ear. "Thanks."

"We aren't expecting any problems, but we will be doing pat-downs at the gate, and everyone on my team is fully equipped to handle any issues."

"I'm sure it will be fine." Our showing list included five couples, two families, and a single woman—all with a history in the Miami area, verified funds, and squeaky clean background checks. The only danger in sight was that of a lowball offer.

"The Hertz family has arrived at the gate." The female voice came through the earpiece, surprising me. I glanced at the man, and he settled into place before the monitors and changed the inputs, all screens changing to exterior shots.

I thanked him and moved out into the hall, carefully returning the hidden door to its place and blowing out a nervous breath.

It was showtime.

Three days and six more unanswered calls to Chelsea later, I pushed a new fertility pill through the foil packet and raised it to my mouth, putting it on the back of my tongue before taking a long sip of water. Through the windshield, I watched as Easton spoke to the yard guy. There was a lot of gesturing in the direction of the hibiscus bush, and Nick nodded. A thumbs up was given. Easton turned toward the car and I placed the packet into my purse and pulled the zipper closed. Setting it down by my feet, I watched as Easton got in.

"Did you tell him about the caterpillars?"

"I tried. I also told him not to cut the bush so far back, but I don't know how much he understood."

"Should I talk to him? My Spanish is a little better than yours."

"Yelling *mi pantalones es rojos* isn't going to help in this situation."

"Ha. I know more than that. And the joke's on you because it's son rojos." I glanced down at my pants. "And I think these are more orange than red."

"I didn't know the color for orange."

I frowned for a minute. "I think it's just orange. Or orange-jee."

"No, it's got its own name."

"No, I think purple is the same way. Purpala, or something like that."

"Whatever. You're proving my point." I pulled up Google translate on my phone.

When we moved to Miami, we had vowed to learn Spanish. I'd bought Rosetta Stone, and spent a good weekend hunched over the computer, sounding out the vowels. But then I'd started a new audiobook, and then baseball had started, and then we started trying for a baby, and learning Spanish was quietly slid to the bottom of a very tall pile, which included a lot of more interesting things.

"Ha! It *is* orange." I turned my screen to show him. He paused, halfway out of backing down the driveway and looked at the proof.

"You didn't change the second language. It's displaying English to English."

"Oh." Deflated, I edited the fields, then watched as *naranja* populated. "Crap. It's naranja. I was way off."

"It's okay, love. I love you for so much more than your brain." He patted my knee in support.

"You're funny," I sniped, closing down the browser. "Besides, you don't have to love me for my brain. You can love me for the three offers I have on the Olive Line Trail house." I beamed at him.

"I still can't believe you already have offers."

"I told you it would go quick. Assuming they accept one of them." The De Lucas should. Our best was over list price, with a fifteen day close and no financing contingency. Assuming they didn't freak out over the control room, or find asbestos in the walls, it was virtually guaranteed.

"When will you know?"

"They said they'd let me know by morning." I refreshed my email for the third time, hoping they had made an early decision. Nothing. I switched over to Facebook.

I scrolled past a cat meme and at least four posts with people at the beer festival. "Everyone is at that beer thing. Look, Amy and Aleja look like they're back together." I showed him the photo. "We should have gone. We still could. We have the tickets."

"I thought you were trying to lie low from Chelsea."

"I am." I scratched at an itchy spot on the inside of my knee. Pedicant Entertainment was the main sponsor of the beer festival, which was how I originally landed two VIP tickets. Last year, we'd gone as a group—fourteen of us holding down a VIP balcony just off the stage and chugging beers every time the cannon fired. This year we'd had similar plans, our tickets and calendars set months ago.

I hadn't officially been uninvited, but considering the last text I'd gotten from Chelsea called me a *cunty dickwaffle*, it probably wasn't a good idea to show up at the VIP tent and flash my tickets. While I wasn't exactly sure what a cunty dickwaffle was, it had cunt and dick in it, so it probably wasn't good. Though, as Easton had so support-ably pointed out, it also had *waffle* in it, and who doesn't love waffles?

"Well, you need to make up with her fast," Easton said. "The Katy Perry concert is next weekend. I know you're willing to miss out on beer, but don't tell me you're skipping the musical event of the decade."

"Don't make fun," I snapped at him. "You know how much I love Katy. And... I don't know. A lot can happen in a week. She could forgive me or kill me, and I honestly don't know which is more likely."

A reminder flashed across my screen, interrupting my view of an aban-doned baby elephant cuddling up to a German shepherd.

Kurt in town

I turned toward Easton, watching as he tapped his fingers against the steering wheel, bobbing his head slightly to the music. "That, uh, guy from the website is in town tonight."

"The guy you sent me screenshots of?"

"Yeah. He offered to meet us for a drink, if we wanted to."

He looked over at me. "Do we want to?"

"I don't know." I sat back against the headrest. "I feel like we have so much going on right now." A month ago, I was researching how to make my own face masks. Now, I had Chelsea pissed at me, had landed a major client, hooked up with said client, and was trying to fit in drinks with a complete stranger who was willing to be my husband and my sexual guinea pig.

"Are you attracted to the guy? What's his name? Ken?"

"Kurt." I pulled up the swinger website and logged in. "Let me show you his picture."

The page was slow to load, and I eyed a hooker on the corner eye our Range Rover, her hand lifting to shyly wave at Easton with super-long red fingernails. "Not happening," I muttered, scrolling down and clicking on OrlandoC11's album.

Easton chuckled. "Didn't even consider it."

"This is him." I passed over the phone. Easton glanced up at the red light, then swiped through his photos. "None of his dick?"

"Nope. Should I have asked him for one?"

"Maybe." He handed back the phone. "Considering that we're potentially meeting him for sex, I think it's probably the norm."

I had thought about asking Kurt, had prepped myself for it with each email communication, but then chickened out each time. It just felt tacky. Too aggressive. Wouldn't he have offered pictures of his dick if he felt comfortable sharing them?

"Ask him for one." Easton moved into the left turn lane. "Panera or Subway?"

"Uh, Panera. You want me to ask him for one right now?"

"Either you can ask him, or I can ask him, and I feel like it's going to be hella awkward coming from me."

"Yeah." I pulled up his latest email.

Hey Rachel. Just landed at MIA. If you guys want to grab drinks tonight, lmk.

I hit the REPLY button and stalled. This was the same issue I had had before.

Sounds great. We're still figuring out our plans. Btw—I never saw a photo of you naked. Do you have one?

It sounded ridiculous. I read it aloud to E, and he shrugged. "Great. Send it."

I backspaced over the last two sentences.

You don't have any nude pics in your profile. Do you have any?

I hit *send* before I chickened out, then blew out a big breath. "Done."

"It's cute how stressed out you get over stuff like that." He pulled into a front spot and put the SUV into park.

"It's not cute, and you're annoying. Just for that, no bakery item for you."

He snorted. "Right."

"I'm serious. I'm gonna tell Tina you're not allowed to have one." I opened the door and got out, narrowly missing a clump of pigeon poo.

He met me at the front of the Rover and threw an arm around my shoulder. "Tina loves me. She'll sneak one in with my sandwich."

"Tina loves my Yelp review," I informed him, waiting as he held open the door for me. "Yelp reviews trump sex appeal."

"We'll see." He grinned down at me as I stepped past him and through the doors.

The double chocolate-chip cookie that Tina (horny bitch) had given E was gone, a crumble of it stuck in his facial hair, a swipe of chocolate smeared across one finger. I picked up his hand and licked the evidence away and he gave me the sort of cocky grin that made me horny as hell.

Outside, a Rolls pulled up and parked, the driver stepping out and coming to stand in line. E nodded to the car, visible through the wall of plate glass windows. "Bet that's Kurt there. Getting his chicken and rice bowl to go."

I grinned. "Chicken and rice, huh? Couldn't have given him a more manly meal?"

"It's Panera. I think they make you check your balls at the door in exchange for a cookie. Why do you think he sent that guy in?" He nodded to the driver, who was gazing up at the menu.

"It's a little sexist, assuming that it's a guy in the car. Maybe it's a woman."

"Fair point." He leaned back against the booth and threw one arm over its length. "I think Nicole had a Rolls."

I picked up my chip bag and yanked it open with a wee bit more force than necessary.

"No—" He shook his head. "It was a Bentley."

"Oh good," I said. "I was worried it was something ostentatious."

"Hey now, we looked at Bentleys once. Remember that white convertible you test drove?"

I bit a barbecue chip in half and nodded. "It had terrible gas mileage."

"Horrible," he agreed. "Plus, the body style was"—he held his palm flat and tilted it from side to side—"*okay.* Nothing compared to your car."

"I didn't want to point that out, but I agree completely. And the personal concierge service was so annoying. I mean, who wants a complete stranger offering to help them find things or book dinner reservations?"

"Or call an ambulance if you're in an accident," Easton added.

"Exactly!" I threw my hand in the air. "Way too pushy."

The driver took a to-go cup from Tina and walked down to the drink fountain, giving us a polite nod as he passed. I waited until he passed and then stuffed another chip into my mouth.

"Did the guy email back?"

I checked my phone, my pulse quickening as I saw the new email. "Yeah. And..."—I looked up at E—"there's an attachment." No message, just an attachment. I clicked on the icon and waited for it to download. Under the table, my heel began to shimmy. "I'm nervous," I confessed to E. "It's like—"

I was going to say that it's like waiting until Christmas, but then the image loaded and I completely lost that thought process.

27

The man with the biggest dick either of us had ever seen sat at a four-top in the bar, his enormous dong tucked into a pair of dark green jeans. I double-checked the color and notated the white high-top Nikes, which was an interesting choice when paired with the red plaid flannel top. *Flannel*. In Miami. In September.

"You look like your pictures." Kurt smiled. "That's good. Most people don't. Or they do, but it's an old pic and they're forty pounds heavier or with way more miles, if ya know what I mean." He had a Wisconsin accent, the lilt similar to a sorority sister I'd had who'd chewed a lot of gum and wore a fanny pack, despite strict instructions from our social chair to *burn that thing to hell*. "I don't get it," he continued. "You's a good-looking couple. Why don't you just find friends in Miami? Why get on the site?"

I stared at him, fascinated by the fact that this guy belonged to the polite emails and the gigantic penis. GI-GAN-TIC. I'm talking about circus freak. Must-be-surgically-enhanced big.

Easton's knee nudged mine and I had no idea what I was supposed to say. "We're new to all of this," he said. "And..." He looked at me quizzically, and I realized he'd forgotten my fake name.

"Rachel," I provided.

"Right, Rachel doesn't want to go to a club."

"Fair enough. You should learn her name though." Kurt grinned, and a mouthful of veneers were exposed.

"Is your dick naturally that big?" I leaned forward, keeping my voice low. Beside me, Easton let out a cough. "I mean, I just don't understand how it—"

"I know, right?" He grinned. "It's surprising, because I got small hands. And everyone says the hand and the dick size have to do with each other, but they don't. And yeah, it's all me. Granted, I do stretch it."

"You what?" Easton, who was mid-bite into a cheese stick, paused. "You *stretch* it? What does that mean?"

"Penile traction device," he responded, sounding out each syllable as if we were wanting to write it down. "You got to go to a doctor to get it. I, myself, I use Andropenis, but there are lots of options out there." He pointed to E. "Do your research. You need to find one you feel comfortable with and that fits into your schedule."

"What do you mean, fits into his schedule?" I moved my stool closer to the table.

"Well, you know. These things take time. It's not just bim-bam-boom, you got a big dick."

"How much time?" I pressed.

"Well"—he glanced around as if to make sure no one was listening

—"they say six hours a day. But I think nine hours is the sweet spot. Nine hours is..."—he held up his thumb and forefinger in an okay sign—"BAM. Good to go."

"I'm sorry, did you say nine hours *a day*?" Easton squinted at him.

"Ideally."

"For how long?" I asked.

"Oh, not long. That's the beauty of it. Four months. Four months, and you get anywhere from two to three centimeters in length—that's what the doctors say—but I got a full inch and a half." He beamed.

"I'm sorry, how can you fit nine hours of this in every day?"

"Well, you can do other stuff while wearing it. I'm an accountant. Every tax return I filed last year?" He paused and winked at me. "Prepped it while in the device. Honestly, it cleared my mind a little."

"Yeah..." Easton said slowly.

"So you had a big penis already? And you got an extra inch and a half by using the traction thing?" I asked.

"Well.... and the injections."

"Holy shit," Easton muttered.

"The injections are just for girth. I added two and a half inches in circumference over the course of two years. It's actually an acid they're injecting. Hyaluronic acid. I can email you that. I know it's a bitch to remember."

"That's okay." Easton waved off the offer. "No one's putting a needle anywhere near my dick."

"Elle?" The high-pitched voice came from behind me. "Elle Ribbenham, is that you?"

Oh *shit*. I slowly turned, wincing at the sight of Keri McIntyre, our pledge class president who—last I'd heard—was in New York working in finance and dating some Saudi oil heir. "Keri," I said carefully. "What are you doing here?" Seriously. I chose a shithole bar in Model City for the express purpose of not running into anyone I knew.

"Oh, I'm just in town for the night." She still had the thick Southern accent. "And Easton North, look at you!" She reached out her arms and flung them around his neck, squeezing him tight. I looked behind her, half expecting to see our entire executive team, but she was alone. "That's right, I forgot you two got *married*! So, you're actually Elle North now. Just like that Kardashian baby!"

Thanks, Keri. Got my social security number and address handy? I'm sure this guy with his penile traction device and farm-boy fashion sense would love to have that too.

"Oh, I'm Keri." She turned her attention on Kurt and panic erupted in my chest. "I'm sorry to interrupt you guys, I just haven't seen Elle since college! Of course she looks exactly the same."

"Oh, stop." I watched in desperation as she took the stool next to Kurt.

"No, really. Elle, you look exactly the same. It's your skin. You've got such great skin." She clamped a hand on Kurt's arm and peered at him. "How old are you?"

"Keri—" I protested.

"Forty-two," he supplied, treating us all to another bright show of his teeth. I opened my wallet and fished out two twenties.

"Now, see. I never would have known it. You moisturize, don't you?"

"We should be going." I eased off the stool and placed the cash on the table. "Kurt, I'm sorry to rush off, but thank you so much for, ahh, helping us with our accounting questions."

"Happy to help," he said, smiling broadly. "Email me anytime."

"Oooh, are you an accountant?" Keri leaned in closer to him, seemingly unconcerned with our departure. I watched her hand settle on his thigh and wondered how far from the mystery meat it was located.

"It was good to—"

I cut Easton's goodbye off at the knees, pushing him toward the door. "Go," I mumbled. "Just go."

"Wow." I held Easton's hand as we moved through the crowded parking lot. It had rained while we were in the bar, the cling of moisture still thick and muggy in the air. We paused to let a pregnant woman with a Winn-Dixie cart pass. I was momentarily distracted from Kurt as I realized how little I had thought about a baby recently. Even with taking the hormone pills, I just... hadn't.

Easton stepped over a puddle, keeping his boots clean. "Yeah. What are the chances Keri would be there?"

"I know. And why did she stay behind at our table? I think she was into him!" I headed to my side but Easton followed, trapping me against the SUV as he leaned into me.

"I love you so much." His voice was husky, his eyes warm. He cupped my face and stared down at me, then lowered his mouth to mine for a kiss. I surged into it, clutching at his shoulder as I rose to my toes for better access. From somewhere to our left, someone let out a wolf whistle, then laughed. Easton's arms tightened around me, then he reached to the side and opened my door. "Careful," he warned. "The sidestep is slick."

I navigated past the not-so-slick sidestep and up into his Range Rover. He closed the door and gave me that smirk—the same one he flashed the first night we met, in a dark side street of a bar, when he'd offered a ride to me and a vomiting Chelsea. It still had the same effect—a warm rush of exhilaration and attraction.

"So." Easton pulled out of the lot. "I take it that you're not interested in giant penis guy."

"Kurt," I clarified. "And no. Definitely no." The photo he had sent me had looked like a fat sausage—the shaft jutting out almost a foot from his skinny body. I had opened the photo up three times during our ride to the bar, unsure if I was afraid or interested in the disproportionate appendage. After hearing Kurt's enthusiasm for genital mutilation—and meeting him in general—I could safely say that I was not interested in seeing, touching, or interacting in any way with it.

Easton took the ramp for the 441. "What do you think he's telling Keri about us?"

"No idea." He glanced over at me. "You worried about it?"

I chewed on the end of one fingernail. "Not really. I probably should be." I could remember a time when my social heartbeat rose and fell around what Keri thought of me. Now, with everything going on, the concept that Kurt might tell her something... I didn't have the emotional bandwidth to handle another concern. Maybe that was why I hadn't been hyper-focused on a baby. Not enough time or energy.

He pulled my hand into his lap and squeezed it. "I'm glad you weren't interested in him. The thought of you doing anything with him..." He shook his head. "It didn't do anything for me."

"Why not?" I turned my hand over in his, curling my fingers around his.

"I don't know. I'm still working it out. But when we were sitting there, talking to him—I was bored. Also, freaked out by his science project of a penis, but literally fucking *bored* at the thought of you doing anything with him. And I think it's because I didn't see him as competition."

"Did you see Aaron as competition?"

He shook his head slowly, his eyes on the road. "Not really, no. But I think I needed the comfort level I had with Aaron. I don't think I would have been okay with what happened otherwise."

"Well, I'm not sure you're going to consider any of the other guys on the site as competition," I said, thinking back through the hundreds of messages we had received. Kurt had been the only one who hadn't been too old, too ugly, too young, or too creepy to consider. "I can keep looking."

"Or we can go back to the De Lucas." The suggestion was quiet but deadly, each word shooting over and hitting me in the chest. A stab of hope. Arousal. Trepidation. Fear. Too many emotions to properly sort out.

"What do you mean?" I asked carefully, my finger halting in its caress of his palm.

"I don't know." He came to a stop at the light and looked over at me, his profile lit red by the signal, his face devastatingly handsome against the shadows. "You liked them, right?"

Brad's touch . . . each brush electric against my skin. Hands skimming up and down, around my nipples. The heat. His fingers flexing, lifting, cupping . . . Possessive. Confident. Exhilarating. His warm breath against my neck, my breasts. "Ask your husband if I can touch you."

"Ummm... yeah." A lot. An ocean's worth of arousal.

"So, maybe we do something with them again. Something more."

I thought of my lunch, scheduled for this Tuesday with Julia, and warred over how to respond. Our post-De Luca fight was still fresh in my mind, plus there was the issue that Brad and Julia may not want to hook up with us. "I don't know." I reached down and undid my first heel, flexing and stretching the foot as soon as it was free. "I felt like that ended badly with you and me."

"It ended badly because I was insecure." He sighed. "I need to get over that."

"*Are* you over that? I mean, it's only been a week." And it wasn't like anything had changed. I still hadn't fully forgiven him—if that was the right word—for the Nicole debacle. Not that it was his fault, but *still*. A wasted trip to Los Angeles. Countless calls with her. Hours of research and wining and dining and bullshit, bullshit, bullshit—only to have her make a big investment and cut Easton out of the payday. Well, Easton cut himself out of the payday but STILL. A fresh bloom of anger erupted in my chest. I yanked on the other heel and tried to smother the emotion.

"I could be over it. I think"—he paused, and I could see the indecision on his face before I heard it in his voice—"I think I *need* you to fuck him."

"What?"

"I've been thinking it over. I feel like I'm running from it if you don't. I need to know how I compare. And look, if he pleases you better than I do, then I'll learn how to fuck you better."

He gripped on the steering wheel, the veins along the back of his hand bulging. I looked away as the radio softly played the strands of a Dave Matthews song. "That's crazy. I'm not judging a contest between you two. And he's a person. A married person. He's not a ride at the fair that I can hop on because you want to know how I like it."

"Look, I wasn't worried about Aaron. And at FSU, half those guys had drunk dick or came in a few minutes. I've never had much competition." He glanced at me. "Maybe I'm sloppy. Maybe I've relied on my dick too much and never really learned my stuff. But *that* prick?" He shook his head as if in disbelief of Brad De Luca. "He knows his shit. I was fucking intimidated just sitting across from him. And when he had his hands on you, his mouth on you?" He swore. "I *felt* you, Elle. I had my mouth on you. You responded. And you came so hard. You were damn near quaking against my mouth."

"But that wasn't just him. She—" I took a deep breath and tried to sort through the emotions I'd felt. "You made this sound when she took you in her mouth. It's a sound you make with me sometimes, when you really like what I'm doing. And it triggered something in me. I thought I would hate it. I thought I would be furious and insecure and jealous. But instead, it was like a fire, one that made me crazy turned on. It made everything else—his touch, your mouth, the experience... more. And it was watching them together, her reaction, knowing they could see us—it was everything, and experiencing it with you—that's what I loved."

I looked at him. "What happened with Aaron was more than a normal night between me and you. But that wasn't him. It was you—you trusting me to do that. You giving that to me. Us sharing that together. And if you have sex with Julia, I think it would be hot even if she sucked in bed. I think just the experience of you having two girls instead of one—it would be more. And..." I faltered as I suddenly realized that the idea of that no longer scared me. Our night with Aaron had been one of the hottest of my life, but I'd never attributed that to Aaron. I had immediately filed it in its own category in *our* sex life. I pulled on the seatbelt and tried to find my way back to our conversation. "Does any of that make any sense?"

"Yeah," he admitted. "I felt that—all of that—when I watched you with Aaron. And maybe it'll be the same with this guy. But I need to know. And... if Brad doesn't want to fuck you, or they don't do that, then fine. But right now, I'm fucking intimidated, and I hate feeling like I'm not good enough." He drove faster, and the Rover's left tire shuddered over the center line before he brought it back. "You *want* him. I know you do, and I can't give you a nice house, or a secure life, but I can give him to you."

It sounded like the biggest, most fucked-up risk in the world. I sank back into the seat, and I tried to figure out which stick of dynamite to grab first.

"You already give me what I need. Okay? So stop all the bullshit about that. If I needed to fuck him, I'd tell you that I needed to fuck him. But I don't. Would I like to? Sure. I'm sure you'd like to bend over Julia and take her for a ride too. We're human. We want pretty things and you and I are pleasers. We like to please and we like to have someone fawn over our shit while we do it. But this moment isn't when we need to throw Brad Fucking De Luca into the mix. You were right, what you said last night. They have their shit together. They know what they're doing. We are lost damn ducklings, wandering around sex city unescorted and Kurt is a perfect example of why we need to just chill out for a moment and regroup." I held out my hands in a calm-down gesture. "Why don't we take a break and just... step back from everything. Go back to normal for a few months."

He pulled into our driveway and parked, leaving the engine on. "Is that what you want?"

"I have no idea what I want," I replied honestly. "I'd really like you to just make an executive decision so I can go back to scrolling through Pinterest and bitching about your dirty clothes being left on the floor."

His grin appeared for a brief moment, then he sobered. "Okay. Are you ready for the executive decision?"

"I'm ready. Wait." I reached forward and flipped off the radio, killing the background noise. "Now I'm ready."

"We'll take three months off. No visiting swinger sites, no dirty talk about threesomes, no bringing up anything about any of it."

"Three months," I confirmed, my heart sinking a little at the prospect, which had seemed like such a great idea, just seconds before.

"Three months. Starting right after you have sex with Brad De Luca."

28

The tequila, I decided, was entirely to blame. That, and Chelsea's continued refusal to answer my calls. Plus, the fact that I was eighteen hours away from lunch with my biggest client, one where I planned to ask to have sex with her husband. Tack on the accepted offer now on file on the De Luca house, and I was feeling a dangerous combination of drunk, lonely, cocky, and panicked.

Would confronting Nicole Fagnani help any of the above? Here was three tequila shots worth of let's-find-out.

"Stay close," I tore a twenty-dollar bill in half and passed one side of it to the taxi driver. "I'll give you the other half when I come out."

"You kidding me?" The man shot me a look like I had just pissed on his seat.

"What? Not good? I thought people do that." I saw it in a movie once. There, the guy had seemed smooth and smart.

"You think I have scotch tape in my glove box? How'm I supposed to spend this? I gonna give McDonalds two halves of a bill?"

"I don't know... don't you have some tape at home?" I glanced at the meter, which had just ticked up in cost. This conversation was getting expensive.

"Do I look like someone that keeps my drawers at home stocked with scotch tape?" It was a valid point. He had a lizard tattooed up his neck, the tongue of it curling along one cheek. From the smell filling the car, I doubted if he even had soap at home.

"Okay, give it back." I held out my hand.

"I'll trade you for another one. A whole one." He held the half bill just out of reach, as if worried I would squelch on the deal.

"If I give you the entire twenty, then what's to stop you from just leaving?"

"There's fourteen dollars on the meter. I'm not going anywhere."

I took back the half of the twenty with a sigh, then reluctantly passed forward an intact bill. I wasn't entirely sure *we* had scotch tape at home. "Okay. I won't be long."

My phone rang and I fished the slim device out of my back pocket, cringing when I saw Easton's name on the display. He had been out with Aaron, watching the game and mending the awkward tension that my Chelsea-confession had created. I thought I'd have a few hours of alone time to drown my sorrows in margaritas, maybe catch up on Gossip Girl reruns and that half-tub of Mint Chocolate Chip in the fridge.

Only... the margaritas hadn't exactly mellowed me out. Instead, they'd fueled my rage at one giant tennis slut. Which was why I was climbing out of the taxi and staring up at Nicole's giant iron gate, gauging my ability to climb it. Sober, there was at least a five percent chance I'd make it over. Now? My likelihood had fallen into the negative percentile.

I went for the keypad instead, pressing the call button and leaning over, putting my mouth close to the speaker.

"Can I help you?" a sharp male voice crackled through the speaker.

"I'm here to see Nicole."

"Your name?"

"Elle North. She knows my husband." It was a gamble. I thought about adding a threatening line, something along the lines of *tell her she better talk to me or else*, but I'd used up my badass moves with the ripped twenty, and that hadn't exactly gone smoothly. I wasn't prepared for this guy to call my bluff when I had nothing else up my sleeve.

The gates, shockingly enough, began to part. I walked unsteadily up to the massive Mediterranean home, and ran through a cliff notes version of my speech, which had sounded really good in front of my bathroom mirror, but was quickly falling apart in my head.

"Elle." Nicole stood on the front steps, a pink bathrobe wrapped tightly around her large frame. "I'm glad you're here. Come in."

I paused, surprised. *She was glad I was here?*

"Look." Nicole spoke before I had a chance to. She closed the ingrained wooden door that would look killer on our house and turned to face me. "I owe Easton and you a massive apology."

"Yes, you do." My anger was deflating quickly at the ashamed look in her eyes and I struggled to hold onto it. "What you did—"

"It was criminal, I know. And it's even worse because I've been in that situation. I've been that girl." She looked over her shoulder and I realized there was a woman, standing in the dimly lit foyer. Not quite the security team I had envisioned, unless the security team wore Miami Heat T-shirts and mesh shorts. "This is Jessica, my girlfriend."

The surprise must have shown on my face, because she pulled the neck of her robe up self-consciously. "Yeah. I screwed up a lot of things on that flight."

"I'm going to head to the den. Give you two some privacy." She nodded to Nicole and to me, then left, her lanky frame towering over both of us.

"Wow," I said quietly. "She's tall."

"Tall, and still upset with me." She gestured toward a low bench tucked into the curve of a grand staircase bigger than Chelsea's guest house. "This has been hard for her."

I was surprised she even told her about it. Then again, everything about this visit—her wet hair, make-up free face, crestfallen expression, the girlfriend—all of it was a surprise.

"There's absolutely no excuse for what I did." She settled onto the bench beside me and the robe gaped at the knee, revealing blue pajama pants and bare feet. "I was drinking, and afraid of the opportunity and feeling..." She tilted her head. "Feeling like a little girl in a man's world. Everyone we'd met with that weekend had been men. My agent. Easton. The MGM rep. The game designers. And all of them —including Easton—had spoken to me as if I was made of glass. Or... like I was twelve and dressing in my big sister's clothes and makeup, pretending to be grown-up and they were going along with it to be nice to me. I didn't feel like anyone there really cared about me. What I wanted. What I thought. I started in this world when I was fourteen, and my manager and agents and parents made all of my decisions. I was this commodity—a brand—and other than being told where to go, and when to practice, and who to play... they didn't have use for me. None of them looked at me as anything other than a cash register until my coach put his hand up my shirt one day and really looked at me. Wanted me. And for something that had nothing to do with tennis."

My stomach twisted and I could feel the third margarita revolting at the thought. "Nicole, you—"

"On the plane," she said quietly, "I was drinking and I had this really weird moment where I felt like it was happening all over again. My life being controlled. My self-worth reduced to just a commodity. My future and money being decided for me. And I had this ridiculous craving for my coach. I needed someone to look at me as someone other than Nicole Fagnani, the tennis player. I needed to be seen as a woman. Desired as a woman. Craved." She let out a helpless laugh. "And he was right there. And I just... I just wanted to feel a reaction from him. Proof that I wasn't just a paycheck. It was so, so stupid of me." She brushed a hand over her cheek, wiping away a tear that had fallen.

"Easton doesn't look at you as a cash register," I said quietly. "But, to be honest, part of my anger *is* over the lost commission. Commission he lost just because he's a good guy. He's still new in wealth management and has had some trouble getting his foot in the door. You—you were a big deal to him. And I know he wouldn't have pushed you for this deal if he didn't think it was the right thing for you. And..." I groaned.

"Whatever. It's done. It just hurt him—in more ways than one."

"You're right. He is a good guy.

I knew that the minute he pushed my hand off of him. And when he walked away from the commission and turned me over to his boss." She met my eyes. "I know he doesn't want anything to do with me, but I can't let what I did slide. I've been calling him but he won't answer. Please, Elle. Help me."

As much as I wanted to take a check from Nicole for the commission,

I couldn't. That was something between her and Easton, and I'd stand by whatever decision he made with it. But I did think he needed to hear what she had just told me. It was up to him whether he wanted to give her a second chance.

"I'll have him call you tomorrow," I promised. "But... there is one thing that you can do for me."

She raised her brows. "Anything."

29

I was still hungover from the margaritas, my stomach flipping in protest as I sat across from Julia De Luca the next day. She looked stunning in a bright green sundress, one that showed off her olive skin and dark hair. I watched as she delicately cut into a giant blueberry pancake, then shoved a wedge of it into her mouth with the gusto of a linebacker.

The new sushi restaurant had been closed, so we'd ended up at IHOP —a transition she had enthusiastically accepted. Upon arrival, she'd grilled the waitress about their syrup brands and distributor, then ordered enough food for two.

She noticed me watching and gestured to her plate with her fork. "Want some? I have plenty."

"Oh, no. But thank you. I'm trying to do keto." I gave an apologetic smile.

"Yeah, Brad's doing that. Except that he cheats and drinks Coke, which I'm pretty sure throws the ketosis thing completely out of whack." She blew at a strand of hair that had fallen into her face. "So, how's everything?"

I tried not to stare at the giant diamond that screamed at me from her ring finger. "Good. I have the buyer's inspections scheduled for Friday. I'm coordinating it with Martha, she's prepared and is working with the security."

She nodded as her delicate jaw worked through a bite, then she took a sip of milk. "Great. But, I was actually asking about you and Easton. Did I totally freak you out the other night?"

"Oh!" I inhaled sharply. "No, absolutely not." I shook my head. "No, it was fine."

She gave me a tentative grin. "It's okay, Elle. I'm a wife, just like you. You can tell me if it freaked you out."

I relaxed a little, picking up my fork and scooping a little of my eggs onto the end of it. "Honestly, it didn't freak me out. I thought it would. I was prepared for it. But it was hot. And it was something that I could give him, to kind of make up for the"—I glanced around to make sure that no one was in earshot—"threesome we did with his friend."

She was shaking her head before I even finished talking. "You don't need to make up for anything, Elle. If that's what the experiences are —one for him, one for you—then they won't work. He needs to be into watching you be pleased as much as he's into getting pleased."

"I think he is." I flushed and took a small bite of the egg, which was too runny for me. I chewed. "I mean, we'd never talked about being with a girl, until we had that conversation at your house and all... you know. All that happened."

"Personally, I'm very selfish in our sex life," she confided. "It's why Brad doesn't fuck other women."

My thoughts stalled around the statement. "You don't?"

She shook her head, and another big square of fluffy pancake disappeared between her glossy lips. She chewed, taking her time, while my heart sprinted around my chest in equal parts joy and despair. *Brad doesn't fuck other women.* She swallowed, then continued. "We used to do it in the past and had a really bad experience with this one girl." She wrinkled her face, as if she'd smelled something rotten. "She was the one who pretty much told half of Miami our sexual business. It took me a while to recover from her, and we stopped doing anything with anyone for a while." She picked up her milk and I thought of our three-month break, the one that was going to start right after I slept with Brad. *Ha.* We were such cocky idiots.

"So, you just meet with men? Single men? Or..." I tried to think of another scenario.

"Pretty much. Or a couple, and we have same room sex, or Brad does some stuff with the wife and she pleasures me. It turns me on to have him make them come, I'm just not down with him actually fucking them. At least right now." She peered down at her plate. "Wasn't this supposed to come with bacon?" She twisted in her seat, looking for our waiter. "Sir?" She lifted her hand and the man all but tripped over a family of four to get to our table. She explained the bacon predicament as I struggled to pierce a wobbly piece of sausage in half with the edge of my fork.

"But, anyway, mostly just threesomes with a guy. That's my favorite, and then you don't deal with the egos and relationship dynamics of a couple." She picked up a strawberry with her fingers and popped it into her mouth. "But, you know, every couple is different. I know wives who love to watch their husbands fuck. *Love* it." She shrugged, as if we were talking about whether to get a minivan or sedan, or what yoga class to choose. "You've got plenty of time to figure it out. Try different stuff and be honest with each other."

She fell silent and I felt the need to say something, anything, to contribute to the conversation. "We, uh, think we're going to take a break. For a few months. After our next one."

She nodded. "Not a bad idea. Who's your next one going to be with?"

I hesitated. The question felt deeply personal, even though it wasn't, not considering we had no "next one" lined up, no confidences to break. "I'm not sure. We, ugh, met someone from SwingLife but he was really weird. And the other guys on the site—"

"Suck so bad," Julia chimed in, giving me a pained look. "Close that account. Trust me. And pull off any photos that you have on there as soon as possible. You can't control who downloads and does what with that content. Brad had a legal conniption when he read their terms and conditions." She laughed. "I'm pretty sure he's the only person who's ever read that encyclopedia of crap."

Yeah, I'd scrolled through the fine print with a flick of the wrist, then agreed to it all. Which, in hindsight, seemed incredibly stupid, since I was trusting them with my most private thoughts, communications, and photos. I gave up on cutting the sausage and just stuck it in between my back incisors and ripped it in half. "So..." I chewed through the piece, then swallowed. "Where am I supposed to find these people then? I know there's a club, over by the airport..." My words trailed off at Julia's emphatic head shake.

"Don't go there. Again, that's an uncontrolled environment. Cameras. IDs at the door. There's too much exposure possibilities."

It was starting to feel helpless, and I felt an irrational irritation toward Julia, who was really great at hogging her husband and shooting down ideas, but horrible at actually providing solutions. I stuck the remaining piece of sausage in my mouth and realized exactly how ridiculous I was being. Julia De Luca wasn't my personal sexual concierge service. She was my seller. I should be focused on selling her house, not drilling her for tips on picking up strange men for group sex.

"Who are you wanting to meet up with next? A single guy or a girl? A couple?" She pushed the pancake plate to one side and took her side of bacon from the food runner who approached. "Thank you so much."

I waited until the man had left. "A guy."

"Okay, a guy." She nodded, but her focus wasn't on me. She stared off into the other side of the restaurant, and I watched as her fingertips tapped absentmindedly along the table. "I might..." Her gaze came back to me and she hesitated. "I mean, I don't want to get all in your business or anything..."

I leaned forward and waited.

"But, I might have a guy for you. Someone I'd feel really comfortable recommending. He's single and totally professional. No drama. No bullshit. Shows up, does the job and leaves." She wiped her palms off with each hand and then showed me her palms, as if to demonstrate his clean performance.

"He's, umm..." I cleared my throat and straightened my knife beside my spoon. "Good?"

Her smile widened. "He's *very* good. And big." A playful gleam appeared in her eyes. "Like your husband. Who, by the way, is ridiculous eye candy. Is he a good fuck?"

A blush heated my cheeks, one that was paired with a surge of arousal and pride. "He's an incredible fuck," I admitted.

"The cocky ones normally are." She grinned, then snapped back to business. "Now, I don't want to push this guy on you, but if you're interested, just let me know. I can have Brad text his number to Easton."

"That would be great, if you could. We don't really know what we're doing," I confessed.

She snorted. "None of us do. We just learn really quickly what *not* to do. And I'm not trying to preach at you, but Easton needs to be the one who does all the communication with the guy. And if you hook up with a single woman, you do all the communication with the girl. Otherwise, it gets messy and starts feeling sketchy." She reached across the table and gripped my arm, making sure I was listening.

I was. I was soaking in all of it, terrified that I would forget something crucial and screw it all up later.

"You have to *vigilantly* protect your relationship at all costs." She held my gaze. "Do you understand?"

"I think so." But no... not really. There were so many rules. So many dynamics. I was supposed to vigilantly protect my relationship—but diving deeper into this world seemed like the opposite of that. Look at the night we hooked up with them and the subsequent fight we'd had. Granted, maybe that tension had come from the event with Nicole, but still.

She smiled, and the intensity faded from her giant brown eyes. "It'll be fine. Oh, and, Elle?"

"Yes?" I asked nervously.

"Tell Easton to tell him you want the *doctor's experience*. He'll know what that means." She winked at me, then reached for her purse and signaled for the check.

30

"Okay, let's walk through the plan. E?" I turned to E, who was trying to get a chunk of gum off the bottom of his shoe. "E, pay attention."

"What asshole spits their gum out on the sidewalk?" He scraped his Nike across the pavement. "Jesus."

"Don't say Jesus." I returned my focus to Aaron, who looked despondent. "Aaron. Try not to look like your dog just died."

His glum look turned into something more of a glare, but that was okay. I'd take mad over mopey all day long.

"Okay, whatever. Look pissed. I'm trying to help true love find its way and you guys aren't helping."

"True love?" Easton groaned. "Stop labeling this. The man just got through a divorce."

"Okay," I countered. "I'm trying to help two friends who are physically attracted to each other but are afraid to admit their connection because they're stubborn and freaked out about the teensy-tiny threesome we had." I glared at E. "Happy? True love was a helluva lot shorter."

"Let's not use the word teensy-tiny in any sexual activity that involved me." Easton rubbed his pec with a scowl.

"Or me," Aaron chimed in.

I inhaled for three counts, then exhaled for three counts. Maybe Aaron and Chelsea didn't need a matchmaker. They were already living together, if you ignored the pool and yard between them. Surely they could figure out their way through this snafu and onto the Happily Ever After side.

Except... it had been thirteen days and Chelsea was still ignoring my calls and texts. Aaron had tried to get into the main house to talk to her, only to find that his personal passcode had been deleted and his number blocked from her phone. We needed a grand gesture, something to get her to forgive all three of us while falling back into her crush with Aaron.

Enter Nicole Fagnani. Nicole Fagnani, who—thanks to her new alliance with MGM Entertainment—now had enough pull with Miami Stadium to get Aaron sixty seconds on stage, during Taylor Swift's set change.

Sixty seconds that was going to start as soon as she finished *White Horse* and hustled that cute little booty off stage.

I listened as she sang and if there was a worst song to preface Aaron with, I'd have to search Spotify for hours to find it. The entire thing seemed to be about a man who fucked up and how it was too late for him to come and apologize now. I turned to E, who was already engaged in a level-one bromance with the sound guy. I pulled on his arm. "Are you listening to these words? This is horrible."

He shrugged and I paced over to Aaron, who was leaning against a

Twisted Marriage | 221

wall, watching the audience. "I can't see her," he said, speaking loudly in an attempt to be heard over the giant speakers.

"You know Chelsea. She's in the front row somewhere." That's where our tickets had been. She'd probably given mine to her assistant, or the gay trainer at her gym, or the barista at Starbucks who gave her extra whipped cream.

All sub-par choices when compared to *me* but none of whom slept with her crush, and I could concede that that did knock a friendship a little off-kilter.

"Okay." A short and stocky man wearing a giant headpiece strode up to Easton. "You miked and ready?"

"Yep." Aaron straightened. "Good to go."

"Here's a microphone. It works in conjunction with your earpiece, so it's not necessary, but a lot of people feel better having something in their hands."

Aaron took it and nodded. "Okay."

"Remember. Only sixty seconds. Now, let's go." The man headed toward the brightly lit stage and gestured for Aaron to follow him. As the pair passed me, I met Aaron's eyes and gave him a quick smile. Gripping the brim of his baseball cap, he tipped it at me.

The lights on the stage extinguished, and I saw a glimpse of Taylor running off stage, a trio of attendants offering her water and fanning at her face as if they were a pit crew. A spotlight activated and Aaron stepped into it, the roars of the crowd settling into a hushed silence.

When he lifted the microphone to speak, every single eye in the stadium was on him. I clutched Easton's arm and wondered what Chelsea was thinking.

"They told me I have sixty seconds," Aaron drawled. "Which doesn't seem like enough time to make a woman fall in love with me."

There was uneasy movement in the crowd and a mumble of what seemed to be approval from the thousands of women before him. Easton pointed to a monitor and I moved over, focusing on the close-up view it afforded.

"But that's okay, 'cause I don't need Chelsea Pedicant to fall in love with me. I only need her to forgive me. I'm a guy. We do stupid things, and what I did didn't have anything to do with her. I wasn't even thinking about her because, to be honest, I never thought I had a chance with her. And maybe I don't, but if I do, then, Chelsea, I'd like to take you on a date. I'd like to pick you up and take you to dinner and treat you the way you deserve to be treated. Like a lady. Like, maybe..." He glanced down at the floor for a moment, then shyly back up. "Like maybe *my* lady."

"Oh my God, he's running over time." Some bitch with a side mohawk turned away from the monitor and wildly gestured to a grip. "We need someone to pull him off."

"Are you kidding me?" The stocky guy who had escorted Aaron on stage shot the woman a glare. "The audience is eating this up."

And they were. There was a ripple of sighs and awwws and several crude comments screamed out from various corners of the civic center. Then, so close to the stage that I could see the reflection of sequins on her shirt, I heard a loud and unmistakable voice. "Aaron Talbot, I *will* go on a date with you."

On the monitor, Aaron's face widened into an ear-to-ear grin. "You will?"

"Hell yes!" The monitor view changed, focusing in on Chelsea, who was in the process of trying to crawl over a lighting rig to get to the stage. Aaron bent over, offering her his hand, and when he lifted her up and onto the stage, the stadium erupted into cheers.

He looked down, his arms still around her, and when she spoke, it was captured clearly by his mic.

"I think you're supposed to kiss me now."

"Kiss her! Kiss her! Kiss her!" The chant rolled through the crowd. Aaron glanced at the audience, then dipped her back, true Hollywood-style, and kissed her squarely on the mouth.

My jaw dropped. Between the kiss and the speech, I'm not sure why we were even here. Aaron seemed to have the swoony romance act down pat.

"This is going to go viral," the gaffer beside us mused.

"Okay, we're rolling RIGHT NOW with Taylor," the mohawk screeched. "We need lights and start the music. Three, two, one, GO!"

The beat started and I heard the opening lines of "I knew you were trouble" bursting out of Taylor as she swept onto the stage, her smile big, her hand raised. The crowd turned their attention to her, and Aaron and Chelsea faded into the background to everyone except Easton and me.

"You did good," Easton whispered in my ear, wrapping his arms around me and hugging my back to his chest. "Really good."

I watched as Chelsea pulled Aaron down off the stage and toward her seat and hoped it was good enough for her to forgive me too.

31

"Mr. and Mrs. North?" The receptionist peered at us from the far end of the cramped waiting room. "You're up."

I glanced at Easton, then stood, smoothing the front of my white cotton sundress into place. Underneath it, I wore my sexiest bra and panty set, the thong already beginning to stick in between my legs.

Easton waited for me to go and I walked through the crowded area, apologizing as I bumped into an older woman's knee, then high-stepping as I moved over a toddler sprawled out on the carpet. I reached the desk and smiled at the receptionist, who waved a bored hand in the direction of the double doors. "Go through there and to suite 4A."

I pulled on the handle of the double door and entered a wide hall, reassured by the familiar smell of antiseptic and bleach. There were medical suites on both sides, some blinds open, their secondary waiting rooms exposed. I walked past a rheumatologist, a podiatrist, a psychiatrist, and stopped at the door to Suite 4A. The blinds were closed, the suite missing the name plaque that had adorned the other doors. Easton rapped on the door, then tried the handle. It swung open and he stepped inside. I hesitated.

"Coming?" He lifted one brow.

"Yes. I just…" I glanced back down the hall.

He smiled. "Come on." He held out his hand, and I took it. When the door shut behind us, a bell tinkled through the small intake area. I hesitated, looking over the plastic chair, scales, and blood pressure cuff. Past that, a room through which I could see an examination table. A side desk with a computer. A man in green scrubs and a white coat who spun on his stool and stood.

The doctor. Older. Mid-fifties, if I had to guess. He reached out, pumping some antibacterial gel into his palm and I could see the salt and pepper of his hair, the clean-shaven jaw, the rugged cut to his features. He waved us forward with a wedding-ring-free hand. "Come on in."

Easton led the way, moving into the exam room and glancing around quickly before tilting his head at me to come on in. *All clear*.

"Elle, I'm Dr. Loutin. I'll be performing your exam today. Please, take a seat." He gestured to two plastic chairs set against the wall. "Before we begin, I need both you and your husband to sign some paperwork."

He held out two clipboards, and I took mine, sliding a black pen out from the clasp. I glanced at E, who was already signing the bottom, then at the doctor. The man was studying me, his eyes a pale shade of blue, and gave a pleasant smile. "Read over all of it," he urged. "Please. Take your time."

I sat down next to E, and took an inventory of the space. A round jar of long Q-tips on the counter. Another with cotton balls. A box of surgical masks. A package of latex gloves, size large. From a speaker in the ceiling, melodic ocean sounds played. I looked down at the form.

I'd expected a HIPPA statement or release of medical documents form, something fitting with the role-play, but this was a legitimate contract, one that appeared to be created specifically for us.

I, Elle North, understand that Dr. James Loutin is not a medical doctor, and any medical advice that he gives will be ignored.

I, Elle North, agree to communicate with Dr. James Loutin if I am ever uncomfortable or interested in leaving the office. For clarification, the safe word LASSIE will be used. If LASSIE is said, Dr. James Loutin will immediately stop and leave.

I, Elle North, agree that my husband will be present for all activities. I also state that I have not brought any sound or video recording equipment into the experience, and will keep this experience confidential. Dr. James Loutin is held by these same rules, and will not be recording or sharing any part of this experience, except for this contract, which will be held by him for litigious protection. You will also be provided a copy for your safekeeping.

Allowed activities.

I, Elle North, allow for the following activities:

- To be stripped naked

- To be touched and kissed all over my body

- To be penetrated vaginally by mouth, fingers, and/or penis(es)

- To be penetrated anally by mouth, fingers, and/or penis(es)

- To be slapped by open palm (spanked) on my body, but not my face

- To be spoken to in words that some would find demeaning. *For example: Slut, Whore, Kinky*

- To perform oral sex on Dr. James Loutin and/or my husband

- To have sex with Dr. James Loutin and/or my husband

- To have anal sex with Dr. James Loutin and/or my husband

- To have Dr. James Loutin and/or my husband ejaculate on or inside my body or mouth

Dr. James Loutin will wear a condom during all vaginal and/or anal sex. He has been rigorously tested for all known sexually transmitted diseases within the last ten days, and is clean.

I, Elle North, state that I am free from sexually transmitted diseases and that I am not pregnant. I consent to the use of condoms.

I scrolled down the rest of the page, which contained a good bit of legalese but nothing else of interest. Aware of both Easton and the doctor watching, I signed the bottom of the page.

"Good," the doctor said crisply, taking the clipboard from me. "I'm going to step out of the room and let you get undressed. Please put on the gown, open on the front, and be sure to remove all undergarments."

I nodded and he strode to the door, his shoes creaking along the way. I spotted the disposable green gown, folded on the examination table, and stood up. The door clicked behind him and I turned to E. "This is interesting."

"Yeah. The contract surprised me. I mean, he'd mentioned that he'd have a disclosure for us to sign, but I didn't expect it to be so explicit. Turn around."

I pivoted away from him, holding my hair out of the way as he undid the clasp at the top of my dress, then dragged the zipper down. "I liked the contract. It made me feel safer."

"You're always safe with me." He pressed a kiss on the back of my neck. "Do you feel comfortable with him?"

I thought of his calming presence, the careful way he had studied me, his professional and almost distant manner. "Yes. And Julia said he's good, so I trust her." *Very good*, she had said.

He pushed at the straps of my sundress, and it fell to the floor. Unclipping my bra, he skimmed it down my arms, then stepped back, leaning against the wall and watching as I stepped out of my panties, then folded everything into a neat and orderly stack that I placed on one chair. I looked down at my shoes, cork wedges with a tan sash that tied around my ankle. "Should I take off my shoes?"

"Would you normally in a doctor's office?"

I weighed the options, then decided to. Sitting naked on the edge of the examining table, I felt the foreign plastic against my bare bottom, and shifted until I was on top of the paper-covered portion of the table. I undid one shoe's strap, then the other, and passed the wedges to E, who placed them on the floor under the chair. Unfolding the gown, I worked my arms through each hole and then sat back down, my legs hanging off the end, and waited.

It was chilly in the room. Underneath the open gown, my nipples hardened, each shift of movement scraping them against the stiff paper of the gown. Between my legs, I could feel the heaviness of arousal begin, the anticipation agony, my lubrication threatened to drop from between my legs and pool on the table. I squeezed tighter, and stiffened as the metal handle of the door turned a half rotation. It cracked open, and I heard Dr. Loutin's voice from the other side. "Ready?"

"I'll start with a general exam, then we can discuss any problems you might be having." He sat down on the padded stool and rolled over to the table. Pulling a pair of glasses from his pocket, he put them on and focused up at me. "Open your knees a little for me, Elle."

He started with my feet, his fingers working over the bare soles, flexing my ankle, massaging along the pad of my heel and then up the muscles of my calf. He paused in one area, kneading a tight knot, and I watched as his brows knit in concentration. "You have very strong legs. Do you run?"

"No, but I played soccer. In high school mostly. A little intramural in college."

"You still have the muscle tone. That's good."

His hands slid higher, running over my knees, and he produced a tiny hammer, which he used to tap on one, then the other. My feet gently rocked. He nodded in approval and then stood, his warm palms sliding up my thighs, squeezing and manipulating the muscles. "Open wider?"

I did, the cool air sliding in between my legs. I was almost on full display, the open gown covering some, but not all of me. Could he see the wet glisten of need? Could he see my thin strip of hair?

From his place against the wall, Easton coughed. A simple sound, but one that magnified everything.

"Let's go a little wider with those knees, Elle. I want you to really open up and show me everything."

Such a kind, professional tone. No hint of what he was asking for. No tremor in his voice as he pushed gently on my knees until I was almost straddling the table.

"You're very flexible," he noted mildly, then straightened, focusing his attention on my right arm. Between my open legs, my ignored pussy cried out for attention. I glanced at E, whose expression was tight, his eyes smoldering with arousal.

"Lift your arm over your head?"

I followed his instructions, and the change in position caused the gown to gap open, my left nipple almost exposed. I shifted my position, craving some contact against my needy core.

"You can put that arm down. Lift the other arm?"

I obeyed, staring straight ahead as he probed at the muscles of my shoulder and my triceps. He pushed on a ticklish spot and I caved toward the touch, letting out a nervous giggle. "That tickles."

He lowered my arm and nodded. "I need to do a breast exam. Is that okay?"

"Yes."

"Open up your gown for me."

I pulled at the fragile sides, spreading them apart, my nipples painfully hard, my skin heated with anticipation. When his right hand touched my collarbone and trailed a slow line down and over my nipple, I shivered.

"Are you sensitive?"

"Not normally."

His fingers circled my nipple, a wide arch, then a tighter spiral. "But right now?"

I inhaled as his warm palm settled over my pert bud and he squeezed. "A little."

"You have beautiful breasts. They're natural?"

"Yes."

His second hand cupped the other breast, and they moved in concert over my skin.

"One of the things you wanted to see me about was your arousal levels. Is that correct?"

I glanced at Easton, who gave a subtle nod. I met the doctor's eyes. "Um... yes."

"Mr. North, would you mind helping me in this part of the exam?"

Easton straightened off the wall and stepped forward, moving to stand beside the doctor.

"I'm going to keep touching her breasts, and I need you to put your fingers inside of Elle and tell me how wet she is."

Easton reached forward, his gaze tight on mine, and I struggled to keep my eyes open, to maintain our eye contact as he pushed two fingers inside my open pussy. I failed. The intrusion was too much and I gasped, my eyes closing as the doctor's hand pinched my nipple.

"She's wet," Easton bit out.

"How wet?"

"Fucking soaked." He worked his fingers in and out, and I could hear the wet slurp of my skin. "You like that, Elle?"

"Yes," I gasped.

"You like his hands on you?"

I let out a soft mew of pleasure as the doctor gently pulled on one breast. "Yes."

"Keep touching her like that," the doctor ordered, as his thumbs rubbed roughly over my aching nipples. "Mr. North, how often do you fuck your wife?"

I was pumping my hips now, making short jerks against the table as I tried to get more and more of Easton's fingers inside of me.

"Every day," Easton rasped, his gaze flicking from my eyes to the action of his hand.

"Interesting." His hands left my breast and he moved beside Easton. "Let me check her for myself."

Easton's fingers took their time in pulling slowly out of me. He stepped back and I watched as he adjusted himself, his eyes thick and lazy with arousal. I knew this look. I fucking loved this look. This was the look where bad ideas came from. This was the look right before things got really fucking dirty.

The doctor sat on the stool, then rolled toward the end of the bed, his face now level with my knees. "Lie back on the table and open up your legs for me. Hold them at the knee." I did, closing my eyes at the bright overhead light. From the next room over, I heard the muted sound of a conversation, barely audible over the still-playing reception music.

"Hmmm. Beautiful." His fingers spread me open, and I flinched when the tip of one finger began a slow and delicious exploration of my pussy. It rolled along the side of my slit, then flicked over the bottom rim of my opening. It traveled back up the other side, then slowly circled my clit. I arched against the table as he played gently with my swollen bud, the pleasure excruciatingly precise. "You know," he said mildly, as if we were about to discuss a weather update or interesting news bulletin. "Your sex life is much more active than a traditional married couple."

"Is it?" I clutched at the edge of the table, my hips rocking a little, needing so much more. Easton walked slowly around the table, coming to a stop beside me.

"Yes. Most husbands and wives have sex once, sometimes twice a week. Extensive sexual activity can sometimes dilute your body's responses to stimulation." Dr. Loutin pulled me to the edge of the table, then lifted my right foot, placing it in a stirrup that I immediately recognized from every gynecological appointment I'd ever had. He positioned the left, and I felt the brush of his scrubs against my ankle as he moved between my legs. "Elle, I'm going to do a few things and I want you to stay as still and quiet as you can. Can you do that for me?"

"Yes."

He settled back on his stool, rolling closer until he was in between my legs. His finger began to swirl in a knot around my clit. "Let's use Dr. Loutin when you address me, okay?"

I closed my eyes as the pleasure grew, my voice a silvery whisper when I spoke. "Yes, Dr. Loutin."

"Good girl. I bet you drive men crazy, Elle." The finger of one hand pushed in between my folds as his other continued in a tight sweep around my clit. "Does she, Mr. North?"

"Men stare at her all the time. I can see how badly they want to fuck her." Easton's fingers traced along the open edge of my gown, pulling the paper further away from my breasts.

Was it true? Did he notice men staring? I hadn't.

"Wow, she's tight." Dr. Loutin's finger pulsed in and out of me and I struggled not to pant. "Now, Elle, I'm going to stimulate your Grafenberg spot, which is located right... *here*. Can you feel that, Elle?"

I let out a low moan when his fingers brushed over the spot. He left my clit and his palm gently pressed on my belly, just above my pubic bone. "Right there," I gasped.

"If she gets any louder, I'm going to need you to put something in her mouth."

Easton's fingers skated over my breasts. "I have something that will keep her quiet." In my peripheral vision, I saw him reach for and undo his belt.

My head lifted off the cushion of the table as the stimulation of his fingers increased, and I let out a louder cry, my legs trembling against the stirrups.

"She's spilling out all over my fingers," the doctor muttered. "I don't have a cloth. Come look at your slut."

I trembled at the name and snuck a peek down to see my husband standing beside the doctor, their attention pinned to my open legs, Easton's dick now hanging out from his pants, already stiff with need. The doctor was also clearly hard, his green scrubs tenting out in an impressive fashion. The sight of both them side by side, turned on by what they were seeing... I clenched my inner muscles around the doctor's fingers, my hips rising off the table, needing more.

"I need to get her juices up before they get all over the table."

"Lick it up," Easton said tersely. "Or I will."

The man glanced at him, his profile so fucking proper. Close-cropped hair. A stethoscope still hanging from his neck. Freshly shaved face. He continued pulsing his finger on my G-spot as if he'd forgotten the mind-blowing task. "How's she taste?"

"Best pussy you'll ever sample in your life."

The man glanced at me. "Look up at the ceiling, Mrs. North and try not to come all over my face."

My orgasm was about to break, my legs beginning to shudder, his words binding me tighter—when his fingers retreated. I let out a cry of disappointment.

Easton chuckled. "She didn't like that. She needs something inside her, badly."

"She can be patient," the doctor said, his fingers returning to their slow and tender exploration of my pussy. "I want to taste her first." He bent over, and the warm wet tip of his tongue lapped across my most sensitive place, starting at the bottom and flicking up and over my clit, over and over again, his mouth sucking across my folds, his hands gripping my hips to keep me in place as I began to buck under his mouth. I craned my neck to watch and saw Easton's hand furiously working over his cock as he watched the doctor thoroughly sample my pussy. I reached for him, wanting him inside of my mouth, and he scowled at me in an almost chiding fashion. *Not yet,* he mouthed.

"I'm going to..." I clutched wildly at the table, my body tightening. "Oh my God, don't stop. Stay on my clit—"

He stayed right there, his tongue swirling over the sensitive bud, round and round, tighter and tighter, a hot circle of pleasure that was binding and expanding through my entire—

I froze as the eruption occurred, my body straining and then breaking as the warm waves of pleasure washed over me. I don't know when he stopped or when he stood, but he was suddenly upright beside me, his face wet, his mouth slightly open as his eyes devoured my exposed body.

The doctor groaned, pulling at the string of his pants and pushing them to the floor. "She's like fucking candy." He straightened and I swallowed at the sight of his cock. Julia was right. He was big. And hard. Very, very hard.

"You need to take her right now or I will," Easton growled.

"Have her ride you. I want to test her gag reflexes on my cock."

Easton pulled my limp legs from the stirrups and grabbed my hands, getting me to my feet. I wrapped my grip around his dick and squeezed.

"Not your hand," he said gruffly, pushing it away. "I need to fuck what he just tasted." The tight expression on his face, one of agonized need... the reverence and command in his voice—the need in me notched a powerful step higher. How had I ever lived without this?

"That's it, right there. Take it all. Show me that you can take it all."

I sank all the way onto Easton's cock and gripped the doctor's thighs, my mouth working as far down his shaft as I could manage. He'd lowered the table almost flush with the floor, which had put my mouth at the perfect height for his dick. My eyes watered as I pushed him further down my throat and he hissed in approval, then pulled slowly out. I looked up at him, his handsome features tight with concentration, his mouth hanging slightly open as he blew out a hard breath, his voice noticeably affected when he spoke. "It's hard not to come with her mouth on you."

"I know," Easton grunted, his hips pulsing beneath me. "Wait until you're inside of her." His hands gripped my waist and I looked down at him, returning my focus to rising up and down on his cock.

"Have you ever been penetrated anally, Mrs. North?" The doctor pressed the control switch and I gripped the table as it moved, Easton and I rising higher, then shuddering to a stop. At the doctor's question, my husband's eyes fell closed as if in reverent prayer.

"Yes." I tightened around E as the doctor moved around to stand behind me.

"Lean forward. Rest your hands on either side of your husband's head." The tremor had left his voice, and I couldn't decide which I liked better—cool and professional Dr. Loutin, or a shaken and aroused version. There was the wet sound of lubrication squirting from a bottle, then the cool feel of his finger working around my tight anus.

"It doesn't feel like it's been opened lately. Keep riding him, Elle." He hand moved along with my movements, probing gently at the rigid hole until the slick tip of his finger pushed inside of me. My ass cheeks clenched and I felt Easton's dick flex in response, his hand settling on my butt cheeks and pulling them apart for the doctor. "How long has it been?"

"Umm…" I lifted and fell, my gaze on Easton's face, which had gone dark with pleasure.

His finger went farther inside of me. "How long?"

"A few weeks," I gasped.

"Two months," Easton corrected. "Put another finger in her. She's getting so fucking tight around me."

Two months? I struggled to focus on that number. Had it really been that long? Between my cheeks, a second finger worked tightly in beside the first, the pain sharp and unique. I lifted higher and slowed my movements to give him more access.

"Have you ever been double penetrated, Elle?"

"No," I moaned, a new world of pleasure opening up as he worked his fingers apart, stretching me open, my body burning around his touch. "I can't take you both. You're too big."

"You can take it," Easton urged, his mouth tearing across my collarbone, nipping and sucking at the skin as he kneaded handfuls of my ass in his fists. "Please, Elle. You have no idea how badly I want this."

But I did. I knew because I wanted it, and probably more than he did. My body was coming apart at the idea, my craving laced with apprehension over their size. But I liked it when my husband begged and I feigned further reluctance. "I can't," I gasped.

"Relax your ass. Breath out slowly. Big breaths."

I couldn't relax, not when the pleasure was wrapping tight cords around his fingers, my body already crawling toward the edge of a monster orgasm. There was another squirt of lube, and I stiffened in place when a third finger wedged into the tight hole. "No, please—"

"Please, what?" He was moving closer. His dick poked the back of my thigh, and I couldn't figure out what I was begging for, only that I wanted it *all*. "Is this what you want?" There was a shift, a push, an expansion, and I don't know how he managed to exchange his fingers for his cock, but he was inside of me, pushing deeper, Easton was frozen still, and *holy shit*, this was the sort of thing that someone should have told me about ten years ago.

"Stay still, Easton," I gasped, clawing at his chest, unable to move even enough to look down at him. "Just—give me a moment."

"Her ass feels incredible. She's a fucking sexual thoroughbred."

"I know. I'm the luckiest man on earth." Easton ran his hands tenderly over my breasts. "You lead the movement, Elle. When you're ready." His touch was soothing and reassuring, his voice calm despite the shudder that ran through it. "But fuck, baby. You've never been so tight. It feels...amazing."

I tested the movement with a slow lift up, which withdrew both of them almost out, my range of motion stopped by Dr. Loutin's firm grip on my ass. I lowered down, and both of them responded audibly, the groan and flex of their voices giving me the courage to move again, quicker this time, my pleasure flexing in time with the small bounces of my hips.

"Okay stop." The doctor gripped my waist. "Easton, fuck her from beneath. Slowly first, then as hard as she can take it."

"I—" I started to protest, the words dying as Easton spoke up from beneath me, his fingers pinching the tip of one breast.

"Trust us. We won't give you more than you can handle." He tightened his grip on me. "Stay still. Both of you."

With the stiff meat of the doctor's cock filling my ass, I stayed in place as Easton slowly thrust his hips up, sliding the thick rod of his dick in and out of me, his pace quickening as I began to adjust to the double penetration.

"Holy shit," he gasped.

"I'm close," I cried. I stared down at him, meeting the fierce look of domination and possession in his gaze, then pinched my eyes shut as everything in my body snapped into a thousand shards of pleasure.

32

"I can't believe it's not even dark outside." I lowered the sun visor and slumped against the seat, stretching out my legs. "There should be a rule against being that kinky before six p.m."

"Are you hungry?" Easton shifted into reverse and began to back out of the spot.

"Starving. Pei Wei?" I watched a couple as they left the medical building and wondered how close their appointment had been to ours. When we had left, the office next to ours had been full of people and I had flushed, wondering if anyone had heard anything.

"Pei Wei works for me. Want to call in an order?"

"Yeah." I dialed the number, then put the phone to my ear. In the time it took me to place our order and give our credit card number, Easton returned two business calls. I ended the call and settled back in the seat, listening as he spoke about a potential market dip in medical marijuana stock.

I was pleasantly sore, my ass aching the most. I was also a little buzzed, my body still humming from the experience. Julia and I had spoken about that at lunch—the high that came after the sex, a unique feeling of sexual invincibility. I had felt it after Aaron and after the De Lucas, though that peak had been destroyed by our fight. I glanced at Easton, grateful that the insecurities that had emerged after Brad hadn't come back.

He ended the call and glanced at me. "That was fucking hot."

"Your call?" I asked innocently.

"Funny." A light spattering of rain began to fall and he turned on the windshield wipers. "I thought he was good. Respectful but still masculine. What'd you think?"

"The setup was hot. It felt real, and that..." I blushed. "That was really hot for me. Plus, he was good. I liked his dick. And he knew what he was doing."

"It was nice that he came practically on demand."

I had ended my "exam" on my back, my limbs weak, my body twitching with the aftershocks of pleasure as the two of them stood on either side of the table, their dicks in hand. Easton had muttered that he was close, and the doctor almost instantly come, his rope of come hitting me across the breasts, a splatter of it on my cheek. Easton had followed suit, his release more focused on my mouth, and I had lifted onto my elbows to take him, and then the doctor, into my mouth and sucked them both dry.

I shifted in the seat so I was facing him. "Do you think you'd be okay, just meeting with guys? Not doing any threesomes with girls?"

"Babe, after what just happened, I'm okay with anything you want. You could bring up fucking a banana peel and I'd jump into action."

I laughed, but could see that there was something else.

"You... you didn't like what you did with Julia?"

"It was okay. But we also fought afterward. And I know that was mostly about Brad, but I'm not sure that's what I want. In that scenario, I liked it. But I'm worried, in a different scenario, I won't."

"Then we won't do it," he said with a shrug. "I don't want to do anything you aren't fully on board with. But we can figure that out later. We said three months, right? Who knows how you'll feel then."

Three months. I had *completely* forgotten about our three-month hiatus after this event. I nodded. "Right. You're right."

Three months. It felt like both a blessing and a curse. Three months to figure out our future. Three months to return to a normal life. Three months for the drama to cool, and our relationship with Chelsea to mend, and our sex life to reconnect to normality.

Three months. A blessing, I decided.

"You seem deep in thought," Easton mused. "Having second thoughts about your Pei Wei order?"

I scoffed. "Never. But, come here." I reached over and undid his seatbelt, then tugged at his shirt. "Hurry, before the light changes." I leaned forward, and he leaned forward, and our kiss met in the air above the center console.

"I love you," he whispered. "You're everything to me, you know that?"

"Same here," I whispered. "You're all I need in life."

The light changed green, but we stayed there a moment longer, one final kiss deeper, before we broke apart.

33

"Okay, so I'm still really mad at you." Chelsea stood on our front stoop, two grocery bags in hand. "But, I am also equally impressed by Aaron's apology speech, which you had an apparent hand in setting up, so I've decided that it's okay."

It was a bit of a grey area in terms of forgiveness, but she smiled, and I was ready to have Chelsea back in my life, even if she was still smarting on the edges. I hugged her, and she returned the gesture, her movement slightly hampered by the groceries she still carried.

"Here, let me get those." I took them from her and peered into each one. "What is this stuff?"

"I was cleaning out my fridge and couldn't stand to throw it all out. You're still keto, right?"

"Still keto. Here, come in so I can shut the door. The air conditioner is being temperamental." I carried the bags into the kitchen and started to unpack the contents, growing less hungry with each new item. Brussel sprouts, chia seeds, and olives hit the counter, followed by a glass jar containing chunks of coconut. "Were you eating this stuff?"

"Kind of. I was buying it and looking at it. But now I'm off that. I'm only putting into my body what it wants to eat." She looked around. "Where's E?"

"At work. They're doing some team-building rah-rah thing." I loaded some of the items into the fridge, then moved to the pantry, dubiously eyeing some organic flax seed crackers before sticking them onto the shelf next to E's extra-cheesy Doritos. I shut the pantry door and turned back to her. "Chelsea, I am really sorry. You had every right to be upset, and if I'd had any idea that—"

"I know you wouldn't have done anything with Aaron if you'd thought that I liked him." She grimaced. "It was like, the one secret I was actually good at keeping."

I let out a soft laugh. "No joke." Curiosity got the best of me. "Why *did* you keep it a secret? Why not tell me?"

"I don't know. I kinda did. I was dropping hints like crazy. And I asked you if you thought it was too soon to make a move on him."

"You did?" I frowned, certain I would have remembered that.

"Yeah. I think you thought I was joking. Or just, you know, being 'Chelsea'." She put air quotes around her name and fell silent.

I balled up the empty bags into my fist and came around the counter to give her another hug. "I'm sorry. Easton and I kinda were exploring things sexually, and it was right at the time when Aaron was staying here, and my hormones were out of control from this fertility—"

"Stop." She held up a hand. "You don't have to explain your sex life to me. And if you and Easton are stepping outside of the box, then seriously—more power to you guys. Seriously. Ignore all of that terrible stuff that I said about swingers and monogamy and married people being boring." She inhaled. "I just... don't want you to experiment any more with Aaron."

I shot her a look. "You know you don't have to worry about that. You just said you knew we wouldn't have done that if we'd known—"

"I know, I know, but I just had to say it so that I wouldn't have to ever think about it again."

"Listen to me." I put both hands on her shoulders. "I will never ever ever touch Aaron or be naked in front of Aaron, or do anything with Aaron that I wouldn't do with my grandma sitting beside me. And you know how judgmental my grandma is. Okay?"

"She really is a judgmental bitch," Chelsea admitted. "Remember when she called me a hooker for wearing a tube top?"

"I remember." I laughed. I squeezed her. "Okay? Do you feel comfortable now?"

"Yes. But I do have an important and completely inappropriate question to ask you."

"Is it about Aaron's penis?"

Her mouth dropped open. "What?! No! I wouldn't..." she sputtered through a few more useless adjectives before dropping into the closest stool. "Yes. Tell me everything. Length, width, stamina. Because I got to tell you, Elle, I really like him. And you know I'm picking about my penises. So before I go tossing my heart into his soulful eyes—"

"I'm not going to tell you anything about his penis." I folded the paper bag up and stuffed it under my sink.

"What? Come on! I told you all about Easton's dick before you even met him."

"And that was a gross invasion of his privacy." I folded my arms over my chest. "I'm not going to do it."

"Give me a hint." She picked up the cucumber and slid her finger along the length of it. "Just tell me when to stop." She moved about six inches down the shaft and glanced at me. Moved another inch. Paused. Moved another inch. Paused. Moved another inch. Her eyebrows raised. She kept going.

"I'm not telling you." I snatched the cucumber from her and opened the fridge door, tossing it into the produce drawer. "And thanks. Now I'm going to have that visual when I eat it."

"I'll pay you to tell me. Come on. Fifty bucks."

"My moral compass doesn't have a price tag. At least, not since Easton agreed to take Nicole Fagnani back as a client. You should have returned my calls last week. I might have spilled everything for a Subway gift card back then."

She pouted. "So, it's ugly. Is it like a curly fry? Or wait, it's tiny, right? Like a baby carrot?"

"Are you hungry? What's with all the food references?"

She sighed. "I'm starving. Have you eaten lunch?"

I grabbed my purse. "Let me lock up Wayland and we'll go. You want to drive?"

"I guess." She reached out and hugged me, the impulsive gesture catching me by surprise. "I missed you, Elle."

I set my purse down and squeezed her back. "I missed you too. Like crazy. Even when I didn't want to." She started to pull away and I tightened my grip on her, my mouth close to her ear. "It's not ugly or tiny. I think you'll be very pleased."

She whooped out a celebratory yelp, one that sent Wayland into a barking fit, and had me laughing, despite the plummet my morality had just taken.

"Now come on," I insisted. "For once, I'm buying you lunch."

34

Easton found me on the back porch, my feet resting on a bag of dog food, a glass of wine in hand. "Hey." He bent over and brushed his lips against mine.

"Here." I pulled my bag of chips off the adjacent chair and patted the cushion. "Sit. You can watch your son make a complete fool of himself."

"What's he doing?" He settled into the chair and worked at his tie, loosening the knot and lifting it over his head.

"He's terrified of that container." I held out my glass of wine and he took it, tipping back the glass and taking a generous sip of the chilled white chardonnay—a recommendation from Julia De Luca which was excellent and cheap, a winning combination.

"This is good," he remarked. Glancing at the darkening yard, he whistled for Wayland, who glanced his way, then returned his tense attention to the empty gallon of weed killer, which had blown off out of the recycling container and was lying on its side in the yard.

"You can have some of those chips if you're hungry."

He picked up the bag and grimaced. "Kale potato chips? Where'd these come from?"

"Chelsea stopped by. We grabbed lunch and made up. All is forgiven."

"Wow. I forgave Nicole, Chelsea forgave us, Aaron might actually get laid... things are looking up."

"Don't forget about my closing next week," I pointed out. "The De Luca house will officially put me on the map. Julia already referred a friend of hers to me."

"Why were they selling that house? Are they buying something else in town?"

"I think there's some kind of drama with Brad's family. I asked, and they didn't really answer, so I dropped it. But if they do buy something else, I think they'll definitely use me again."

"Of course they will." He reached out and grabbed my hand. "Congratulations, baby. You know, we never did go out and celebrate that sale."

"We went to Roadhouse, remember? You ate too many of the peanuts and got all puffy?"

"No, we needed to do a proper celebration. Something like old times. Smith & Wollensky... or maybe Joe's Stone Crabs." His eyes lit up. "Come on. This was a huge sale for you. You need to be properly wined and dined. Buy a new dress. Let me get you flowers. Order too many desserts and have drunk sex in the limo."

"Oh there's a limo?" I raised my brows and laughed as he pulled me out of my chair and onto his lap. "You know I'm no good in limos."

"You won't fall asleep in this one," he vowed. "I have all sorts of filthy ideas to keep you awake."

"Let's let it close first," I negotiated. "I don't want to jinx anything."

"You can't jinx this," he whispered, nuzzling the crook of my neck. "This is the beginning of everything. Can't you feel it? Our lives, coming together?"

Wayland let out a low growl, then bolted away from the bucket with a terrified whimper as a gust of wind rolled it a half-turn to the side. I laughed, calling him to me, and he scurried over, his tail pinched between his legs.

"Don't let him—" Easton's warning was cut off as Wayland crawled into our laps, his feet pistoning into my thighs as he worked his way in between us and laid back, exposing his belly.

"I can't breathe," Easton wheezed. "You guys are too heavy."

"DOWN." I pointed to the floor and Wayland opened his mouth, his tongue lolling out one side.

"Go on." Easton heaved him off in a tumble of paws, ears, and tail, and I smiled as he hit the ground and immediately sprinted into the dark. "Okay, where were we?"

"You were telling me that this was the beginning of everything." I settled back onto his lap and curled against his chest, my head settling against his shoulder.

"It is," he said softly. "I know it is."

"I think you're right." I lifted my chin enough to kiss his neck. "And okay, I'll let you shower me with praise and expensive food in a candlelit setting."

"In a new dress," he reminded me.

"In a new dress."

"Followed by filthy limo antics."

"Don't promise what you can't deliver."

He growled, his arms tightening around me. "Oh, I can deliver, Mrs. North. Should I give you a preview of the action right now?"

"Absolutely." I grinned against his kiss. "But you should probably take me inside. I have a tendency to be very loud when I come."

He heaved to his feet, keeping me cradled in his arm. Clicking his tongue against his teeth, he gave me a heated look. "What did I do to deserve you?"

I traced my finger over his lips. "Don't be grateful. I don't know if you know it, Mr. North, but you married a very dirty woman."

"I know exactly what I married. I *love* what I married, and I'm going to give you everything that dirty little mind wants." He shouldered the door open and carried me into the house, his mouth peppering mine with fierce kisses. "The good. The bad. And the filthy." He deepened his kiss, pulling me tighter to his chest as his mouth crushed against mine.

"Promise?" I whispered, when we moved into the bedroom and he carefully laid me on the bed.

"I swear." He lowered himself on top of me and I closed my eyes, surrendering to his touch, his kiss, and his promise.

I knew one thing. My husband always delivered on his vows.

Especially the filthy ones.

AFTERWORD

Wow. I haven't loved a couple this much since Brad and Julia, back in 2012 and 2013. If you haven't read the Innocence trilogy, I urge you to read it! If you liked this series, you will love their story, which is just as dirty and with even higher stakes! Start with Blindfolded Innocence.

I do think I'll write another book in their story, but I can't guarantee it. I hope this gave you enough of a complete ending to close their chapter in your head. I was very torn on whether to give Elle a baby at the end. If I do write a third book, I think I'll address her fertility there. I am of the strong personal belief that a woman doesn't have to have children in order to be happy, and know that Easton and Elle have a wonderful future ahead of them with, or without, children.

Now, I'm off to celebrate the completion of a good book. My celebratory process normally ends with me stumbling into bed, sleep-deprived and mildly delirious. Tonight, I am anxious to spend time with my husband. After living in Elle and Easton's romance for the last three months, I'm anxious to return to my own. Instead of one dog, we have three. Instead of Chelsea, my best friend couldn't get past the steamy prologue of Filthy Vows before blushing and turning away. And instead of Easton, I have my husband, who blows all my fictional heroes out of the water with just one cocky grin.

Thank you for picking up this novel. Thank you for following me on social media, and subscribing to my crazy email updates, and for leaving reviews and recommending my novels to your friends, and for considering my releases when they pop up on retailer shelves.

Your support allows me to write new novels, and pour my heart and energy into new books. Thank you from the bottom of my heart.

Until the next novel,

Alessandra

ABOUT THE AUTHOR

Alessandra Torre is an award-winning New York Times bestselling author of twenty-two novels. Torre has been featured in such publications as Elle and Elle UK, as well as guest blogged for the Huffington Post and RT Book Reviews. She is also the Bedroom Blogger for Cosmopolitan.com. In addition to writing, Alessandra is the creator of Alessandra Torre Ink, a website, community, and online school for aspiring authors.

If you enjoy Alessandra's writing, please follow her on social media, or subscribe to her popular monthly newsletter, where she hosts a monthly giveaway, along with writing updates, personal photos, and more.

www.alessandratorre.com
alessandra@alessandratorre.com

f facebook.com/alessandratorre0
🐦 twitter.com/readalessandra
📷 instagram.com/alessandratorre4

ALSO BY ALESSANDRA TORRE

Looking for another sexy read?

Hollywood Dirt. (Now a Full-length Movie!) When Hollywood comes to a small town, sparks fly between its biggest star and a small-town outcast.

Blindfolded Innocence. (First in a series) A college student catches the eye of Brad DeLuca, a divorce attorney with a sexy reputation that screams trouble.

Black Lies, the New York Times Bestseller. A love triangle with a twist that readers couldn't stop talking about. You'll hate this heroine until the moment you love her.

Moonshot, the New York Times Bestseller. Baseball's hottest player has his eye on only one thing—his team's 18-year-old ballgirl.

Tight. A small-town girl falls for a sexy stranger on vacation. Lives intersect and secrets are unveiled in this dark romance.

Trophy Wife. When a stripper marries a rich stranger, life as a trophy wife is not anything like she expects.

Love, Chloe. A fallen socialite works for an heiress, dodges an ex, and juggles single life in the city that never sleeps.

CPSIA information can be obtained
at www.ICGtesting.com
Printed in the USA
LVHW042202300420
654814LV00005B/1400